PERIL IN THE
HIGHLANDS
A D.C. DENISE KELLY STORY

JAMES GLACHAN

A NEW BEGINNING

DENISE Kelly got out of her Hillman Avenger and stretched her back. It felt like all the muscles had fused together and getting some movement back into them felt so good.

She deliberated for ages over whether to stop somewhere for a break or do the 7-hour journey in one go. In the end up she chose to drive straight through, apart from stopping near Perth to refuel her car.

She parked across the road from the Glenfurny Police Station. She almost felt like she was going on holiday as she drove up from Ayrshire, but this was anything but. This was a posting to the other side of Scotland and a chance of a new start to her career, a new beginning.

The police station seemed quaint with its freshly white-washed walls and dark blue woodwork and door. Indeed, the whole town seemed to be small and picturesque. She expected policing here would be about chasing poachers or making sure the pubs shut at the correct time.

It seemed a world away from what she had left behind and would hopefully be the re-charge her body and mind needed.

She checked the Avenger's doors and boot were securely locked as all her worldly goods were in it. Surely it would be safe parked on the road beside the police station but, knowing her luck recently, the whole lot could be nicked.

She tried the police station door but found it was locked. At first it just seemed unmanned, turned out it was actually part-time. Closed until 3 pm, according to the notice pinned on the front door. She smiled when she read it.

"We are open between 9 and 10 am and from 3 to 4 pm. In case of an emergency out with these times dial 999."

She checked her watch; it was only 10 past 2, a while until opening time. Policing by appointment. She smiled and shook her head at this, what a different way of life. When she left her old home that morning it was March 1973, looks like 7 hours later she had arrived sometime in the 1950's. She briefly wondered if they knew the Second World War was over.

First things first, her rumbling belly reminded her she hadn't eaten since setting out just after 7 o'clock that morning. She left the car and walked down the street looking for food. The first shop she came too was a general food shop, according to the sign above the shop.

The sign had block letters informing her that H.Samson and Son were Purveyors of general foods. How quaint, she thought. The sign might have been impressive when fitted, but it looked like it hadn't seen a lick of paint in over 20 years.

Looking in the window, she was a strange window display for a food shop, it was full of cleaning products. Flash, tide and almost every other cleansing product available but pride of place seemed to be given to a pack of brillo pads which were on a pedestal in the middle of the display.

Denise then mused that the last shop window she had looked in was Frasers in Glasgow about a month previously. It had an amazing display of perfumes that would cost her the best part of a week's wages for even the smallest bottle, a world away from brillo pads.

In her reflection she saw she was smiling, a smile being a rare visitor to her face in the past few months.

She looked past the display into the shop itself to see if they did take-away food. She could see there were three people in the shop and even through the thick plate glass Denise could hear raised voices from within.

The front door opened and a young girl, who seemed to be little more than a teenager, emerged crying. She turned and walked past Denise, walking up the hill without looking back.

Denise hoped she wasn't heading for the police Station; she would have a wait.

Her police instinct told her to go straight into the shop and try to pick up the vibe of what was going on.

There were only the 2 people left in the shop, probably a married couple judging by the apparent aggression, and both being dressed in matching grey nylon overalls. The woman, behind the counter on Denise's right was pointing at the man as she entered.

'Pregnancy isn't an illness! You need to let her go now, Hugh!' she screeched.

Hugh, Denise reckoned, was the H from the sign, although more likely he was the "and son" part.

'How can I do that, sack a girl because she is pregnant.'

Seeing the customer, she never answered, just clammed up and stood silently, smiling falsely at her.

Denise quickly picked up that the girl had failed to turn up for work that day blaming her pregnancy, obviously not the first time she had used the excuse either.

The moaning woman who was standing behind one of the counters was in her late 50's and had the weirdest hairdo, pure grey on the sides and jet black down the middle. Denise thought it looked as if a skunk had been dropped on her head.

Responding to her presence, skunk-head quickly flicked on the charm switch.

'Hello lass, what are you after?'

'I need something to eat. Do you do pies or sausage rolls?'

'Of course, we do, my dear. Over on the other counter.'

Denise turned to the opposite counter and saw it had an array of stodgy buns and other bakery products. Her stomach turned over at the thought of food. As she walked over to study the goods on offer the shopkeeper crossed the shop.

The old wooden floorboards creaked beneath the shopkeeper as she walked. Denise hadn't realised she was so fat, mainly because seeing her away from the counter it seemed to her the skunk woman's head was too small for her big torso.

Out of the corner of her eye she saw the big woman growl at Hugh as she walked past, making her now certain he was her husband, who now stood silently against the far wall with his arms folded, like a cigar store Indian.

Back behind the food counter the woman was now charm personified.

'Now dear, what do you fancy?'

'Are those mince pies?'

'No, mutton?'

Back home in Ayrshire they called mutton pies mince, but she wasn't here to argue. Not while her stomach was screaming for food.

'Yes, I will have a pie. Can I have one of the buns with pink icing on it too.'

Denise paid and walked slowly to the door. She knew the woman was still raging and was waiting to unleash her bile on her husband who stood waiting on it. You don't have to be nosey to be a good policewoman, but it helps, was always her mantra.

As she opened the door to leave she paused and heard the woman unleash her rage again.

'She was a useless, lazy girl before, now she is a lazy, useless pregnant girl.'

5

Leaving the shop, Denise spotted a bench straight across the road and thought it would be an ideal spot for her food. She could also watch the shop, her interest now piqued by the events in there.

The food was great. Maybe because she hadn't eaten for nearly 8 hours by then, but it was fresh, tasty and cheap. She would be a regular there from then on, she was sure.

As she ate, she kept an eye and an ear across the street at the shop. Even from her perch a distance away on the other side of the road, she could still hear muffled voices. She was certain they were still having a shouting match, and it seemed she was winning.

Although she wasn't there to judge what Hugh had said was true, how bad would it look if he sacked a girl when she was pregnant? Especially in a town where everybody would know each other's business.

Denise had just finished eating when a police car drove slowly past. No surprise it wasn't going fast, it was an ancient Morris Minor, resplendent in light blue and white police livery.

Time to meet the local police, she thought, as she headed back up to the station.

When Denise tried the police station door it was locked again, although the police car was in the car park, and she was sure she could see the someone walking about inside. She rapped on the door.

This brought no response, so she knocked again. Louder this time, a right policewoman's knock.

The constable, who had been driving the car, looked over the counter to see who was disturbing him. He shook his head then walked slowly round to the front door as if it was a big bother to him.

Meantime, while waiting, Denise rummaged through her handbag for her warrant card. It was the last thing she thought she would need today.

The constable appeared and stared through the glass at her.

She held the I.D. up. Closed at first, then opened so that he could see who she was. Even then he seemed reluctant to open the door for her.

'Could you open the door please,' she said exasperatedly through the glass.

He disappeared back round to the office and came back with a big bunch of keys. The constable opened the door a crack and stuck his head through.

Denise was taken aback, she expected to be invited in.

'Hi, I am D.C. Denise Kelly. I have to report here tomorrow.'

'Okay, I will see you tomorrow. We open at 9 o'clock.'

The constable went to close the door again, but Denise stuck her foot in, something she learned early on in her career, but didn't think she would ever need to do it at a police station.

'I am a fellow officer, I thought you would at least invite me in.'

The door opened a bit, and she could see the dumb cop was wondering what he should do. Obviously, this wasn't in the manual he worked to. All the time Denise looked round the entrance for a hidden camera, she was beginning to think this was secret filming for Candid Camera, the T.V. show where hidden cameras catch you getting set-up in funny situations.

The door was then opened fully, and the bobby walked away, grudgingly saying, 'You better come in.'

The station itself was also like a throwback to the previous century. It was on one level, the 2 cells on the left- hand side and to the right, over the counter, was a cosy office with an inviting coal fire burning. Beyond this there were a couple of doors, no doubt housing a detective's office and possibly a toilet and kitchen.

'I am here to shadow Detective Sergeant Les McCall. Is he not working today, I thought I could meet him and introduce myself?'

The constable, who Denise guessed was about 40 years old, had thinning red hair that was now mellowing to a mixture of fair and grey, he wasn't much taller than her and his belly was bursting out of his uniform. Probably fitted him when it was new, but that must have been a good few years ago.

He plodded over and clicked on an ancient looking kettle.

The copper's face was flushed with red, a complexion she had seen in the few people she had met so far up here in the Highlands. She saw now his belly was also overhanging his belt by a good few inches, it was clear there were no yearly fitness test up here, she thought.

'McCall doesn't do Mondays,' he finally said. 'Fancy a cuppa?'

'Oh yes, I could murder a cup.'

She smiled at the pun, being police, but it was wasted on her present company.

The P.C. sat down as he waited on the kettle to boil. He didn't offer any chat which surprised Denise, who hadn't taken him for the strong silent type. Boy, she knew this would be very different from Ayrshire. She thought it might be a different World up there, but it seemed this was more like a different planet.

'So, how many of you work here at the station?'

This was immediately met with a furrowed brow. Denise was glad she started with an easy question.

'There is me. Oh, I haven't introduced myself, I am P.C. William Lambie but folk call me Billy. There is old Andrew MacCallum, he is a bit of a weirdo. He is due to retire next year so is taking things slowly. Then there is McCall. He is a good copper.'

He nodded then added, 'When he is here.'

Denise felt like asking him to rewind a bit, old Andrew is a bit of a weirdo he said. If he is compared to yours truly he must be a right fish she thought. What had she landed herself with here, she thought again? Two weirdo P.C.'s and what sounded like a Detective Sergeant with a drink problem.

'What brings you to Glenfurny?'

Denise was surprised when Billy finally asked something, especially when it was probably the last question she wanted to answer.

Denise had deliberated what she should say about why she volunteered to move across the country. Did she want everyone to know she was leaving a broken marriage because her police officer husband couldn't keep his truncheon in his uniform? No, she decided, not just yet.

'I saw the advertisement for a year-long post here in the Highlands. It seems there is a shortage of officers up here. Thought it would be fun.'

'Fun? Right,' Billy said, shaking his head as he got up to make the tea as the kettle started to whistle.

Denise didn't like the way he said either word. Maybe he wasn't as thick as she thought.

'Sorry, I have no sugar or milk, we drink it black.'

Denise winced at the thought, black tea, ugh. She needed fluids; she would just need to drink it black. It tasted as bad as she thought it would. There would need to be changes, milk and hermesetas for a start maybe even biscuits.

'So, did you know I was coming?' Denise asked.

'No,' he said blankly.

'Did the Detective Sergeant not mention it?'

'No. Not for my pay grade to know.'

'But surely we all have to work together as a team.'

That just got a knowing look and shrug from her minion before he took a drink and hid his expression from her.

'Anyway, what is the Detective Sergeant like?'

'Oh, he will like you,' Billy said, raising his eyebrows slightly for a second then breaking into a mischievous grin.

That wasn't what she expected to hear. For some reason she thought he would say something like he was a good cop when he was sober. Maybe she was reading her new superior wrong, maybe he wasn't a serious drinker after all.

'So why does he miss Mondays?' she asked, trying to get a better angle on McCall.

Billy's head went down, as if guilty about talking about him.

'He is fond of the women,' he said quietly.

That hung in the air between them. Denise was sure Billy wasn't going to open up any more about Les, so she changed tack, hoping to meander the conversation back to her mentor to be.

'Are you married?'

'Not yet.'

'Oh, right. Are you seeing somebody?'

'No, not yet. Someday.'

'Right. So, you are planning to meet somebody and get married someday.'

Billy nodded and smiled as if this was a simple plan and an obvious thing to be doing. He just hadn't started on his plan yet.

'It's complicated, my mother doesn't keep well. I need to spend time with her.'

Their stimulating conversation was interrupted by the

phone ringing.

The P.C. looked at the clock and shook his head. It was nearly 5 o'clock, too near stopping time for his liking. He didn't hurry to answer it either, just walked casually over to the phone in the corner.

'Hello. Okay Liz, calm down. Right. When was this? Are you sure he is dead?'

Suddenly Denise's interest went up a few notches. Although from what she had encountered there so far it would probably be somebody's pet cat, dog or even budgie.

'Have you phoned the Doctor? Right, that's good. Now stay calm, I will be there shortly.'

THERE'S BEEN A DEATH

Although P.C. Lambie had appeared calm on the phone, when he hung up and turned round, Denise noticed the colour had drained from his face. It had lost its ruddiness.

'That was Liz Wilson at the guest house. She just found Sergeant McCall; he was dead in his bed.'

It was no wonder he was in shock, she thought.

'Oh God. I better come with you.'

'But you are not on duty yet.'

'Tell you what, I won't tell anybody if you don't.'

It was meant to be a joke, but the P.C. didn't laugh at that either.

'I will need rubber gloves and an evidence bag,' Denise said, being ever the professional. 'I don't have anything with me.'

Lambie thought about it for a minute. 'There are some rubber gloves in the kitchen.'

Denise just shook her head. 'It's okay, I have some in my car.'

'You have a car,' Lambie said, surprised.

'Why, did you think I flew up here on a broomstick?'

Again, the joke fell flat.

'Never mind,' she said, 'I will get you outside at the car.'

Denise rushed down to her car and got a couple of pairs of

gloves and a small evidence bag from the sports bag she kept her work stuff in.

She was still waiting outside the car for a few minutes before P.C. Lambie appeared.

'I had to go a place,' he said, a bit embarrassed.

At least some of the colour was back in his cheeks.

Denise wondered at first if the P.C. had been sick at the thought of seeing a dead body, surely he had been involved in a sudden death before. She settled on him needing a number 2.

The P.C. opened the car and leaned over and popped the door lock for Denise to get in. She sat back and reached for the seat belt.

'Is it far?'

'No, not really.'

The car pulled out of the police station car park, turned the corner and stopped at the next building. Denise was still fumbling for her belt but felt silly when she realised the car was so old it didn't have seat belts fitted.

Lambie killed the engine. 'We're here.'

'Next door.' She was exasperated again. 'Why did we not just walk?'

'Ah,' he said, 'It's about image. People need to know there is an incident and we are in charge here.'

'My dad told me that,' he added proudly.

Denise shook her head at this. Getting out she followed the P.C. as he walked up to the front door. It opened before he even knocked it.

The landlady, who stood waiting on them was a woman of about 60, who looked pale and drawn. Denise reckoned she had been a looker in her day, but it seemed life hadn't been good to her.

'Oh Billy, thank God you came so quickly.'

'All part of the job, Elizabeth.'

'Hi, I am D.C. Denise Kelly,' she said introducing herself. She stuck out a hand, but the landlady just nodded. She did not look happy to see her.

'He is up in his bed,' Liz said, letting them both pass.

Lambie headed up the stairs, obviously knowing the way.

Before she went up the stairs Denise spotted somebody nosily looking through from the end of the hall, which she supposed was the kitchen area. Denise thought she recognised the face, which surprised her because she didn't know anybody in the town yet. Maybe

Denise followed the P.C. up the stairs. As she followed him up the stairs she was met with the unmistakable aroma of what had to be boiled cabbage, drifting upwards. Memories of horrible school dinners left her hating the stuff.

Walking slowly, having to copy the P.C.'s laboured pace, she couldn't help but notice the threadbare carpet on the stairs. The magnolia-coloured paintwork had probably been white when it was fresh. The wallpaper was peeling in bits too, the truth was it looked like the whole place needed a spruce up.

Outside the bedroom, on the second landing, the P.C. stood back and let his superior lead the way. So much for her not being on duty.

The bedroom door opened easily and swung forward revealing a tidy room. The only thing out of place was the lump in the bed that was obviously the body of the deceased policeman.

Just as she walked in the room the doorbell downstairs rang.

'That'll be Doctor Harkins,' P.C. Lambie said. 'He just lives just down the street.'

'Hope he could get parked okay,' Denise said, but again her

attempt at mirth was wasted. Maybe not the best time for humour anyway.

'Maybe we should wait on him,' he went on.

Denise, however, had walked over to the bed, perplexed by what she saw. Over the course of her career, she had seen a few bodies dead in bed but this one was positioned in a very strange way.

Pulling back the covers it was easily to see why. Les was lying on his side, but his legs were bent and slightly open. He was naked except for a pair of underpants. It didn't look natural; something just didn't add up to her.

Then she saw his neck. The curtains in the room were drawn, making the room dark. The dull 60-watt bulb didn't help, but it looked to her that his neck was bruised. Normally, if she was on duty she would have her pocket torch with her.

The inspection was disturbed by voices at the door. The Doctor had arrived outside the room. She was impressed at the punctuality.

Denise wasn't impressed by him when he walked in. He looked as if he should have retired about 20 years previously. He had a shock of white hair and big bushy grey eyebrows that resembled huge blond hairy caterpillars. He wore glasses with lenses that were so thick they looked like something you would use to put in sunlight to start a fire.

He was wearing a crumpled suit that had seen better days, and it had the remnants of all his meals from that day down it in small portions.

Denise stood back and let him past. He whiffed strongly of embrocation although she wondered if it was actually embalming fluid she smelled.

Doctor Harkins pulled back the covers.

'Oh dear, oh dear,' he said then tutted as he touched certain parts of the body.

'Such a shame in one so young,' he went on.

Denise walked back to the doorway where Billy Lambie stood alone.

'Heart attack do you think?' Billy asked her.

Denise shook her head. 'No, I have seen plenty sudden deaths, this isn't normal, there is something strange here.'

'We will see what the Doctor says.'

After a full study, including using a rectal thermometer, the Doctor walked over and joined them.

'Death was sometime last night. Natural causes I would say. I suspect he suffered a heart attack.'

Denise shook her head and looked over at her P.C. who nodded in agreement with the quack.

'What about the bruising on his neck?' she asked him.

'Bruising?' The Doctor looked bemused, then he walked back over to the body. Taking his torch back out of his old-battered Gladstone bag he shone it on the dead body's neck area.

Denise followed him and looked over his shoulder for a better look than she had earlier now the torch light played on it. The view wasn't any better, the beam from the torch was as bright as the old doc.

'Oh, I see. No, I think this is just blood that has collected post-mortem.'

'Why would it gather in his neck area? I still think it looks like bruising to me. We will need a post-mortem.'

The Doctor held his hands out. 'Go ahead but they will just tell you what I have said. Heart attack. No need to give you a certificate then, if you want a second opinion.'

The Doctor walked out and said something to Lambie before stomping away, obviously miffed that his professional judgement was being questioned by some meddlesome fresh-faced female.

'Billy, what do we do now then?'

He too seemed miffed with the newcomer who had just appeared and was now poking her nose and interfering in something that seemed straight forward to everyone else.

Denise noticed his attitude but didn't have time to deal with that now, she was sure there was something strange here, putting it mildly.

She knew what would have happened back in U Division and thought it would be the same here but wanted to be sure.

'Well, constable?'

'We will need to contact the local hospital, the Lawson Memorial, and they will send the van to collect him.'

That sounded the right thing to her.

'Okay, you go and do that. I will stay here and secure the room.'

'Secure the room. Do you think he was murdered?'

'Do you know anybody that can strangle themselves?'

'Strangled? No, the Doctor assured me it was a heart attack. Can't be a murder, we haven't had a murder here in 30 years.'

'With a doctor like that, I am not surprised. Certainly, looks like that to me. Look, you go and phone the hospital. Before you leave ask the landlady to come up. I need a word with her.'

'Can I go after that. I need to be home for my tea. Mother will have it ready, and I need to check she is all right.'

'Sure, I can wait. Come back first and tell me how long will it be before they are coming for the Detective Sergeant.'

When Billy left, Denise put her disposable gloves on and had a quick look round Les' room. Like the rest of the B and B it was tidy but needed refreshed. There was a wardrobe. In it was his dress uniform and two dark suits, obviously his work clothes and three pairs of shoes in the bottom. Nothing else.

She patted the suits down and found his notebook in the inside pocket of one of the suits. She put it in her evidence bag, hopefully this would be good reading at a later date.

There was a small drawer unit which had a portable telly on it. Beside it a net of satsumas which had been opened and one removed.

There was a small bin beside the bed. Denise looked in it to see if the peel from the fruit was there. It was, along with a few bundles of used tissues. Along with the two foils sachets from condoms. Investigating further, she found the bundles were in fact packages with the used condoms in them. She gagged at the discovery and was glad she had her gloves on.

Denise heard the stairs creak outside the room. Denise went to the door and found Mrs. Wilson was just getting to the top landing.

She had the look of somebody who had just reached the top of Everest only without the elation. In fact, she looked as if this was the last place in the world she wanted to be.

The landing was bare except for an old wooden cane chair outside the deceased Detective's room.

'Take a seat,' Denise offered.

The landlady sat awkwardly.

'Relax. I just need to ask you some questions about D.S. McCall's movements over the weekend.'

Liz Wilson looked utterly scared.

'Look, it's not an interview. You aren't a suspect or anything, I just need to find out about the Sergeant's movements.'

This still didn't seem to make any difference to the interviewee.

'When did you see Les last?'

'I saw him go out about 7 o'clock last night. I heard him come back in just after 10 but didn't see him.'

'Was he alone?'

'Yes. I can tell by the creaking stairs. And he didn't fart.'

Denise thought nothing would surprise her on the job anymore, but this just did.

'Sorry, run that past me again.'

'I live in the apartment downstairs. I hear everybody coming in because the stairs creak. When Les comes in alone, when he reaches the first landing he stops and farts. Always does it if he is alone. I think it's the beer that does it. But never does it if he has one of his fancy women with him. Must hold it in for later.'

The landlady said "fancy women" as if it left a bad taste in her mouth, that she thought they were something worthless, dirty, of lower class.

'So, he was alone. Who else lives on this landing?'

'There are two boys who are builders. They are working at the big hotel. They are in rooms 1 and 2 downstairs. Two elderly ladies, Miss Gilks and Miss Hall live across the landing in 5 and 6 and my daughter is next door here in room 7.'

'Next door. She might have heard something. I will need a word with her. In fact, I will need to speak to them all.'

'Is that all you need from me,' the landlady asked, keen to escape. 'I have the teas to sort.'

'Oh, no, there is something else.'

The landlady looked surprised at the way the D.C. suddenly said that. Truth was, Denise just realised she had nowhere to stay that night. The events had taken over and she hadn't even thought about it until then.

The Highland police force, in an example of their efficiency, had informed her in her letter telling her to report here, informed her there wasn't police accommodation available and she would need to make her own arrangements.

'Do you have any spare rooms?'

The landlady scratched the back of her neck, taken aback, this was probably the last thing she expected to be asked.

'Yes. I have a room on the landing below, room 4, just below this one. It's ready to be let. Why?'

'Well, as it turns out I have nowhere to stay tonight. Is it en-suite?'

'En what?'

'Has it got its own bathroom?'

Liz smiled, holding back a laugh, considering the circumstances that surrounded them.

'No. It's shared like here; 1 bathroom between 4 rooms, we are not the Ritz. If you are finished with me here I will go and get it ready.'

'Is your daughter in just now?'

Liz nodded.

'Right, could you send her up just now so that I can have a quick word with her too.'

Liz suddenly looked worried. 'Oh, she is not in trouble, is she?'

'What? No, I just need to ask her a few questions, like I asked you. You know, if she saw or heard anything last night or this morning. Being next door, she might have heard something.'

The landlady nodded, satisfied, and headed quickly down the stairs.

Denise realised the events of the day were having a toll on her. She sat on the chair pinched her nose, she felt a bit of a headache coming on and wondered if every day would be like this. Not the quiet backwater she expected when she arrived a few hours ago.

The stairs beneath were creaking again announcing the imminent arrival of someone. Denise expected the Wilson girl, but it was P.C. Lambie who appeared. His face was redder than usual, and he was breathing through his arse. She wanted to ask him ironically if he ever went jogging, but now wasn't the time.

He stopped on the landing but couldn't even speak for a few minutes as he struggled to get his breath back.

'They will be here to pick D.S. McCall within the next 2 hours,' he eventually managed to get out between pants and heavy breathing.

'Two hours?' the Detective Constable said exasperatedly.

The cop nodded, hinting that this was the norm for this neck of the woods. He then he stood guiltily, waiting to be excused.

Between his heavy breathing, the stairs could be heard creaking again. This time a familiar face appeared. It was the girl from the food store, the one who was pregnant, lazy and useless. It must have been her sneaking a look from the kitchen when she first came in. That was where Denise knew her from, the shop.

'Right, you can go,' she said to P.C. Lambie. 'See you tomorrow morning at 8.30 sharp.'

'But.' He started to complain at the thought of the early start but thought better of it. After all, it was surely his duty to stay with his deceased colleague's body so with the D.C. volunteering, he couldn't complain. He just nodded in agreement and headed down the stairs.

'Right, and I want to see P.C. MacCallum there too,' she called after him.

The constable, who was already at the first landing, waved

back at her. She hoped for their own good that meant they would be there. The general apathy at the station was already starting to grate on her, even though she hadn't even officially started work yet.

The landlady's daughter had stood quietly on the landing waiting her turn to be interrogated.

Now they were alone, Denise got up from the chair and offered the pregnant girl the seat. The girl shook her head and refused to sit.

'No. I will just stand,' she said very quietly.

'Are you sure?' she said, hinting at her condition, her pregnancy clearly showing.

Denise, not having much experience of pregnancy except from a few friends, reckoned she was about 7 or 8 months gone.

Denise was surprised when she refused again, the poor lass looked tired. Her not sitting bothered Denise, it seemed strange she wouldn't take a seat. What was really annoying her was it meant they were talking at almost eye-level. Denise was only a couple of inches taller than her, whereas if the girl was sitting, Denise would be towering over her, giving her a position of superiority, an old police trick.

'So, I am Detective Constable Kelly. What's your name?'

'Susan. Susan Wilson.'

Susan was so nervous she could hardly speak.

'Don't be nervous. It's not a police interview, I just need to speak to you because you stay in the room next to Detective Sergeant McCall. Now, when did you last see or hear anything in the room, say from 10 o'clock last night?'

'I saw him lying in his bed this afternoon when mum asked me to come up with her. Les hadn't appeared all day and she was worried about him.'

'Yes, your mother told me that. What about before then?

Last night or this morning?'

'I heard him going into his room last night just after 10 o'clock I think it was. I could hear some noise so he must have put the T.V. on. I must have dozed off shortly after that. Never heard anything else from his room last night or this morning.'

Denise paused. She wanted to break the ice before continuing.

'I saw you today at the grocer's shop. You work there, right.'

She nodded. Denise then used another old police trick, pause and don't speak. The person you are interviewing thinks it's their turn to speak so they carry on talking.

'I have been working there since I left school.'

'Right. What age are you, if you don't mind me asking?'

'No, it's okay. I was 19 last week.'

'So, you have been there, what 3 years. I will tell you something, you don't look 19. I take it you and your boyfriend are starting a family soon.'

Susan looked down and rubbed her swelling belly.

'I don't have a boyfriend.'

That seemed all she was willing to divulge.

'Did you ever go in Les' room?'

'Yes.'

Denise said 'Oh.' Simply that, not implying anything but leaving it hanging to be interpreted however Susan wanted to take it.

'No, not for that,' she said, repulsed at the thought.

The obvious implication he could be the father of the unborn quickly quashed.

'Sometimes I help mum do the rooms or to get his washing. Mum does his laundry. That was all I ever went in for, I never went in when he was there,' she added.

'Oh, I didn't mean you and him,' Denise said, making a face, as if it was a gross suggestion, then smiling.

The girl smiled along with her.

The reason she asked that was because she had to cover all bases. After all, if Les McCall was such a lothario he could have swept a young innocent off her feet, and into his bed. Although that seemed as far from the truth as there could be.

'Anything else you think I should know?'

'No, I don't think so.'

'Right. If you do think of anything, let me know. You know where I will be.'

'Are you working here in Glenfurny now?'

'For my sins, yes.'

The girl smiled again. Denise smiled back, looked like she had a connection to the place now.

'Could you do me a favour,' Denise asked. 'I need the spare key for the door to lock it while I get my stuff from the car.'

'The key is on the sideboard.'

'Yes, but I need all the keys so the room can be locked and secured so that nobody has access to it.'

Without saying anything else Susan turned and headed back down the stairs.

Left on her own, Denise looked at the chair. There was something about it that bothered Susan, she thought it was important but couldn't put her finger on it. Yet.

Denise had been on quite a few murder cases, but this didn't have a feel of that, but it was definitely in the "unexplained" category. She went back into Les' room. She was sure there were clues as to what had happened here, but she couldn't find them. The post-mortem would hopefully help to point her in the right direction.

The Doctor had re-covered the body with the bedclothes when Denise suddenly had another thought- should she have asked for a pathology team? She had made the call not to, now it would be on her head if she was wrong. However, if he had been murdered she would be taken to task about it, not the good start to her career there she wanted.

She went back to looking over the room but was disturbed by the creaking stairs, giving away that somebody was approaching. The room door was open, but the person stopped short from getting too close.

Denise went out and found Susan waiting patiently out on the landing. She handed over the spare key and turned to go.

Denise checked the key was the same as the one she had picked up from the sideboard and turned to thank her, but she was already out of sight in her hurry to leave. Still, Denise didn't have time to think about her, she still had to empty her belongings from her car.

THE YELLOW PERIL

Denise opened the boot of the yellow peril. That was the name she gave the car when she had inherited it from her father and was bright canary yellow with a black sunroof. It was so out of character for her father to buy such a bright coloured car, he was conservative with a capital 'C'. Normally his cars were bland, dark colours, not bright yellow. Indeed, the most garish thing she could remember him before the car was wearing a red tie he got as a present when she was a young girl.

She had laughed when she first brought it home and said it was his, she thought he was pulling her leg, but he said one day she would get it. She thought he meant the joke, but less than a year later she inherited the car after his sudden death.

All her belongings were in the boot, except for some clothes lying on the back seat of the car and a few bags in the footwells. Not much to show for being on the planet for nearly 30 years.

She lifted her suitcase out. It was a family heirloom and was closer to being a trunk than a case, it was massive. She thought about taking a sports bag with her on the first trip, but the bag was really heavy and carried it on its own. Strangely it hadn't felt so heavy when she dropped it in the boot that morning.

Luckily she was just across the road from the B and B and hadn't too far to struggle with it.

The door to her new room was open when she finally dragged the heavy case up the stairs. She was welcomed by a citrus fresh smell, obviously the landlady had sprayed something lemony in the air to mask any staleness.

The key was in the lock, so she dropped the case off, locked the door behind her, and went back to her car for more.

Back at the car and her luck changed. As she was deciding what to take next a works van drew up outside the boarding house. Two lads got out and were going into the house. Denise wasn't the kind of girl who liked to play the damsel in distress, but after carrying the heavy case she decided to cash in on her feminine attributes.

'Excuse me guys!' she called over as they went to go in the front door.

The lads turned and saw who was calling. Without another word they crossed the road to get a closer look at her and see what she wanted.

'Could you do me a big big favour and help me take this stuff in.'

The two lads looked to be in their twenties and must be the two boys the landlady spoke about earlier.

One was tall, with long blonde hair the other shorter with short dark hair. Both looked quite fit and muscular looking although their clothes were all dusty. Denise wasn't bothered about getting a bit of dust on her stuff if it meant not having to humph it all up to her room.

The lads quickly looked her over. They saw a pretty woman with short, dark bobbed hair. Not as tall as the blond guy but a bit taller than the shorter one. She was wearing jeans and t-shirt that she seemed to fill out nicely, and a short black jacket.

The lads looked at each and agreed with a nod this was a bit of nice eye candy.

'Where is your stuff going?' the taller one asked.

'The boarding house,' she said pointing across.

'I am moving into room 4.'

'Sure,' they said, exchanging eye-contact with each other, pleased to be getting in her good books and happy she would be a new neighbour.

They delved into the boot and grabbed as much as they could and took the bags she had already taken from the car.

They managed to get everything, leaving only the clothes from the back seat Denise had piled in, mainly jackets and work suits. She grabbed them and followed the eager lads into the house.

They must have virtually run up the stairs because she didn't catch up with them until they were waiting outside her room. Unlocking the door, she let them in past her.

'Put them down anywhere,' she said. 'In fact, put them there on the bed.'

As she put the clothes down beside her other stuff, the lads saw her ceremonial uniform which was sitting on the top of the pile.

'Are you police?' the short one asked seriously.

'Yes,' she said, nodding and smiling as she spoke.

'Aw, that's a shame. I hoped you were one of them kisso-gram girls,' he added with a mischievous grin.

Denise laughed with them, but they stopped when she said- 'In fact, I need a word with you both.'

The two lads looked at each other guiltily, wondering what she wanted them for.

'I am sorry I have to tell you Detective Sergeant Les McCall died either last night or some-time today.'

The lads looked at each other, shocked at the news.

'No way, lecherous Les,' the shorter one whispered, then added 'dead.'

'Really, he's dead,' the taller one echoed, surprised at the news.

'Yes. Mrs Wilson found him this afternoon. Did either of you see him between 7 o'clock last night and this morning?'

They looked between each other before the blonde lad spoke again.

'We saw him in the pub last night. Came in about 8 o'clock. He was with a woman, but she left about 9. He stayed for another an hour or so then left on his own.'

The shorter lad nodded in agreement.

'He wasn't drunk but didn't look happy he'd been jilted.'

'Did you know who she was?' Denise asked.

'The woman. No, never seen her before. Not local, I don't think. I hadn't seen her in the pub before anyway,' blondie continued, seemingly having taken over as the spokesman for the pair.

'How did he die?' the other lad asked.

'We don't know yet. Just waiting on the undertakers coming to take him away.'

'You mean he is still up the stairs,' the shorter one said, shivering at the prospect of a dead body being on the premises.

They were interrupted by the doorbell ringing downstairs.

'Hopefully that's them now,' Denise said.

'I hope so too,' the blonde lad added before leaving to go to their own rooms across the landing.

Denise watched the mortuary guys put the body in a body bag and carry him out the room and down the stairs.

Although he had never met the guy she felt so sad for him. Or maybe it wasn't him she felt for, more because she saw this could be the way she ends up years down the line, dying sad and alone in a crumby bedsit like this one.

She locked the door behind her and stopped to wipe a tear from her eyes.

Next thing she would have to do was settle up with the landlady. She found her in the dining room, collecting the empty plates from the evening meal.

They went into the kitchen and settled up for her months' rent as they had agreed.

'Would you like something to eat?' Liz asked, after the money was sorted.

It was something she hadn't even thought about since her late lunch as the adrenalin had kicked in and events had kept her going. Now it was mentioned, the thought of food and the wonderful heady aromas of food, still noticeable in the kitchen, had her stomach rumbling.

'Yes please.'

'It's only lamb casserole and mashed potatoes.'

Only, Denise thought, it sounded heavenly.

'Sounds great.'

'Sorry, but there is no boiled cabbage left.'

'I will live,' she said smiling, dreading the thought of the horrible green stuff she smelled earlier being dumped on her plate.

In the dining room the others that were left were finishing their puddings. The lads were already finished and were away leaving the 2 older ladies left.

Before they disappeared Denise grabbed a quick word about Les and whether they had seen him last night or this morning. Not surprisingly, neither had seen him since tea-time on the Friday night. They kept themselves to themselves they were keen to add.

They left soon after, gently nodding to her as they left, leaving her alone in the empty room. Something told her she would need to get used to her own company, sitting alone would be the norm for her, for a while at least.

After her dinner Denise retired to her room. She found a notebook in one of her bags and noted down everything that had happened and what she had gleaned from the residents.

Happy with her recollection, sleep suddenly caught up with her. Without even washing she stripped to her underwear and slipped under the covers and into an instant sleep.

WAKEY WAKEY

Denise picked up the phone. The voice was instantly recognisable. What once was cheeky, almost sexy in a way, and made her heart flutter was now utterly repulsive to her.

"Hello darling, good news. I have just heard your immediate superior has left the constabulary. Not to worry, they called me and asked if I would come up and take over from him. I said yes. We will be back together again. I have missed you. No. we have missed you, I have missed you and the Cyclops has missed you too."

Denise jerked awake, soaked in sweat although she definitely wasn't warm. There were nightmares and nightmares, but this was the worst ever.

Why dream about her ex-husband John? She hated the dirty cheating bastard and thankfully had managed to not give him a second thought since arriving in the Highlands.

She should have known there was something wrong with him when she found up he gave his penis a name. He called it Cyclops because it only had one eye. Weird or what?

She lay in the dark waiting until her racing heartbeat returned to normal. According to her watch it was 3.07, a strange time to be wide awake like she was now.

She needed to take her mind off her cheating rat of a husband, so she focussed on Les' room. What had she missed?

Then the nagging thing at the back of her head seemed to click. Her room was the same as the room above. The only difference was she had a chair in the corner, there wasn't one upstairs in Les' room. Yet there was one in the landing above. Could the one out in the hallway be from Les' room, and if so why? She had to look at his room again.

Dressing quickly with the clothes she wore the previous day, she slipped out of her room and headed upstairs. She walked carefully up the side of the steps and found they didn't creak as much as going up the middle of the treads.

In Les' room, she walked over to the same corner of the room where her chair sat. Even in the dim light she saw the imprint of 4 quite deep indentations where a chair had sitting for a long time. She had been right. The question was why had Mrs. Wilson taken the chair out and why was Susan so scared of it? Questions for the next time she spoke to them.

Denise arrived at the police station at 8:30 prompt. Surprisingly the door was open and both P.C.'s were present. The kettle had already been boiled and there was tea on the go.

P.C. Lambie was making the tea. The other cop was busying himself setting the coal fire although the room wasn't cold.

'P.C. McCallum, I presume. Pleased to meet you. I am Detective Constable Denise Kelly. Hopefully we can work together.'

The older guy looked up from the fire hearth but never spoke, merely gave the slightest nod.

'So, P.C. Lambie, any idea when the post-mortem is?'

'No.'

'Have you tried phoning the hospital to find out?'

'Thought it was too early.'

'Too early. You two might be part-time but the rest of the world works 24-7. What did they say at headquarters when you told them?'

This time the P.C. looked guilty. 'You never said to phone

them. I thought you would do it.'

'I never said!' she shouted at him.

She had tried to hide her rage, but it was getting harder by the minute. 'Can you not think for yourself? We have had a senior police officer die and you never thought about phoning headquarters to tell them.'

Lambie bowed his head.

'Who do you usually report to?'

'Chief Inspector McKelvie over at Inverness headquarters.'

'What's his number?' Denise asked, trying to hide the anger in her voice.

'It's at the top of the blotter,' he said, without looking over at her.

Denise dialled the number and waited nervously as it rang. How could she put this diplomatically, she wondered?

'McKelvie,' he answered, almost immediately and with a masterful voice.

'Good morning sir. This is Detective Constable Denise Kelly. I have reported for duty at Glenfurny this morning.'

'Oh yes, one of the secondments from down south. Ayrshire isn't it? Great to have you on board. How can I help you?'

'Well, I am sorry to have to be the bearer of bad news. Detective Sergeant McCall, who I was supposed to be here to shadow, unfortunately was found dead yesterday.'

'McCall. That seems sudden. I spoke to him last week and he seemed to be in fine health. How did he die?'

'Well, the local doctor said it was natural causes, probably a heart attack, but I wasn't so sure. I have asked for a post-mortem. His body is at the local hospital now.'

'Right. Oh dear, this is bad news. Not the start you imagined for your first day.'

'No Sir. Well, actually, I was involved yesterday. I was here at the station to introduce myself when his landlady called the incident in.'

'I see. Listen, I am tied up with meetings this morning, but I will be over there before close of business. If you need anything else just call. If I am not here, it will go straight through to my secretary, leave a message with her.'

After she hung up, Denise then turned to Lambie again.

'What is the number of the local hospital where D.S. McCall went?'

'It's at the bottom of the plotter, it's under Lawson Memorial.'

Denise looked at the plotter again. It was filled with all sorts of numbers including the local pub. Denise phoned the hospital and was eventually put through to the morgue. She found out the post-mortem was due at 10 o'clock and asked for the results would be faxed through to the Glenfurny police station as soon as it was written up.

Denise hung the phone again then a thought came to her. The dead policeman would need to be formally identified.

'Don't suppose any of you know who Les McCall's next of kin is?

'No, but I know he had a sister in Dundee,' Lambie offered. McCallum just nodded.

Denise phoned McKelvie again. This time it went through to his secretary. She explained the local police in Dundee would need to contact his next of kin and he would need to be formally identified.

By the time she made all these calls her tea, which now had milk and sugar in it, supplied by Lambie, was cold. As she stood at the kettle with her back to the door, it opened, and the bell rang telling of someone's arrival and somebody breezed in.

'Here, I heard shagger McCall was dead. Is that why you two are in early?'

He hadn't seen Denise, who turned and cleared her throat. The intruder was the local postie, standing with a handful of letters and whose face suddenly went crimson.

'Sorry, I didn't see you there.'

'That's obvious. What if I had been a grieving relative of D.S. McCall? It would have been nice for the family to know his nickname was shagger.'

'Sorry.'

Denise tapped the side of her head then her mouth. 'You know you should employ that before you use this.'

Firmly chastised, the postie put the letters on the counter and walked out sheepishly with a red face and another apologetic sorry.

Denise waited until he was clear of the building before bursting out laughing. The other two coppers joined in; this would be a story for the pub later the men thought.

There were 2 letters addressed to McCall and a magazine in a plastic bag. The magazine was The Police Insider, the in-house magazine for the police force. It reminded Denise she would have to re-address her copy of the magazine, something she had forgotten all about when she walked out on her rat of a husband.

She opened the letters; he wouldn't be doing it now. One of the letters for McCall was informing him that Denise would be joining them that day, although it was dated nearly a week before. The other told him he was due his yearly medical and had to phone to book it. Too late for that, she thought.

'Do we have a typewriter?' Denise asked. She was surprised to find out they had one and Lambie showed her through to the back office.

The office was small and cramped, although calling it an

office was a bit of a stretch. There was just room for a table and chair, a filing cabinet and a safe fixed to the wall.

On the table was an ancient looking manual typewriter that was covered with a plastic case which in turn was covered in dust.

'Right, I will need to type up my notes from yesterday and today. Looking at this museum piece I could be a while. If you could I would like a fresh cuppa every hour.'

Lambie nodded and left her to it.

Denise was quite happy to be alone for a while. Although the typewriter frustrated her at times. The biggest annoyance was that there was no indication that she was nearing the end of the page before she ran out of paper. It wouldn't have happened on her electronic machine she had back in Ayrshire.

When Lambie arrived with her first cup of tea she was more than half-way through her report. After her tea though it seemed to go downhill. First the ribbon stuck then the machine decided to start typing the same letter twice. If the office window had opened further the typewriter might easily have ended up outside on the ground below.

She was just finished, up to date, when the second cuppa arrived. This time it was the older P.C. who brought it.

'Where's Lambie?' she asked.

'There's one of those fax things coming through,' he answered.

'What? Why did you not tell me that first, is that not more important than a cuppa?' she asked incredulously.

'He will bring it through as soon as he gets it.' Then the old policeman just shrugged and walked away.

Denise took a sip of the brew before taking it through to the front office to see what the fax was about, saving the P.C.s the trouble of walking through. She was sure it would be from the hospital.

Denise found P.C. Lambie reading the report and struggling to understand it.

'Heart attack?' she asked, almost certain that was not the answer.

'Don't really know,' he said.

'Give me it here.'

Denise took the report and skim read it.

'What does it say?' Lambie said, suddenly interested in police work.

'Asphyxiation probably caused by tourniquet around the neck.'

Denise felt exhilarated as she read it, she knew it wasn't a heart attack or a collection of blood on his neck, after he died, as old Doc Harkins had suggested.

'Traces of citrus in the mouth area though nothing found in the stomach.'

Curiouser and curiouser she thought, although something was niggling at the back of her head again. It was ringing a bell deep in her psyche.

'Signs of ejaculation which might have been just before demise.'

That surprised her, there was no traces of it when she saw him.

P.C. McCallum had seemed to be following the report so far was now confused. 'What does that mean?' he asked.

Before Denise could say anything Lambie answered. 'It means he came as he went.'

The two men laughed at the thought. Denise never noticed; her mind was concentrating her thoughts.

'Got it,' she announced, clicking her fingers.

The Eureka moment. That was it, Denise thought. She was sure this rang a bell; she was sure she had read about this kind of experience before. It wasn't something back in Ayrshire, she must have read it in a previous edition of the Insider.

McCall got the Insider every month, but she hadn't seen any in his room. She wondered where he kept them.

'Lambie, where did McCall keep his Police Insiders?'

'After he read them they are dumped in the magazine rack, we use that stuff to kindle the fire.' Lambie pointed to the corner of the room where the stuffed magazine rack sat.

Denise hurried over and got down on her knees at the rack, looking through the magazines and old newspapers still there. She was looking for a specific article in one of the recent Police Insiders although she wasn't sure when she had read it or what edition it was in.

She kept skimming the magazines, tutting when she finished each one and the article she was after wasn't in it. When she picked up the last one in the rack she didn't fancy her chances were great in finding what she was after.

BINGO!

Bingo! There it was. In the last magazine was an article about a London CID report mentioned a case of a man found alone in his bedsit. He had an orange in his mouth and a belt tied round his neck that he had been pulling while masturbating to enable him to achieve a heightened orgasm. Erotic asphyxiation it was called. She was certain that was what McCall had been doing when he died.

Lambie seemed to be right for once. In this case, it appeared that the Detective Sergeant had died as he came.

The question now was, why was he found lying in his bed? She presumed Liz and Susan Wilson had found him sitting on the chair and moved him into the bed. They would have more questions to answer now.

Denise lifted the magazine and popped it under her arm.

'Billy, go over to the boarding house and ask Liz Wilson to come over and answer a few questions.'

P.C. Lambie looked dubious. 'What if she says she is too busy?'

Denise knew what he meant. She reckoned she could be domineering to somebody as nice as him and would easily fob him off. Denise wasn't going to let her.

'Then arrest her.'

'Arrest her,' he said, raising his voice slightly, shocked at the thought. 'For what?'

'You are a policeman, use your imagination.'

Lambie put his jacket on and got ready to leave slowly, it was obvious it wasn't a job he wanted to do.

When Billy left, Denise told P.C. Mc Callum he had to go without saying anything, when his colleague arrived back with Liz Wilson. He had to go and pick up Susan, wherever she was, and bring her in. Then he had to put her in the other cell to wait until Denise finished interviewing her mother.

It was the old man's turn to be troubled by the request.

'What if she is working in the shop? Rita won't be happy.'

'If that's the owner of the shop, I don't think she is ever happy,' Denise said. 'Just find her and bring her here.'

He still looked dubious.

'That's not a suggestion, that's an order,' she said, starting to lose patience with him.

He just put his jacket on slowly but said nothing in reply.

Denise planned her strategy while waiting on Lambie and her landlady coming over. Initially she though, arrest her straight away and put her on the defensive. Give her the chance to confess to what she had done because Denise was certain she knew the truth. If she wasn't complicit, threaten her with charges.

Liz Wilson arrived 10 minutes later, just ahead of the P.C. and looking every inch the accused. She walked in slowly and with her head bowed.

There were no interview rooms at the dated station, so D.C. Kelly invited her to take a seat in the first cell.

Before she joined her, she nodded to P.C. Mc Callum to go out and get her daughter Susan, wherever she was.

Denise changed her mind when she looked at the woman sitting on the bunk before her. She looked so down. Running the B and B would be hard for her, but for a woman twice her age it must be 10 times harder. That made her decided to start as good cop, after all it was her landlady she was talking to as well. No point going in heavy and arresting her. Not yet anyway.

'Mrs. Wilson, we have just received the post-mortem report on your boarder, Detective Sergeant Lesley McCall. The facts from it do not tally with the story you told me yesterday.'

She let that hang in the air but emphasised the pronunciation of the word "story" to let her know what she thought of her fiction. Denise was almost certain that she now knew exactly what had happened the 2 nights previously, she just wanted it confirmed. If Mrs. Wilson admitted putting the body in the bed and tidying up the room it was job done.

The terrified woman sat silently, staring at her hands.

Denise had to put a bit of pressure on.

'What you told me yesterday was off the record. Now we are on the record, this is official.'

Again, she let this hang in the air.

Liz Wilson seemed to shrink as she sat on the bench in the cell.

'I told you last night what happened.'

Before she spoke any more, the front door to the police station opened and Susan and P.C. McCallum walked in. The girl still had her grey overall on.

Liz looked up and saw the new arrivals, as they walked past, then looked to the floor.

'This is on the record, it is official,' Denise re-iterated, then waited.

Liz looked at her hands then spoke hoarsely.

'Could I get a drink of water.'

P.C. Lambie was standing at the counter pretending not to watch or listen but went for a cup of water when D.C. Kelly looked over at him.

Liz sipped the water then started talking.

'Les didn't come down for breakfast. That wasn't unusual on a Monday if he spent the night with one of his women. God knows what he got up to with them.

I knew he went up alone the night before and was worried he was ill when he hadn't surfaced all day. That wasn't like him at all. He liked his food.'

Denise said nothing, let her get on with it, although deep down she was getting excited because she was sure her theory was about to be proven correct.

'Susan and I went up to his room after lunchtime. When I opened the door the room was in darkness. It was quite scary. There was something dark in the corner. As I got closer I realised it was a body.'

'It took me a few seconds to realise it was Les. He was sitting in the chair in the corner. He had a black plastic bag over his head and shoulders. I spoke to him then touched him gently, but he was cold and stiff to the touch.

That was when I realised he was dead and had been for a while.'

She stopped again to compose herself and take another sip of water.

'His thing, you know, was out but was wrinkled up and there was a big dried white stain on his boxer shorts.'

Liz's hand was shaking even more as she lifted the mug to her mouth for another tiny sip of water.

'Are we in trouble?' she asked, tears filling her eyes as she spoke.

'Not if you are now telling me the truth this time,' Denise said.

Although Denise believed Liz was telling her the truth now, she didn't know if she was telling her the whole truth yet. After all, it wouldn't be her decision as to whether she would be prosecuted or not.

Liz swallowed hard and sniffed then continued her story.

'I took the plastic bag off, and something fell out. It was a satsuma that had bite marks on it. He was just sitting there. He was like a statue, not moving. He had a belt round his neck and his tongue was sticking out. It was horrible looking. I had to stop because Susan started crying.'

'When I looked in the bin bag there was a lot of his dried stuff in there too. It was like dandruff flakes when I shook it.'

She stopped to get her breath back.

'I didn't want him to be found like that, so we put him into his bed and got rid of the belt, the satsuma and the bin bag, then we phoned the station.'

Having relieved herself of the burden, she started sobbing.

'Why did you put the chair from his room into the top landing?' Denise asked, the thing that had puzzled her the most.

'I, I had to clean it. There was stuff on it, you know body fluids, if you know what I mean. Afterwards, it stank of disinfectant after I cleaned it. If I left it in the room the smell of it would have made it obvious it had been tampered with. Even Billy would have noticed something was wrong.'

'Why did you put him in the bed Liz? Why didn't you leave him the way you found him?'

'I could say it was to preserve his dignity but really it was because I am struggling enough with the boarding house. I thought if something like this came out it would be in the newspapers, and that could ruin me altogether. I don't know what he had been doing, but I knew it was not normal. '

'You are right there, definitely not normal' Denise said as

she patted her on the shoulder.

When Liz's crying subsided a bit she spoke again.

'Susan had nothing to do with this. She only did what I told her.'

'I know, but obviously I still need to speak to her.'

Liz looked at her, understanding now why her daughter was there.

'Right, Liz, I will write this up and need you to sign it.'

'Am I definitely not in trouble?' she asked between sobs.

'I am sure you know my report will need to go to people above me, but I will be recommending no further action. However, it won't be my decision.'

'What could they charge me with?' she asked, bottom lip trembling now.

'Realistically, you could be charged with perverting the course of justice.'

'That sounds really serious,' Liz said, looking at Denise with sad, pleading eyes.

'It probably sounds worse that it is, you could get a fine at worst,' Denise reassured her. 'For now, though, we need to keep this between ourselves.'

Through her teary eyes the landlady started chuckling gently.

'Do you think I want this to be public knowledge?' Liz sniggered.

Denise joined in and managed a laugh as well, even though it was still a very serious situation.

'Can I stay when you speak to Susan??'

'No. Best you go back home. Don't worry, I won't say or do anything to stress her, what with her being pregnant.'

'Okay,' the boarding house owner said, relieved.

Liz got up and smartened herself up before leaving the cell.

'Thanks,' she said, realising how differently she could have been treated by the policewoman.

'Only one more important thing to ask,' Denise asked as her landlady left the cell.

Liz turned, a fresh worried look on her face.

'What's for tea tonight?'

Liz laughed again, relieved and cheered up. 'Lamb chops and chips.'

'Oh my God, a couple of weeks of this and I will be double the size.'

With that the couple walked out of the cell laughing.

Susan had been sitting in the other cell waiting her turn.

'Susan, just tell the policewoman the truth,' Liz called through to her daughter. 'Everything is going to be okay,' she added.

Susan appeared from the second cell. The relief on the girl's face was immense.

'Do you mean everything is okay?' her daughter called back.

'Yes love, as long as you just say what happened yesterday,' her mother said.

Susan walked out of the cell and ran up and cuddled her mum.

Denise, the hard-faced cop had to hold back a tear at the tenderness between mother and daughter, something she never really had from her mother growing up.

Denise repeated the interview process with Susan, who confirmed her mother's story, and told her she too would also have to sign a statement later.

Susan opened the station door to get back to work a lot happier than when she had arrived there and a huge weight off her young shoulders.

As she went to leave Denise called her back. 'If your bosses say anything about you taking time off to come here, tell me later. I wouldn't mind having a few sharp words with Rita.'

A broad smile broke out on the young girl's face, glad to know she had an ally in the town.

When the three police were alone again, Denise reckoned it was time for lunch.

'What do we do for food? she asked.

'I go home for lunch,' Lambie said, almost guiltily.

Why did that not surprise her? She looked at the older cop. He nodded in agreement, he obviously did too.

'Well, you better get off. I have my report to write up. On the way back could one of you nip in and get me a sandwich somewhere.'

'Sure,' Lambie said as the crime fighting duo quickly headed out the door.

Denise sat at the fire and wrote her notes up. She always worked that way, planning what she wanted to write. That was easier than typing something then reading it back and finding it didn't make sense.

She woke when the bell on the front door rattled. With the comfy seat and the cosy heat from the fire she had dozed off. Being wakened in the middle of the night and struggling to get back to sleep, especially after her nightmare and the thrill of possibly solving the mystery of the chair, had added to her tiredness.

P.C. Lambie arrived bearing gifts. His mother had made her two lovely salad sandwiches. She devoured them and washed them down with a big mug of tea.

Billy looked at the half page of notes his new boss sat on the counter.

'You have been busy,' he said sarcastically.

'What have you done today?' she spat back.

In her whole career she was always being assessed by men and compared to men. That meant she had to work harder and longer hours than any of her male colleagues. Being judged like that by a fat, lazy plod hit a nerve.

'Do you know at 3 o'clock this morning I was in McCall's room trying to work out what had happened to him. I haven't slept since as the things in this case have been rattling about in my head as I've tried to make sense out of this chaos. I bet you haven't even given this case another thought when you were off duty.'

Then she added, 'really, what have you added to the case?'

Lambie was quiet for a moment then a thought came to him.

'I said he went as he came,' he said smiling, as if they couldn't have cracked the case without him.

'Right, I will give you that,' Denise said, smiling and it changed the atmosphere between the two.

'I better finish my report in the office, won't nod off in there. Still need tea every hour Billy,'

'Yes boss,' he said with a mock salute.

'I am not your boss,' she replied.

The P.C. nodded but she was higher rank, in his eyes that was the same.

Two hours later her report was complete and faxed to McKelvie, then she waited for the man himself to make his appearance.

A CHIEF INSPECTOR CALLS

Chief Inspector McKelvie walked into the police station as if he owned the place. There was an air to the man that said, I am in the room, pay attention and listen to me.

He took off his fancy hat and flattened his full head of black hair.

Denise smiled to herself. If she was asked to make up an identikit of what a Police Chief Inspector would look like, this guy in front of her would be it personified. Over 6 foot tall, he was clean shaven but had a strong chin. He held himself smartly, proudly showing his strong frame that carried little or no fat.

His piercing blue eyes took in the scene before he spoke.

'Afternoon gents. And to you Detective Constable Kelly. Welcome to the Highlands Police force. I think you will find us a friendly bunch. It will be more of a family feel than the bigger forces down south. Mind you, you have had a strange introduction to how things are here.'

There was no handshake proffered. Was it because she was a woman? Unfortunately, that was the way her mind always worked now.

'You could say that. I take it you got a copy of the report on Detective Sergeant McCall's death I faxed through.'

'Ah.' McKelvie said.

It wasn't what he said but the way he said it that had Denise wondering where this was going.

'We received the post-mortem result and your report. What I have done is ordered the body to be collected and taken to Inverness. There will be another post-mortem tomorrow. That will say D.S. McCall died from a heart attack.'

Denise wouldn't have been given a bigger jolt if she was hit with an electric cattle prod. What the Hell was going on, she thought?

'But my report! It wasn't a heart attack. It was erotic asphyxiation!'

Denise's outburst was because she had put so much work in and solved a strange case and now all her good work appeared to about to be swept under the carpet.

McKelvie raised a hand towards the Detective who he could clearly see was aggrieved.

'I know you are upset. I know your report is good, in fact it's excellent. However, who will it benefit if we make it public? The force? Oh, the force is big enough to take a wee bit of adverse publicity but what about his family? They probably know he is a womaniser but to kill himself seeking sexual gratification. What would that do to his family?'

He paused for a moment for effect, the way she would do herself.

'Imagine if it was a member of your family?'

With her father dead she had no immediate family left but a thought came to her, what if some horrific, historic fact came out about that her father had done something unimaginable like this. Although she knew that would never, ever happen, a revelation like this would have killed her.

McKelvie looked Denise straight in the face.

'On a personal note, what do you think this would do for your career?'

He paused, letting her think about it then gave her his take on it.

'There would be publicity that would follow the rest of your career. You would be the erotic asphyxiation woman. I have seen people's career's being finished with cases like this.'

Denise churned this over in her head.

'I would like a new report tomorrow saying simply that Detective Sergeant Leslie McCall was found in his bed, subject to a fatal heart attack. Tomorrow it is up to you to submit your report, either re-submit a copy of the first report or send me the new report. The decision about what report I receive is up to you.'

The top policeman paused before continuing.

'So, D.C. Kelly. Which report do you think we should go with?'

Denise looked down as she spoke. She was deeply disappointed but when it was laid out like that she knew her superior was right.

'D.S. McCall died of a heart attack.'

'Good decision. Now you will get the new post-mortem report tomorrow as soon as it is done, and I expect your report by close of play tomorrow. In fact, I will come over and pick it up personally. Is that okay?'

'Yes sir,' she grudgingly agreed.

'Good. Carry on team,' the Chief said, before leaving as quickly as he had arrived.

Denise turned to the other two who looked as surprised as her.

'Well, what do you think?'

Lambie shrugged. 'Suppose it's better for everybody.'

His older colleague just nodded.

'Right, but the thing is, you can never as much as whisper a word of this. By that I mean ever mention it, even to your family.'

This time the two of them just nodded.

Denise thought for a minute.

'To make sure, you will both sign the bottom of the new report along with me, we will all be in it together.'

As Denise walked over to the boarding house she still had mixed feelings. Her detective work was spot on, and she solved a curious case. Although she knew it was the correct thing to do for those left behind what about police integrity. Her excellent report being bagged would leave a bitter taste in her mouth for a very long time. She would copy the report the next day as an insurance policy. McKelvie might be the big boss, but how did she know she could trust him?

When she let herself in the to the boarding house the first thing she did was look out Liz and Susan. They were in the kitchen putting the final touches to the evening meal.

Denise walked in and closed the door behind her. There was little chance anybody else walking in, but she was letting them know she was there on business.

'Chief Inspector McKelvie, my immediate superior, turned up today and informed me D.S. McCall died on Sunday evening from a heart attack.'

'What? You mean,' Liz said, then burst out crying. Susan cried too then cuddled her and they stayed like that for a few minutes.

Liz tried to dry her eyes but started sobbing again.

'Do we still need to sign a statement?'

'What for? You simply found him dead in bed.'

'We won't be charged?'

'No, it's over. As far as we are concerned, there can be no

charges because nothing happened apart from natural causes.'

'Thank you Denise. That's such a weight off my shoulders.'

Denise herself now felt a bit teary, mainly because she felt guilty that this was the result she didn't want and how much it meant to her landlady and her daughter.

'Right, when's dinner? That smells great.'

The new post-mortem report arrived just after 9 o'clock the next morning. No mention of satsumas or sperm or chocking to death. Denise had written her new notes out the night before. She had been interrupted when Liz brought her a portable t.v. from the room above. Denise thought it must be from the room above, Les' telly. He would have been the last one to touch the dials. She couldn't bring herself to switch the box on and just continued with her report when Liz left. Doubted she could ever watch it after where it had been.

Denise lifted the fax from the machine in the office while the two P.C.s, Lambie and McCallum had settled down in the office. Denise started to realise this would be all they would do if she didn't do something.

'Right gents. Today I suggest you walk the beat.'

The two guys were aghast, they looked across at each other before turning to face the D.C.

'Chief Inspector McKelvie is coming over today for the new report. What will I have to tell him if he asks what you two have occupied yourself with today?'

'Can we finish our tea first?' Lambie asked.

'Yes, then out for the morning. The whole morning, not just a 10-minute stroll round the block.'

Denise reckoned she wouldn't be getting any lunch sandwiches from Billy's mum today.

Back in the office, Denise rattled out the new report. It took her more than an hour using the decrepit old typewriter. This was the first time she hadn't felt any pride or joy when a report was written up. She still mused about whether she was right to agree so meekly to change the report, or even agree at all.

When she finished the report she started writing a list of what she needed for the office with an electric typewriter top of the list. There were other things, the store cupboard looked as if it was administered by old Mother Hubbard. She also listed things that were needed to get the station a bit moderner.

After that she decided she would walk round the village. Hopefully she wouldn't find the other two cops lounging somewhere else.

It was a lovely, bright summers day. After being cooped up in the tiny office for what felt like 2 days straight, it felt good to get some fresh air.

The town seemed idyllic. Maybe this was the place to get away from it all. Funnily enough, there hadn't been a single phone call to the station reporting any trouble for the past 2 days. Maybe things heated up at the weekend.

Denise looked in the window of the general grocers where she had visited on the Monday. Susan was behind one counter and the older woman at the counter opposite. Her stomach growled at the thought of food. but it wasn't even 11 o'clock, too early. She would nip in on the way back up if she didn't find anywhere else to get food.

A few doors down the street was the local pub, The Pheasant Plucker. An old-fashioned pub that had a black timber frame with white painted panels, from the outside it was exactly what she thought the local pub in a small highland town like this would look like.

As Denise passed the front door, the main door was open and from the noise within advertised that it was already open for business.

Opening the fancy glass inside door, she was met with the real old-fashioned bar she imagined. Sitting along it were about half a dozen men and one woman. The large clock behind the bar showed it was only ten to eleven, ten minutes before opening time.

When Denise stepped in the conversation stopped and a few heads turned to see the new arrival.

'Is that the right time?' she asked the barman, looking at her own watch, as if innocently wanting a time check.

The barman was a cheery soul, smartly dressed, hair shiny with brylecreem, no doubt, and a big thick bushy moustache. He twirled the end of his moustache and tightened the knot on his tie. Denise wondered if this was some kind of mating display. If he expected this to work on somebody half his age he was way off the mark.

'Yes dear. Spot on with the radio this morning.'

'Oh, and do you have a special opening hours here?'

'Och no,' he said, before adding, 'the local constabulary turn a wee blind eye to that kind of thing, if you know what I mean,' he said, winking knowingly.

'Would you like a wee dram yourself?'

'No. I don't drink while I am on duty.'

Suddenly it was like an old Western scene, where the bad guy walks up to the bar. Everything went silent, and all heads turned to face her. She half expected a ball of tumbleweed to roll past.

She smiled. 'I might see you all again tomorrow at this time, but I really hope not.'

Then she turned and walked out, imagining the topic of conversation after she left. She laughed to herself as she walked away. After the previous 2 days she had suffered, it felt good to have a laugh.

She continued walking down the High Street. After a few houses, the next business was a garage. She could see a couple of mechanics working on an old transit. For a moment Denise thought about introducing herself but something about the set-up didn't sit right with her. She pretended to be looking in her shoulder bag as she glimpsed across at the garage.

The owner of one of the cars being fixed arrived just as Denise was watching.

There was a lot of head shaking from the older mechanic, who was probably the garage owner. Denise watched as they walked into the office then the owner walked out a few minutes later, MOT certificate in hand, then drove off. As the car passed Denise couldn't help but notice the exhaust was blowing blue smoke, obviously burning oil.

Denise had grown up with a father obsessed with cars and even she knew there was something fishy going on here. She would need to look into it at a later date.

Within less than a mile of the police station, it was apparent to her the whole town was operating with little or no regard to the Law. That would soon change now she was here; she was certain of that.

McKelvie arrived just after 3 o'clock. MacCallum and Lambie were back in the front office with Denise, awaiting the Inspector's arrival.

When he walked in, they all stood up, giving their superior his place.

'Relax,' he said, but until they left they knew they couldn't.

'You got the new, sorry, you got the post-mortem report this morning?'

He directed the question at Denise.

'Yes sir. I have written up my report.' With that she handed him the new report she had written up.

'I didn't fax it when you said you would be coming over.'

'Good work, Detective Constable.'

Quickly, the Chief Inspector skim read it. Satisfied, he had another question for her.

'What about the copy of the other report? You have kept a copy?'

This hung in the air. The Chief Inspector, who had already witnessed the quality and standard of his new officer's work, knew she wouldn't have only made one copy of the report. However, another copy could be the smoking gun in the future if knowledge of this minor cover-up emerged.

'It's in the station's safe,' she said reluctantly.

With that she left to go to the office to retrieve it.

As Denise opened the safe, a small unit bolted to the wall in the office, the door behind her opened. It was the Chief Inspector, who had followed her through.

Quickly, she retrieved the document and locked the safe. What he didn't know there was another copy of the report in the strongbox along with D.S. McCall's notebook she put there for safe keeping. She didn't let her superior see in, he would have wanted the other copy destroyed too plus she wanted to study the contents of McCall's book personally when she had the time. She was sure there was some useful info contained in it. There again, it might just have a load of women's phone numbers.

The Chief took the file from her and looked at her very seriously. 'D.C. Kelly, I must say I am surprised and delighted by the quality of your work.'

Denise Kelly was gobsmacked by the compliment. Back in Ayrshire all you got from the bosses was complaints, never praise.

'I am also pleased you see the difference between big city policing that you left behind and the community policing that we do here in the Highlands.'

Denise smiled. Oh, she was pleased to be complimented but also thought it funny to hear Irvine being described as big city. It was a New Town and just that, a big town, mind you, but a town just the same.

'You were supposed to be shadowing D.S.McCall but I will propose you take over the running of this station at present, until other arrangements can be made.'

Denise was aghast. She hadn't expected that.

'I am sure it is well within your capability, Detective Constable. You haven't any objections to this?'

'No sir. I have already passed my Sergeants exams and have been used to working with added responsibility back in the big city, as you said.'

'Going forward, I will need to discuss the way forward here with my fellow superior officers, but that's not for just now and we will keep you informed.'

Nodding, the Chief Inspector turned and was heading out of the office.

'Sir, before you go.'

He turned and gave her his full attention.

'I realise we eh, turned a blind eye in this instance. With community policing.'

The Chief didn't agree but didn't say anything to deny it either and waited for her to continue.

'But what about other things. Say pub opening times and dodgy MOT's. How do we police them?'

The Chef Inspector smiled. 'With the full force of the Law,' he said, before adding, 'We don't want lawlessness. However, if the occasion calls for it we should use common sense. If there is anything, and I mean anything at all that you aren't sure about, I am only a phone call away.'

'Well, speaking of that, there is one other thing. I have made a list of the stationary and other items we need to run an efficient station.'

She handed him the list of goods and sundries she had written earlier. The Chief Inspector gave it a cursory glance, nodding as he quickly perused it, then put it on top of the other files she had handed him. With that he left the office and the station, leaving her now in full charge of the cop shop and the two worthless P.C.'s. she had under her command.

This was not what she imagined her new career would be when she volunteered. She thought she would be based at Headquarters in Inverness, part of some crack investigation unit or the serious crime squad. Her own office maybe, a flat in the centre of town, exciting night life, fancy restaurants, cocktail bars, and a chance to meet a nice guy who wasn't a policeman. She couldn't be further from that the dream here in Glenfurny.

ANOTHER NEW BEGINNING

Denise left the boarding house with a spring in her step. Although there were more than a few questions to be answered about exactly what her role would be going forward, she was keen to make the right impression.

She had a feeling her two underlings wouldn't be happy with her, especially after she had drawn up some plans the previous evening about how she wanted to run things.

The police station lights were on, so somebody was there even though it was only 8:30, half an hour before "opening time."

Like the previous morning, both P.C.'s were present and the kettle was just coming to the boil.

'Just in time, tea boss?' Billy asked.

She smiled. Last time he called her that she had baulked at it, now it was for real.

'Please. Should I be bringing biscuits?'

The coppers looked at each other and smiled but said nothing. They didn't seem to object to the suggestion either.

They settled down with their drinks and Denise decided to jump in feet first and share with them with the part of her plan that involved them.

'How would you feel about working alternate days?'

When she had written it down she had thought it was self-explanatory, work one day off the next. It was simple, it wasn't exactly rocket science.

However, the 2 men just stared blankly at each other before Billy finally spoke.

'What do you mean?'

'Well,' Denise tried to explain, 'for example if you worked Monday you would have the Tuesday off then work Wednesday and have Thursday off. When you are off Billy, Andrew will be working.'

'Why?'

'So, we have cover for every day. Policing shouldn't be part-time like we are doing here.'

Andrew seemed to have worked it out quicker than his young workmate. 'You mean you want us working weekends?'

'Yes. But you will only work one day each weekend, unless you want to swap with each other and work alternate weekends.'

Andrew put his tea down and folded his arms, showing defiance.

'We don't do shifts,' he said indignantly.

'It's not shifts, it's days but by splitting it we provide weekend cover.'

'Ah, then that is the same. In addition, we would be entitled to shift allowance. Headquarters have already told us we were strictly dayshift workers. Monday to Friday, 9 till 5.'

'When was this?' Denise asked.

'If I remember correctly it was in March 1964.'

'That was 9 years ago. Things have changed since then. What happens at the weekend?'

'They have to dial 999. Dingwall deals with it.'

Denise pulled a hand through her hair. When she was a

child, maybe 20 years ago, that was the way things would have been done. It would seem things hadn't evolved up here as fast as back in Ayrshire, or the rest of Scotland.

She never thought the guys would have been against the idea of change, but after all this time she should have realised they would be set in their ways. McCallum especially, as he coasted to his retirement. The question of it them getting extra money never entered her head.

Although headquarters had refused them before, she felt McKelvie would back her, he seemed keen to help her get things working better there. She would have to run it past him later.

'So, if I get the go ahead to get you more money would you consider it?' she said, hoping for a compromise.

Andrew smiled, as if he had won a small victory. 'No, we are not interested.'

She looked over at Billy Lambie. He hadn't said anything to his before colleague, who had answered for them both, spoke up.

'Billy, is that what you think?'

Billy stared down at his tea. He probably knew no matter what he said, it wouldn't be popular with one of the other two.

He didn't get a chance to answer because the station door was suddenly flung open. A dapper gent stormed in and rang the bell on the counter although he could clearly see the team were staring at him.

Denise put her cup down and walked over to the counter. Before she could speak the gentleman beat her too it.

'I am Stewart Urquart. I am the estate manager at the Drumbaggen estate. My farmhands have reported to me that we are losing sheep. It would appear to be at a rate of 1 every 8 days. Now, let me tell you these are some of the finest pedigree sheep in the Highlands and are very expensive. We are losing a lot of money.'

The estate manager had the air of an ex-military man. He was dressed in tweed and check and no doubt had plus fours, like a country gent, and Denise was sure he was the type of man who wouldn't suffer fools gladly.

'You are saying what, they are being stolen?'

'Yes, rustled.'

'How many sheep do you have?'

'Over 500.' He held up his hand, as if to stop the D.C. asking any stupid questions. Then he took a small black notebook from the inside pocket of his jacket.

'To be exact we have 521 at the last count which was yesterady,' he said after consulting his book.

'This rustling has been going on for about 2 months now which is why we have been doing regular counts and know exactly how many sheep we have.

We have obviously been trying to catch the thieves ourselves, but our estate is too large to cover with the staff I have, especially at night.'

'If it has been going on for about 2 months, why wait until now to report it?', Denise asked.

'What to Tweedledum and Tweedledee there and the Mad Hatter who unfortunately has just passed away?' He pointed over her shoulder to the 2 P.C.'s., still sitting, supping their tea

'No,' he continued, 'I spoke to my friend Chief Inspector John McKelvie last night about this when I heard there was a new police.'

He paused then, as if saying woman was a hard thing.

'A new police constable was stationed here, and he said you had arrived with a very good reputation.'

'So, if it's every 8 days, when do you expect the rustlers to strike next?'

Denise said rustlers instead of thieves because when she joined the force 10 years previously, she never expected to be out chasing "rustlers."

'The last one went missing last Friday, so we expect another loss over the weekend but probably tomorrow night.'

'Okay. Well, I am new to the area. Could you show me on the map your estate?'

There was a map of the local region on the wall just inside the office. Denise lifted the counter flap and let the estate manager in.

He raised his hand and pointed a neatly manicured finger over the outline of the estate, it seemed to cover most of the map.

'That is a very large estate, I am sure you would appreciate how difficult it would be for us to police it.'

'Well, I am sure with you in charge we will soon get a result. You know Chief Inspector McKelvie speaks very highly of you, so I will leave it in your capable hands.'

With that he turned and marched out. As he left he turned and said, 'Carry on chaps.'

He paused, realising his faux pas but turned and carried on out without correcting himself.

Denise walked over and wrote up in the daily book the details of their conversation. She had refrained from looking round, she could only think of her two P.C.'s as Alice in Wonderland characters and she was scared she would laugh out loud in front of them.

Behind her she could hear the men muttering to each other, probably about Urquart.

'Right,' she said when all the details were complete, 'this changes things. I need a volunteer to do nightshift tomorrow night with me.'

P.C. McCallum sat shaking his head, arms still folded in defiance.

'Why?' the younger officer asked, as if oblivious to the conversation Denise just had with Urquart.

'We are going on a stake-out.'

'Wow. A stake out. Real police work,' he said excitedly.

That was it, she had her volunteer.

McCallum just sat and continued shaking his head.

Denise walked over and studied the map. The amount of area Urquart had pointed out would need about 50 officers to stake out. She remembered a bit about map reading from school but there was a dotted line on the edge of the Drumbaggen Estate.

'What is this dotted line?' she said.

Without any prompting, Lambie walked over to her side.

'That will be the old Roman road. There are the remains of an old Roman fort at the top of it.'

'The Romans? Don't be so stupid, the Romans never settled this far north!'

Denise and Billy turned and faced Andrew; they were surprised at the old cop's animated outburst.

Now he had her attention he was keen to educate with his local knowledge.

'You have never been up there Billy, have you?'

Billy shook his head.

'There are the ruins of an old farmhouse up there and the lines on the map are the old farm road. You would need a 4x4 to drive up that road now. It was driveable up to about 5 years ago, but it's rutted and overgrown now. When I was a lad it was still a working farm, I knew the lad whose family owned it.'

He paused. 'That was Gemmel's farm, Tommy was their son's name. Got shot and killed in the war. He was their only kid, his parents never really recovered from that.'

The old cop then leaned over and put more coal on the fire and sat looking in the grate watching it.

When Denise realised that was all they were getting from the senior man, he had another question for him.

'Have we got a map of the district. You know, like the one on the wall. I fancy spending the rest of the day exploring the area.'

McCallum got up as if it was a bother to him and produced a map from one of the drawers beneath the counter.

Denise spent the day driving about the area in the yellow peril. The car needed a drive as it had been idle for the 4 days since she had arrived in town.

She found the old road they spoke about and drove up as far as she could. Parking up she walked a bit further on up the road. She could see there had been some vehicles using the road, obviously tractors or vehicles suited to the rough terrain beyond.

She had a hunch she was on the right track. Driving back down the road there was a sort of lay-by, just off the track and hidden by the surrounding undergrowth. That was where she planned to park up the next night to see if her hunch was right.

FRIDAY NIGHT: SATURDAY MORNING

Friday night and Denise was in her room, settled for a quiet night. Her only entertainment would be the small portable brought from the room above. She realised how stupid she had been, she still had both sets of keys for Les' room, so the television couldn't have been from there. It also dawned on her she would need to clear the room and gather the D.S.'s possessions to be sent to his next of kin.

Switching the telly on she had to waggle the aerial in every direction possible before a slightly crackly picture appeared. She put the old wooden chair in front of the telly and prepared to be entertained.

A few minutes later there was a quiet knock on her door.

She opened it to find the blonde builder from across the landing.

'Colin and I wondered if you fancied going down to the pub for a drink?'

'Sorry. I am all set for a quiet night in.'

'But it's Friday night. Nobody should be sitting in on a Friday night, especially a pretty young woman like you.'

She smiled at the compliment but wasn't swayed.

'How can I go out with a couple of guys whose names I don't even know?'

'That's easily remedied. I am Andrew West, but my mates

call me Andy. My other half is Colin', he motioned over his shoulder to his mate who was standing a fair bit behind, looking desperate to get to the pub, 'but we call him Coco.'

'Coco,' she said smiling. Thinking back, she had a few nicknames herself at school but thankfully none that she carried into adulthood.

'Well?' Andy asked again.

'I don't know Andy; it's been a long day. In fact, it's been a long week.'

The young man looked very disappointed.

'Look, we are working tomorrow morning, so we are only going out for a few drinks. Besides, I bet you don't know many of the natives. They are a colourful lot. It will be a chance to get to know some of them.'

'Okay, give me 10 minutes to freshen up.'

'Right, we will wait down the stairs,' he said as a big smile broke across his face.

Denise suddenly felt like an 18-year-old again, as if she was getting ready for a date. Of course, it wasn't a date, he was probably not 20 yet, she was nearly 10 years older. But it was nice that somebody would think about her and realise she would be stuck in her room.

She quickly did her make-up and changed her top. Normally her work clothes were very conservative, all buttoned up, so she picked a top that showed a glimpse of bosom. Not hanging out, she didn't have enough to hang out anyway, but giving just a hint of her womanliness.

The lads were talking excitedly when she walked down the stairs but went quiet when they saw her.

'So, The Pheasant Plucker is it?' she asked,

'It's all there is,' Coco said blankly.

'Don't bother with him,' Andy said. 'He wanted to go to the dancing down at the caravan park. If we went there we wouldn't make it to work in the morning.'

'Oh, is that the park down near the waterside. Is there dancing down there?'

'Yes. It's busy some weeks but other times it's just wee kids. Jail bait all boozed up.'

'What, do you mean there is under-age drinking?'

This suddenly changed the atmosphere. The lads stopped talking and looked at each other. They just remembered who they were talking to, the police.

Denise realised she could quickly ruin a good night out if she didn't relax the atmosphere.

'Relax lads, I'm off duty. I am not going to suddenly race down there and arrest folk or shut it down.'

As they approached the pub they had to move onto the road as a small dishevelled looking man approached. Staggering from side to side, as he walked with his head down, he was taking up the whole path, and muttered to himself as he passed. He probably hadn't even noticed there was anybody else there.

Denise noticed the two lads shrug, obviously they knew him.

They stopped outside the pub. Even from outside it sounded lively. Coco stepped forward and opened the front door.

Denise loved the wall of noise that spilled out from a busy pub, it seemed to envelop, drawing you into the cheerful atmosphere. Only when she was off duty, of course. While working, the effect was the opposite, something she dreaded.

However, things died a bit when she walked in. Eyes were upon her. Not being a complete stranger to this kind of reception, she walked proudly to a seat near the back of the pub and sat down as if she belonged there.

Andy and Coco walked over with her.

'What are you having?' Andy asked.

That was a thought. It was ages since she had been in a pub for a drink. In fact, it was a while since she had any alcohol at all.

'Vodka and coke. If they will serve me.'

'Of course, they will. We come every night and they serve us.'

Coco and Andy went to the bar together leaving her alone. Gradually the noise levels seemed to be getting back where they had been before she walked in. Still, there were a lot of furtive looks as people came to terms that not only did they have a new cop in the town but also it was also a woman.

The lads joined her with their drinks. Andy settled down but Colin seemed to have ants in his pants and didn't seem happy just sitting.

After a couple of mouthfuls of drink, Coco left them and circulated going round the pub, chatting to folk here and there. At first she thought Andy had told his mate to clear out and not cramp his style, but she soon saw Coco was a butterfly drinker. Not content with being in one person's company for too long before moving on renew another acquaintance.

She wondered if she was the gist of much of the conversation.

Andy was quiet at first. He would talk about the other drinkers without pointing at them but rather describing them in quite funny and flowery terms.

'That bloke, old Archie, him with the tartan bunnet and face like a skellpit arse is always on the seat in the corner. They reckon they will put the chair in his coffin when he gets buried.'

Funnily enough, Denise did recognise the old, red- faced guy who had been sitting in the same spot the last time she had popped in the pub a few days previously.

'Thone old dog wae the boob tube and skirt up her arse, you see the wan, mutton dressed as lamb. Well, she leaves here every night with a different man. Bendy Wendy we call her, for obvious reasons. Boaby daft she is.'

Denise loved the timbre to Andy's voice and the expressions on his face as he spoke. The thought of the woman being so loose with her body gave him a disgusted countenance.

'Coco took her home one night. He didnae just get a nightcap either.'

Denise was also disgusted at the thought of the old cradle snatcher but buoyed by the vodka, wanted a laugh.

'What about you? Have you not been offered her?'

She paused then added, 'affections.'

Although she hadn't known the lad long she was surprised at the utter disgust on his face at the very suggestion.

'With that? It would be like throwing a sausage up an alleyway!'

Heads around them turned as he had raised his voice a bit much in the excitement of the moment.

Denise burst out laughing and Andy joined in. The heads turned away, realising it was a private joke and nothing more but also they weren't going to be privy to it.

For the next hour Andy gave a character assassination of everybody in the pub in his own outrageously funny way. A mixture of the vodka and his patter had Denise laughing so much her ribs were sore. She realised it was just the tonic she needed.

Andy nipped to the loo. Denise had given him a pound for the next round and sat quietly enjoying the happy atmosphere when a dark shadow appeared before her.

'Inspector. Nice to see you again.'

She looked up to see it was the bar owner.

'It's Constable. Detective Constable Kelly.'

She never proffered a hand. Normally she liked to do that and give as manly a grip as she could, letting people know she was no soft touch. There was something about the man that she didn't like. Something that made her skin crawl even by the way he looked at her.

'Oh, it's Constable just now but it won't be long before it's Sergeant then Inspector. I read in the Herald about the great lack of Police there is up here in the Highlands. There was a bit of an undertone to the article implying that women were being fast-tracked to senior positions.'

Denise didn't speak, she had a feeling this guy was a smart cookie, and he had a point to make. He was just taking the long way round to get there.

'I'm not from these parts either. Originally from the capital but I left Edinburgh many years ago. When I came here I quickly fell in love with everything. Especially the wildlife. The deer, wild hare and squirrel then there are the birds. The golden eagle soaring above is such an amazing sight. Then there are ptarmigan and Capercaillie. You know up here is the only place in Britain you will see them.'

While he paused for a breath, Denise wondered what the hell he was talking about. Women police climbing the social ladder then birds or whatever else he was talking about.

All the time he was speaking he was looking straight at her, his eyes continuing to look at Denise as he spoke.

'You know what bird really amazes me? The cuckoo. I watched a documentary recently about them. You will know, of course, that they don't build a nest but lay in another's. The cuckoo them hatches before the host's chicks and throws their eggs out of the nest. Killing the opposition, you could say.'

They were disturbed by Andy, who returned with their fresh drinks.

'I hope you are not implying I had any involvement in the death of the Detective Sergeant? I was down in Ayrshire at the time.'

'Oh no. Lesley was a weak man. His lifestyle would have got him sooner than later. I just think you will take the opportunity to take over the nest and remove the other birds.'

The pub owner then turned and left without another word.

'What was all that about?' Andy asked.

Denise shrugged. 'I think he was implying I was some kind of cuckoo.'

'The cuckoo cop. That's funny. Think I will call you that from now on.'

'Don't you bother, that's the way nicknames stick.'

The nickname might bother her, but the implication that she might use the Detective Sergeants death to her advantage did. The old curmudgeon didn't know the first thing about her.

Andy turned and looked at her.

'Your serious face is funny.'

Denise turned and looked at him. She didn't realise what the pub owner said was visibly bothering her but laughed when Andy pointed it out.

She turned and for the first time they stared in each other's eyes. Andy saw two hazel brown eyes looking at him, Denise saw his were the lightest, brightest blue colour.

They reminded her of the blue seas and skies of the Mediterranean, where she had holidayed less than 6 months previously. All the time they were there, she and her husband John were making love day and night. After it, she found out about his sordid affair with the other officer, and she wondered if he was thinking of his lover when he was screwing her.

Apart from everything else, that was what hurt her most.

Since getting serious with John, she had never as much as thought of another man. Until now.

When they started on their 3rd drinks Andy started to open up about himself.

He was a clever boy, smart enough to have gone to university, but his family couldn't afford it and, in fact, needed him to help finance the family home and his 3 young siblings after his father had drunk himself into an early grave. He sent most of his wages back every week.

He could also have gotten better jobs but preferred to work with his mate, Coco. They had been best mates since the first day of primary school. Coco wasn't the brightest, he confessed, and needed his mate to look after him at times.

Andy now looked at Denise. Her turn she thought, although she hadn't decided how much to let on about her private life.

Before she could speak Andy seemed to realise something about her life bothered her and he made a suggestion.

'Tell you what, let me guess why you are here.'

'Right, go on,' Denise said, 'this should be fun.'

She was keen to hear what her young companion thought.

'You are from the central belt.'

He looked at her from confirmation, which she nodded to, although Ayrshire was a bit further down south.

'What makes you think that?'

'Your accent, of course.'

'I didn't think I had one.'

'Exactly. You are here because you are running away from something, or more likely somebody.'

Denise shrugged slightly but didn't give anything else away and let him to carry on.

'You aren't wearing a wedding band, but although your arms and hands are nicely tanned, there is a white band where your wedding rings should be. So, I would guess you are married and have left your husband.'

'Well done Sherlock.'

Andy beamed proudly.

'I am getting divorced, but I am not really running away. The Highland Police Force were looking for volunteers to come up here for a year, so I jumped at it. It was a once in a career opportunity and felt now was the time to try something different.'

They were disturbed when the pub doors opened, and a couple made their entrance.

Similar to when Denise made her entrance, everybody paused at the sight.

Denise instantly recognised them; it was the couple from the general store. The store Indian and skunk head had walked in. Unlike Denise, they were happy to be the centre of attention. In fact, they cherished it.

Skunk-head, as Denise continued to think of her as, was almost posing as if she loved being in the spotlight.

They nodded and acknowledged a few friends, before heading to the bar where a space was suddenly cleared for them.

'Are they back together?' Andy wondered out loud.

'But they run the shop together.'

'Oh yes, but there has been a terrible atmosphere when they are both in it together. They have been living apart because of the affair.'

'Affair. Who was he going with?'

'Not him, her. Rita was going with Fergus Boothroyd.'

'Who is he?'

'The bar owner. You were talking to him earlier.'

'No way. That's his name is it? Fergus Boothroyd. So, was it a serious thing?'

'Sure was. He moved into the big house with her. Hugh moved out to the flat above the shop. That was about 4 months ago. It was the talk of the town for weeks.'

'Look at them now. Walking in bold as brass and standing at the bar in front of him.'

'Lot goes on in a wee town like this. I am sure you will soon find out.'

'Oh, I already have. This place is more interesting than I thought it would,' Denise said with a smile.

Coco rocked over with another drink for them. He had been circulating the room, talking to just about everybody.

'What's the word, Coco my man?' Andy asked.

'Most think that Les was murdered. He must have been shagging.'

He suddenly stopped, realising who was sitting with them. He thought before going on.

'Everybody thinks he must have been seeing somebody else's wife behind their back and they have done him in.'

'They are so far from the truth,' Denise said, laughing as he spoke. 'Maybe I should just stand up and tell them what really happened.'

Coco got animated. 'Would you?'

'Coco, I was joking. Anyway, he simply had a heart attack.'

'Then why did you ask us about when we saw him last?'

'Because I needed to cover every possibility. What if there was foul play like you said? If you saw a strange man hanging about outside that would have changed things but he simply went home alone and died in his bed. There was no sign of foul play.'

Coco started laughing. It became one of the laughs you get when you can't stop to tell others what you are laughing at.

'Coco, calm down. What are you laughing at, what's your joke?' Andy ordered his mate.

Coco whimpered as he controlled himself.

'Foul play. That sounds like he was shagging a chicken.'

Denise and Andy looked at each other. Although they knew what he was laughing at, and joined in, to them was funny, it just wasn't that funny.

'Who told you?' Denise asked Colin seriously. 'We found a dead chicken in his room. That was why he died, but it was supposed to be a secret.'

'No way,' Coco said, amazed at the revelation, his eyes nearly popping out of his head.

Denise held her laugh for as long as she could but eventually had to laugh. 'Got you there.'

'Aw man, you aren't supposed to be funny, you should be serious all the time, you are the polis.'

Now the other two laughed.

A loud bell clattered. 'Last orders folks,' Fergus called out.

'Oh my God, is that the time?' Denise said, looking at her watch, and struggling to focus on it.

'Want another before we go?' Andy asked.

The two were alone again. Coco was doing the circuit of the pub again, this time telling folk about the chicken and foul play story.

'No. A couple you said, that must be at least 4.'

'Have you enjoyed tonight?'

'What? I haven't had a laugh like this in years. Can't wait to get to my bed.'

'Sounds nice,' Andy whispered.

'On my own I am afraid,' she said trying to let him down gently.

Although feeling so good, the best she had felt in a long time, sex would be an ideal way to end the night. However, she needed to have a good reputation and having a one-night stand with somebody 10 years younger wasn't the kind of reputation that she wanted.

As they left the pub, Andy called over to Coco, who was talking to old mutton dressed as lamb bird, but he waved them away.

Walking up the hill to the boarding house Andy leaned in, trying to put his arm round Denise. She shrugged him off.

'Don't spoil a great night, Andy.'

'What? No, just thought you needed a bit of a cuddle. There is a bit of a chill in the air.'

'Good try, Casanova.'

The rest of the walk seemed to be under a little cloud. Denise just hoped Andy wasn't going to try anything else. He was a strong guy, but she was trained in self-defence techniques and didn't want to hurt him.

Denise put the key in her room door. She could feel Andy's presence behind her. However, when she turned round he was a few feet away, standing awkwardly.

He stuck out a hand to shake.

'Thanks for a lovely night.'

'Oh, come here,' she said, touched by his nice gesture.

The couple cuddled.

'Thanks for a great night,' Denise whispered in his ear.

As they separated, Denise looked into those lovely blue eyes; she couldn't resist.

They kissed. A peck on the lips at first then full-on kissing.

When they broke free, Denise turned the key in the lock and opened the door. Against her better judgment, she took Andy's hand and led him in.

Suddenly there was a loud crashing noise and a scream from directly below them.

Denise suddenly rushed forward and pulled her truncheon from under her pillow. She kept it close when she was most vulnerable but didn't sleep with it under there.

She rushed past Andy as the adrenalin kicked in. She took the stairs in 3 or 4's at a time, bounding down towards the trouble, whatever it was.

The door to Liz Wilson's apartment was closed but opened when she tried the handle.

'Police!' Denise yelled as she let herself in, lifting her truncheon ready to strike immediately if required.

Liz Wilson was standing with her back to her. Somebody was in front of her and had his hands round her throat, chocking her.

'Police!' Denise yelled again.

Her call hadn't deterred the assailant, Denise had no choice but to raise her truncheon and whacked the guy's arm with her baton.

'Let her go!' she screamed.

She recognised the guy now; it was the drunkard who staggered out of the pub as they were going in.

As Denise moved forward, a hand swung round and caught her firmly on her cheek. She wasn't too surprised, and her training meant she had turned from the blow, lessening the impact but she still felt it.

Responding, she whacked the guy's other arm with a heavy

blow from her persuader, as she called it.

She dropped her truncheon and grabbed the man's right arm and twisted it up his back, far enough to have him under her control.

'Who is this?' she shouted to Liz.

Liz couldn't talk, she was holding her throat and crying uncontrollably.

'It's Robin, her husband,' Andy said from behind her.

He had rushed down after her and stood at the living room door.

Wow, this surprised her. For some reason she had thought Liz's was on her own, her husband either dead and she was a widow or had left her. She seemed to have the downtrodden aura of someone who's partner was dead, or as good as.

'Andy, see Liz is okay. This guy is going to spend the night in the cells.'

Denise hadn't her cuffs so kept the pressure up on her prisoner's arm, enough to keep him under her control and keep him moving forward as they headed to the police station next door.

As he squealed and moaned about the pain, Denise read Robin his rights as she informed him he was being arrested. She was going to charge him with assault on a policewoman. If he was found guilty he would almost certainly get a spell inside.

Denise put her prisoner in the first cell and got the key from a hook on the wall and locked him in.

Robin sat on the bunk, rubbing at his arm, yelling at her.

'You've broke my arm you cow. You've got no right doing this. I was having a domestic disagreement with my wife; you had no right intervening.'

'Right, Robin, and you have no right hitting a police officer.'

'How was I supposed to know what you are. You don't look like a policeman.'

'I screamed at you twice.'

After that, Denise switched off to his abuse, she needed to get him out of there, she had her bed to go to.

Alone now, the moment had gone, and the excitement had sobered her up enough to realise bedding Andy was a bad move.

She got the number for the Dingwall office from another corner of the blotter. It rang for ages before it was finally answered.

'Good evening, Dingwall Police, how can I help?'

'Hi. It's Detective Constable Denise Kelly at Glenfunry station. I have a prisoner here and am looking for somebody to pick him up.'

'Pick them up. For what?'

'To take him there.'

'Glenfurny. Right, got you now. The thing is dear, you have cells there; he is your prisoner now.'

'But the station's unmanned.'

'You are phoning from there now, right?'

'Yes, but.'

'But what? You answered your own question. Is there anything else I can help you with?'

'Anything else? You haven't helped me with this,' she said then angrily slammed the phone down. This meant only one thing, she would have to spend the night there. That was the last thing she needed.

In the cell, the loud sound of her prisoner's snoring echoed in the emptiness of the room. Her prisoner had stopped shouting at her and conked out almost immediately.

That just made her night. She wouldn't sleep now, even if she wanted to.

The dinging of the Police station entrance doorbell sprung Denise into action. She must have been dozing but was quickly alert.

In the dim light she could see a shadowy figure holding a club.

First thing she thought was somebody was coming to rescue her prisoner. She was unarmed, her truncheon was back at the Band B, where she had dropped it.

'Denise are you there?', the possible assailant asked.

'Andy, is that you?'

Denise looked at the clock on the wall, she was sure it said 1 o'clock.

'I brought you your truncheon. I was waiting in your room for you to come back.'

Denise thought that sounded sweet until it dawned on her he was obviously just after sex. She switched on a lamp and got up and walked over to the counter. As she took the club from his hand, he tried to hold her hand as she took it.

'Andy son, the moments gone.'

'But I thought.'

Denise interrupted him. 'Look, I have to spend the night here now. Mister Wilson is in my custody, I can't leave him.'

'I could stay here with you,' he offered. Then he turned and looked over at the other cell.

Denise felt appalled that he wanted a fumble in a police cell.

'Andy, son, go to your bed. You have work to get up for in a couple of hours.'

Andy threw her room key onto the counter then turned and walked out without another word, leaving Denise feeling terrible for not letting him down gentler.

The whistling kettle brought Denise slowly from her slumber. For what seemed hours after Andy left she sat in the chair trying to get some much-needed sleep. She struggled to get comfy in the chair and had to listen to a chorus from her prisoner who, when he wasn't snoring, was farting loudly.

She must have fallen into a deep sleep at some time because right now she was coming to and wondering where she was.

Standing before her making tea was Robin Wilson, her prisoner.

'What the?'

Robin turned and smiled.

'Morning. Tea's up. What do you take?'

Denise looked over at the key rack and the cell key was where she had left it. The cell door was lying open.

'How did you get out?'

'That old thing? Piece of cake. Speaking of cake, I could go a piece of cake right now, I am starving. No, a bacon sarnie that would hit the spot. Oh, with brown sauce of course.'

'Mister Wilson, you do realise you are under arrest. You assaulted a police officer. This isn't something you can gloss over. This is a serious charge.'

Robin turned and smiled.

'Look love, my wife and I were having a slight tiff, a wee domestic. Somebody broke into my house and attacked me, I lashed out in self-defence. Any court in the land would side with me. Surely I am able to defend myself and my wife in our own home.'

'One, you weren't defending your wife, you were throttling the living daylights out of her. Secondly, I yelled police before as I came in the door then again before you hit me.'

'Honestly, I never heard you. I admit I was a bit worse the wear for the demon drink. You see I am a deep see fisherman. Every Monday morning, I head off and don't get back on dry land until a Friday morning. After 4 days without a drink, I am afraid I go straight to the pub when I get back to the town. I know I should get changed and have something to eat before I go out but when I used to go straight home Liz always has a list of things that need done. That wasted drinking time.'

'Right. Well, I don't know if Liz told you, but I have moved into the boarding house and I for one will not have any physical violence against anybody in the house, even if it was your wife. That doesn't give you any special rights, in fact it's worse, it's domestic abuse.'

'Okay, you are right. Let's have a cuppa together and you will see I am not a monster. It's just when I get a drink I have been known to get a wee bit out of order.'

Denise had been calm but Robin just pressed the wrong button.

'A wee bit out of order!'

She gritted her teeth before going on.

'Domestic abuse and aggravated assault on a police officer. That's more than a wee bit out of order.'

'You are right. Let's just have out tea.'

Robin then looked about although there was only the 2 of them in the room.

'You haven't got any whisky about. It's just I need a wee bit of something to take the edge off', smacking his lips as he said it.

'Mister Wilson, I think you are an alcoholic. Maybe you need treatment.'

'No, I can't be an alcoholic. I don't have any all week when I am on the boat, and I it doesn't bother me. Not in the slightest.'

They were disturbed by the doorbell clanging. They turned and saw Liz Wilson had entered. She looked tired and drawn, she probably had as good a sleep as Denise.

'I don't want to press charges,' was her opening gambit. She stood at the counter with her arms crossed.

Denise walked over. 'It's not a matter of that. He assaulted me.'

'You were off duty.'

'Whether he assaulted me, Denise Kelly or Detective Constable Kelly is of no matter. He assaulted me by striking my arm.'

Liz pursed her lips and stared at the policewoman.

'If you charge him I will go to the press and say you covered up Les' death.'

Denise realised this was probably why her landlady hadn't slept, deliberating over whether she could risk going to the papers if this strategy didn't work.

'I have a statement signed by 3 officers,' Denise hit back playing what she thought was her ace card.

Denise felt that in any court in the land the word of 3 police officers would be taken against that of Liz and her daughter.

'I have photographs,' Liz said, trumping Denise's ace.

'What? Why didn't you tell me before you took photographs?'

Liz smirked. 'As we agreed, it wasn't natural. I didn't know what I was dealing with, so I took some snaps as a sort of insurance.'

She took a spool of film out of her pocket.

'I haven't got it developed yet, couldn't risk getting it done at the local chemists. The deal, is I give you this, Robin walks.'

A deal. Denise was a policewoman; she couldn't go around doing deals to let people off with charges. Denise, the policewoman from U division in Ayrshire would have charged Liz as well. However, a bit like Dorothy in Oz, who wasn't in Kansas, she wasn't in Ayrshire anymore, she was in the Highlands force.

What would McKelvie tell her to do?

She put her hand out. 'Before I decide, how do I know this isn't just holiday snaps?'

'You will need to trust me the way I trust that you won't go after my Robin on some trumped-up charges after this.'

Liz dropped the film in Denise's hand.

'Come on you,' she said and turned to leave.

Robin sat his half-empty mug on the counter. 'Think the milk is ready to go off,' he said, before hurrying to catch up with his wife.

Denise looked down at the small roll of film. She would get this developed at a later date but right now it was going in the safe. She also knew another thing, first chance she had. she needed to get out of the Wilson's boarding house and find alternative lodgings. Preferably with her own bathroom.

STAKE-OUT

Denise turned up at the station at 9 o'clock and found Billy was already there and studying the map of the town and its surroundings on the office wall.

'I think the rustlers may be using this road here, the old Gemmell's place,' he said, pointing at the map.

'Billy, I already said that yesterday. I have been up there and found out a great spot to watch for rustlers. Is the car filled with petrol in case we have a chase?'

She said this with her tongue very much in her cheek. The old Morris Minor couldn't catch a push bike in a chase. If she used the yellow peril she might have a chance as the Avenger was quite nippy, but she couldn't use her car for official business without permission. Denise had asked McKelvie for a decent squad car and possibly a car for herself, she would need to wait and see what they got.

'You really think we could be having a chase?' Billy asked excitedly.

'If we have picked the right place to find them we will. Right, it's starting to get dark out there, we better get going.'

Denise went into the passenger seat and let Billy drive, let him live out his adventure. She had lived through enough adventures with the force in her career already, he could have his fun.

She soon realised it was a major misjudgement letting him drive, Billy drove like an old woman. A very careful, very slow old woman at that.

'Billy, have you ever been on an Advanced Driving course?'

'No. Is that a real thing, advanced driving courses.'

'Yes of course it is. I have done it. You learn to drive very quickly in a safe manner. Next time I see the Chief I will ask him about it. If I forget, remind me.'

'Great,' he said, grinning from ear to ear. This gave him a bit of a boost and he pressed down on the accelerator a bit. Just a little bit though, Denise wasn't suddenly thrust back in her seat by the g force.

They parked up, eventually, after Billy did what seemed like a 10-point turn to get the police car into position ready for the chase, if it came to that. Denise wasn't sure if the overhead conditions were convivial to rustling sheep that night. The moon was full but there was a heavily clouded sky. The clouds were scudding across meaning minute by minute they could be sitting in the dark then suddenly bathed in bright light.

'So, Billy, how long have you been a police officer?'

'I joined just over 12 years ago. My father was in the force, he was the local bobby, like me, but was totally against me following in his footsteps. When I left school I worked with the local joiner and learned the trade. My father died when I was 23 and the next year I joined up.'

'Why did he not want you to join?'

'He said it was too dangerous. In the end up it was pneumonia that killed him, not the job.'

Denise was surprised Billy was just over 5 years older than her, she would have thought him 10 years older, at least. The easy life for years had clearly taken its toll.

'Have you always been stationed here, in your hometown.'

'Yes, they tend to do that here in the Highlands unless you are a highflyer. Obviously I am not.'

'Don't be too sore on yourself. I think your problem is you seem to be too easily led by P.C. McCallum. You need to start to think for yourself more.'

Although they talked a lot, in-between times there were awkward silences. Mainly because Denise was asking all the questions and taking the lead.

'What about D.S.McCall, how did you get on with him?'

'I don't think he thought much of me. Used me to run errands for him. I also had to cover for him when he sneaked away to meet up with women.'

'So how are you supposed to learn how to be a good policeman if you are just running errands.'

That killed that line of questioning for a while.

'Are you saying he went to see women while he was on duty?'

Billy nodded, although he looked as if he was betraying a secret. Then he told her something that surprised her.

'Rumour has it Liz was one, he was always making excuses and nipping next door a couple of times a week. I don't think it lasted very long. I reckoned he liked the variety too much.'

Now Denise understood why Liz called Les' women floosies, the scorned woman.

That led to another pause in their conversations. Denise waited a few minutes before changing the subject.

'Did you really not know I was coming?' Denise asked, wondering how much he would say. He had denied it before but now he knew her a bit better maybe he would change her story now.

'No, I knew. McKelvie phoned him a few weeks ago and told him. McCall told us you were coming; he was really looking forward to it. Bragged that he would,' then he paused to choose his words carefully.

'He would bed you. Said you would be easy.'

Denise was flabbergasted. 'What made him think I would

be easy?'

Billy went quiet. For a minute Denise thought he hadn't heard the question.

'Billy, why did he think I would be easy?'

He still wouldn't speak up.

'Billy, he isn't here anymore, you don't need to defend him. You don't need to think he has an honour to protect either.'

'He phoned.'

'Phoned who?'

'I think it was the Irvine headquarters he phoned to ask about you.'

'What did he find out that made him think I would be easy?'

'He told us he spoke to your husband. He said you and him split up because you were having sex with half the officers in the station.'

'The bastard. Not McCall, my husband John. He is the dirty cheating scumbag that was cheating on me with a cadet. If the bosses found out he would have been sacked.'

Denise got so angry she excused herself and got out of the car. It was bad enough her husband was cheating on her but blacking her name to the folk at her new station was well out of order.

After 10 minutes she had cooled down and was calm enough to get back in the car.

'Are you all right?' Billy asked, concerned, when she sat back in.

'Sure. So having met me, do you think Les would have bedded me?'

'Well, he was a bit of a charmer with the women, but you are way, way out of his league.'

'Do you believe what my husband told Les; you know about me being a bit of a slapper?'

'I thought so at first, before we met. Now I know you, I know it's not true. You are lovely.'

They were plunged into darkness as another big cloud obscured the moonlight. Denise was glad because she was blushing at the compliment. She needed to go off in a tangent and there was something else that piqued her interest, Susan Wilson.

'What about Susan Wilson and her baby? Could Les be the father?'

'Who Les? No way. I spoke to Susan often, when I was sent to the shop for McCall's lunch. She said he was well creepy, he made her skin crawl, that was her words.'

'So, who is the father of her baby?'

'Nobody knows. She said she went to the dancing at the caravan park and had a one-night stand with a lad on holiday, but she never saw him again. Didn't even get his name, the name and address he gave her turned out to be false.'

'She said it, but do you believe it?'

'I don't know. The only thing I know for definite is it's not mine?'

Denise laughed gently, not as much as to mock him.

'What about the 2 lads from the building site, could it be one of theirs?'

'No. She was pregnant before they were on the scene.'

That ended that subject. Denise felt her throat was a bit dry, she wished she had brought her flask, although she hadn't got round to unpacking it yet. She was also struggling a bit with tiredness, especially after having to doze in the chair at the station the previous night. That was one of the reasons she tried to keep the conversation going. Billy wasn't helping very much.

In the middle of one of the silences, that were getting longer, Billy started yawning.

'Billy, maybe you should nip out and get a bit of fresh air.'

'No, I feel fine.'

'When was the last time you did nightshift?'

Billy blew out as he tried to remember. 'Must have been more than 11 years ago. It was when I was still doing my training and I was based in Inverness.'

Denise shook her head. That was also the end of that conversation.

Overhead it must have been cloudier as the darkness of the night crept in and the spells of bright light got less and less.

Denise opened her eyes and thought she was dreaming. The bright light from the moon had returned and rolling past was a small dark car. Looking out the back window was a sheep.

She wasn't dreaming, it was the sheep stealers going past.

'Billy, quick, start the engine! Get after them!'

'What? Who?' he said sleepily.

Billy had also dozed off and woke with a start when Denise shouted, realising where he was also taking a moment.

'Oh right,' he said, when his brain caught up with what was happening and turned the ignition keys.

After what seemed an eternity, and the third go at starting, the engine sparked into life.

'Follow that car!' Denise ordered. She had always wanted to shout that order but didn't imagine she would be sitting in a Morris Minor when she eventually got to say it.

Billy took the handbrake off, and the car slid slowly forward.

'For God's sake Billy, put your foot down. It's a chase, remember.'

He did and the old car went a little bit faster.

As they turned the corner they could see the other car was at the bottom of the hill a couple of hundred yards away. It now had its lights on and was quickly speeding away from them.

'For God's sake Billy, floor it. There they are well ahead now. Go for it.'

'We will never catch them in this old crate.'

'I know, but if you get close enough I might get a bit of the registration number or at least know what kind of car it is.'

Billy had the Minor flat out and were hitting a scary 50 miles an hour. They were going so fast the whole thing seemed to be shaking. However, the other car was still getting further away. Before they reached the outskirts of town they lost sight of them, then they came to a fork in the road.

'Which way?' Billy asked frantically.

'Left,' Denise guessed.

They drove on but a few minutes before the road broadened out into the countryside where they could see for miles, and it was clear there wasn't another motor car in sight.

'Shit, we've lost them. Turn it round Billy. Back into town, we might see somebody about.'

'I thought we should have gone the other way,' Billy said as he tried another 3-point turn that became a 5 or a 7 pointer.

'Why did you not say then?' Denise asked, exasperated. They lost the thieves because she made a wrong decision. A decision her demented sidekick should have known was the probably the wrong way to go.

'You are the boss, you said left.'

'Yes, but you live here. In a job like this you need to think like the thief, what would he be doing. We got a break because we were thinking like him that's why we were in the right place but lost it because of this banger.'

Billy drove on, back to his normal speed again.

'For God's sake man, you know more about this place but if you don't tell me what you know we won't succeed as a team.'

'Sorry, 'he said, then drove on round the town in silence.

The town was like a ghost town, no sign of life save for the odd stray cat creeping in the shadows. After 10 minutes, Denise had had enough.

'Look, there is no sign of them. Take us back to the police station. Besides, I will need to write this up.'

'Will you write that I didn't help,' he asked, downcast at the result of the nights endeavour and his part in it failing.

'What? Of course not, we are a team. The team failed but because we didn't have the correct equipment, that is, a decent squad car. That's what will go in the report.'

'Right. I will try harder; I want to be a good policeman and do my father proud.'

'Of course, you will, and I will help you.'

BUMP IN THE NIGHT

Denise sent Billy home and wrote up her report and added to the daily journal with an update on the investigation about the stolen sheep. When she finished she saw it was nearly 2 o'clock. She smiled to herself, at least she wouldn't have to stay there that night.

The moon re-appeared from between the clouds as Denise turned to lock the station door. It was so bright it seemed more like 2 o'clock in the afternoon. The policewoman thought she heard something behind her and was about to turn to investigate when she felt something clamped over her face. There was a strong chemical smell then everything went black.

Denise woke with a blinding headache. The pain so bad she couldn't even open her eyes. Her hand ran over the top of her head right over to the back of her head, thinking she must have been thumped but she was surprised there was no wound.

Next, she tried to open her eyes. Even that was a struggle, when she did manage it her eyesight was blurred. It was only through the blurred images that she started to realise where she was. Well, it looked like she was lying on a bunk in one of her own cells.

Denise tried to get up, but the pain shot through her head. She lay back down and closed her eyes. Her head dropped down and landed on the bunk, sending another bolt of pain through her head.

Rather than try and get up she rolled onto her side and tried to work out what had happened. Clearly she had been knocked out and ironically locked up in her own jail.

'Need sleep,' she muttered then allowed herself to drift off again.

Her eyesight cleared when she tried opening them again sometime later. The cell door was closed, maybe it wasn't locked.

When she tried to get up she felt really uncomfortable feeling between her legs. She sat back down and cried. Although she couldn't remember anything, she somehow knew before checking she had been assaulted sexually.

Slowly she unzipped her trousers and slipped them down a bit. She started to peel down her panties. The first thing she saw was that the label, that said Next, was at the front. How bloody ironic.

'No!' she screamed into the darkness. There was no way she would put them on back to front, somebody had removed them then replaced them.

Looking further inside she was scared to find blood, thankfully there was none. She prayed they had simply had their fun and not damaged anything down there. She would need to get to hospital to get herself checked over.

Pulling her trousers back on she managed to get up and walk slowly over to the cell door. She pulled at the bars on the door but, as she suspected, it was locked solid. The keys were left on the counter opposite to mock her. How embarrassing would this look, locked in her own jail in the first week of a new job.

Oh God, she thought, what if word got back to Ayrshire? They would have a field day at her expense. Probably all down there waiting for something like this to happen, waiting for her to fail so they could slag her off and laugh at her expense. That was what made her all the more determined to succeed. To do that, she needed to get out of there first.

A wave of nausea swept over her, suddenly she felt as if she was going to be sick. Her body felt completely drained. Slowly, she walked back over to the bunk and lay down gently again, aware of all her sore bits. She closed her eyes and slowly the nausea subsided.

"Denny. Denny love, time to get up. No, dad, 5 minutes more. Come on, you have work. Work, no, I am still at school. No, you are a police officer now. Come on, get up and catch those criminals that did this to you."

A puff of air blew into Denise's face waking her up with a smile on her face, her father woke her like that when she was a little kid and couldn't get up for school.

'Dad,' she said, looking out to see his smiling face, then reality kicked in. She wasn't in her bed at home, then she remembered her father was dead and she realised she was lying on a bunk, locked in a jail cell, and she had been knocked out, assaulted and probably raped.

She put her hands to her face ready to cry when in her head she heard her father's voice again, this time in her head.

"My wee Denny wouldn't lie there crying. No, she would get up and get out of there and catch the buggers."

She laughed to herself. Her father never swore, buggers was strongest word used and only used it when he was really angry. Although the voice was in her head, it was the kick on the arse, verbally, she needed.

Dawn was just breaking outside and there was enough light in the cell her to let her take stock. Her head still hurt but her eyesight was now clearer. There was still discomfort at the top of her legs but only when she thought about it or moved too quickly.

She tried the cell door again; it was locked solid. She should have insisted Robin told him the secret of his escape the previous morning. The big wall clock told her the time was just after 7 o'clock. Just under a day until she would be saved, unless somebody missed her. Fat chance of that, she thought.

She took her jacket off and squeezed an arm between the

bars as she tried to reach across towards the counter gauging the scale of her task. She was still about 2 feet short of the keys, she only needed something to bridge the gap to reach the keys and her freedom.

All that was in the cell was the bunk. The cushion came off and she tried slipping it between the bars. Bugger, she thought it was too thick to fit through the bars. The bedframe was firmly bolted to the wall, so it wasn't coming off. That only left her with the clothes she had on. Her handbag strap would have been ideal, but her bag was on the countertop too.

Her bra! It was another Eureka moment for her. She quickly took her top and bra off. Excitedly she hurried back to the task and slipped her arm between the bars. Tightly holding one end, she cast the underwear and it landed on top of the keys. As she slowly pulled it back it slid over the keys without making an impression on them.

Denise had started to get excited at first but soon realised the bra itself wasn't going to be any good. The key was big and heavy and on a large steel ring, something that surely dated back the best part of a hundred years.

What was needed was a hook. Nothing, she had nothing like that in there with her. Then another idea came into her mind- one of her shoes, she thought, that might do. If she could get the heel into the ring it would let her pull the keys toward her.

Tying the shoe to one end of her bra she had the weirdest looking fishing device ever. Now she had the equipment, next she needed the right technique.

She tried one way then another. If she wasn't so determined to get out she would have given up after an hour but right then failing wasn't an option. Not now she had gone this far.

Then, like getting 8 draws on the Pools, the heel of her shoe landed a direct hit in the ring. Scared to breath, she delicately pulled her end of the bra. Slowly, very slowly, it moved towards the edge of the counter. Her heart seemed to beat faster as success drew nearer.

It moved very slowly near the edge, then it was on the edge, then with a bang it was off and landed on the floor.

Denise scrambled to her knees and reached across, she was still about a foot short of reaching, but angling from there would definitely be easier.

She was disturbed by a tap tapping. Standing up, she looked around to see where the tapping was coming from. As it got a bit louder and more hurried, she found the source. The tapping was coming from the glass on the front door and Robin Wilson was ogling in at her.

He winked at her then brought his hands up as if he was cupping his breasts.

Denise looked down and was horrified. In her desire to get out as quickly as she could she hadn't bothered, or just forgotten, to put her top back on, her bare breasts clearly on show to her voyeuristic landlord's husband.

Quickly grabbing her top and turning to put it on, it suddenly dawned on her she hadn't put too much thought into who had done this to her. She had imagined it was connected to the sheep stealers, but an old police adage was that quite often the perpetrator of a crime would return to the scene of his crime, to admire his handywork.

Although if it was Robin, he had been admiring something else a minute ago. The station door opened, and Robin walked in and bent down to retrieve the keys.

'What are you doing here anyway?' she asked, with a bit more attitude than was necessary.

Robin looked at the keys then the captive behind bars.

'My wife was worried about you. She thought you had

maybe arrested somebody again last night and had to spend another night here. I just came over to see if you needed something to eat.'

He shrugged then pointed the keys at the lock.

'If you would rather I left you alone I will,' he said, before turning to put the keys back on the counter.

'No, no. I am sorry Robin. I didn't mean to say it like that, but somebody knocked me out last night then locked me in here. I'm not in the best of moods. Could you please just let me out?'

'Of course, love. I was going to anyway,' he said with a wink and a cheeky smile.

Denise picked up her jacket, grabbed her bra shoe fishing combination and other shoe and got out of the cell as soon as the door was opened.

'Tell me something, how did you get out yesterday morning?'

Robin smiled. 'Did you not know there was a spare key on the windowsill?'

'You are joking me,' Denise said, looking at him as thinking he would laugh. Instead, Mister Wilson walked past her, went over to the windowsill and lifted a key from it.

'Do you want this?' he asked.

'No, put it back in case I need it again,' she said, and they both laughed but the laughing just gave her a jolt to her sore head.

'One more thing, you won't tell anyone about this?'

She knew it was a big ask, especially as, just over 24 hours previously, he had been her prisoner.

'What, I can't even tell anyone you have a cracking pair of threepenny bits?'

'Especially that,' she said.

He laughed, but she refrained, aware of the cost.

As they walked over to the boarding house Robin asked her if she had any idea who could have done it. She explained about the sheep rustlers and following them. Then she asked him what he had been up to the previous night.

'Last night, Liz and I stayed in. We watched a bit of telly and had an early night.'

'That's good, no boozing or bad behaviour.'

'You can't be much of a policewoman.'

This got Denise angry. She was ambushed and coshed, that was why she ended up in the cell. How did getting jumped like that make her a bad cop?

'You think so,' she said, again with the attitude.

'Yeah, if you can't tell when somebody's lying. I was down the Pheasant Plucker early doors and stayed there until I couldn't drink anymore, like every other Saturday night. This is an early rise for me, I would still be in bed if Liz hadn't been worried about you.'

'Oh, right, well tell Liz thanks and thank you too. That's one I owe you. Now I have to go.'

'Go. Aren't you coming in for breakfast?'

'No, I have to go to the hospital and get checked over.'

CHECKED UP AND OUT

Denise drove the 12 miles to the hospital with her window fully open. The cold morning air worked wonders. By the time she arrived at the hospital she felt okay. Maybe she was wasting her, and the medics, time but she could be in trouble with her superiors if she didn't get checked out and was seriously ill afterwards.

As she stood outside she gulped hard before entering the large imposing glass and wooden entrance. Her memories of hospitals were all bad, visiting her mother, as she was wasting away from the Cancer that was eating her from within.

Inside though, it wasn't like that hospital, Kilmarnock Infirmary, which was a typical large, Victorian, purpose-built building. This had obviously been a private mansion that was converted to suit the needs of a hospital, probably during one of the wars.

The receptionist asked her a load of questions before finally telling her to take a seat.

After answering each one she thought more and more she was wasting everyone's time.

The waiting room was empty but still she had to wait for what seemed ages. Eventually a young doctor emerged from a door marked Emergency Room.

'Miss Kelly?'

As she was the only one there it seemed a rhetorical question, although she was still technically Mrs. Kelly, but she confirmed anyway.

She walked into a pleasant but dated treatment room where a nurse was waiting who helped her off with her jacket.

'What seems to be the problem?' the young Doctor asked, looking her over as he spoke.

'I was knocked unconscious in the early hours of this morning. Thought I better get it checked out?'

'Best sit down,' the medic said. With that the nurse showed her to a chair next to the inspection table.

Meantime, the young medic kneeled down in front of Denise and shone a torch in her eyes, all the time asking if she had experienced any ill-effects, dizziness, nausea, blurred vision.

She told him about the blurred vision and the nausea when she woke up first time, to which he just nodded.

'Why did you not come in earlier?' he asked.

'I was slightly unconscious,' she said, trying to lighten the mood a bit.

'Do you know who did this? Was it your husband, boyfriend, lover?'

'No, no and no, I don't have any of those.'

'So, you have no idea who did it?'

'No. They sneaked up behind me and next thing I was out cold.'

'Sounds like your assailant was a fan of Sherlock Holmes.'

'Sherlock Holmes?'

'Yes. The means of knocking someone out in his stories was using chloroform. You have described the classic symptoms of being overcome by chloroform, the nausea, dizziness and splitting headache.

You know I am going to have to report this to the police,' he added.

'No need, I am the Police.'

The doctor's eyes widened. 'Really?'

She put a hand out to introduce herself. 'Detective Constable Denise Kelly.'

'Doctor Grant Jamieson, at your service,' he said reciprocating and being surprised at the strength of her handshake for such a small hand.

'Was it only your head was affected?'

Denise pursed her lips. 'Well, no, the thing is, I was wondering if there were any women Doctors on duty. The rest is a bit delicate and personal'

The young Doctor put his hands out as an apology.

'Sorry, we are a small hospital and it's only me on duty today. The other Doctor's won't be in until 9 o'clock tomorrow.'

'Do you think I could make an appointment to see the gynaecologist tomorrow.'

'You are in luck; I am the resident gynaecologist here.'

If there anything Denise didn't want the medic to say, that was it. She closed her eyes and suddenly the emotions, the worry and the thought of exactly what some stranger had done to her body bubbled up within her.

The result was the mask cracked. In fact, it shattered. The façade of the hard-faced cop she normally lived by was replaced by the that of a young, vulnerable woman, who suddenly started sobbing uncontrollably.

The nurse quickly moved closer and comforted her.

'Denise, no matter how bad you think it is, we can help. That's what we are here for. The sooner we deal with it, the sooner we make it better,' the Doctor said when she manged to get back some control of her emotions.

Denise managed to tell them through the sobbing that she thought she had been sexually assaulted.

The nurse handed her a tissue then cuddled her again. She couldn't imagine one of the nurses back in Kilmarnock cuddling like that.

'Come on love. We will go through to Grant's room and get you looked at. He is a great gynaecologist,' the nurse said, smiling.

The nurse, who Denise had guessed was about her age, then helped her up from the chair and led her through a maze of corridors to the Doctor's own surgery.

Having actually said what had been done it brought a huge sense of relief to her. With the nurse's help she stripped off her trousers and knickers and managed to get up on the examination table. Her legs were gently put up on the leg caps by the nurse.

When the young medic walked in Denise felt so vulnerable, exposed as she was in that position. She suddenly hoped down there wasn't too smelly, then there was the grooming. When had she last trimmed it? With not having any sign of a possible active sex life for ages, it wasn't something she had been tending to recently.

The Doctor went to the bottom of the table and started running his hands on the top of her legs.

Denise looked at the ceiling and bit her bottom lip. Here she was, legs akimbo and lying-in front of a gorgeous young man. It was at that moment she realised the biggest problem; she fancied the doctor. Not in an "everybody fancies their doctor" type of thing but more a really, love at first sight thing.

Yet here he was about to get more intimately acquainted with her than usual at a first meeting.

She closed her eyes; how could she be even thinking thoughts like that after what had just happened to her just a few hours before? She was brought back to reality when the doctor spoke.

'Are you sexually active?'

'Not for about 6 months.'

'And you have no idea what was done or who did it?'

'No. I was unconscious then woke up, alone and sore.'

'Right, to start this could be sore but it will feel cold because I have lub on.'

Denise put her hands over her eyes and tried not to think about what the Doctor was doing. She felt a bit of discomfort as he examined her, especially at the internal but he must have been very gentle because although it was uncomfortable, she didn't feel any pain.

After a few minutes the medic whispered something to the nurse.

Denise felt her legs being gently taken off the supports and a towel or cloth placed gently over her nether region. She managed to relax a bit, realising the worse seemed to be over. She looked up and saw the Doctor was looking at her sympathetically.

'Denise, you are right, you have been sexually abused or at least the person did have sex with you. There isn't signs of any trauma and I think he must have used a condom.'

Denise gave a sigh of relief. The thought of pregnancy hadn't even entered her mind until that moment. Now it was brought to mind, the thought of carrying some rapist's bastard child sent a shiver through her.

'I wouldn't imagine there will be any long-term effects, and I am sure you will be back to normal in a week or so.'

'Thank you Doctor, that is such a relief.'

'Right, you can get dressed now, I will give the nurse a prescription and she will give you some strong painkillers which will take the edge off any pain you might be experiencing.'

'Thank you doctor,' she said before following the nurse through the maze of corridors to get out.

Driving back towards Glenfurny and her lodgings, the sun was up, it was looking to be a lovely day. For the first time she noticed how beautiful the countryside was. Sure, Ayrshire had nice country views, but this was on an altogether different level.

Everybody who visited the Highlands said the scenery was stunning, now she knew why.

Round every bend there was another stunning vista to feast the eyes. She wished she was the passenger on the journey rather than driving, so that she could spend more time drinking in the beauty of the countryside before her.

Yet there was a dark underbelly here, something she had found out starkly in less than a week.

WHODUNNIT?

Denise was a morning person but on that Morning she woke even earlier than normal. Dawn was just breaking, and light flooded into her room, she hadn't drawn the curtains the previous night.

Suddenly she got a fluttering in her chest that climbed up into her throat and caused an eruption of tears. What was scrambling her head and emotions was the events of the Saturday morning. What had this guy done to her and why? The violation of her most private parts was the worst thing she could imagine happening to her. Maybe she should just pack up and crawl back to Ayrshire. At least take the day off work, she was owed at least that.

There again, what did that hold for her now? She had no family back there, just bad memories. No home, few friends. What little she had here was as much as she had in Irvine.

She managed to stop the sobbing and got up and made for the bathroom.

The image she saw in the mirror was a washed-out version of herself with red, almost bloodshot eyes.

'Look what this shit had done to you.'

She pointed her first finger of her right hand to the mirror.

'You aren't going to lie about feeling sorry for yourself. You need to get back to work and catch whoever did this to you and make him pay.'

The only after effects of her assault was that peeing was a bit painful, more tingly than really sore, it wasn't as bad as she had hoped or imagined it would be.

She popped a couple of the painkillers and quickly washed. Now with her vigour was renewed, and she was going all out to catch the filth that had abused her and quickly.

Although Denise was early, even for her, the two P.C.'s were already there, she found them looking at the notes she had written on Sunday morning before she left the station for the first time.

'Thanks for not dropping me in it,' Billy Lambie said, pleased it was only the Morris she said was at fault.

Denise smiled. 'We are a team. We lose as a team, and we will win as a team.'

'What I don't get is this note at the bottom.'

'What note?'

'It says "stop now", in capital letters. The writing looks different to the rest.'

Denise hurried round to the other side of the counter as fast as she dared and took the book from Billy. She read it and looked at the other two policemen. She had wondered how much she should tell them about her experience after Billy had left her. No point in keeping secrets now, she decided.

'Sit down. Both of you.'

The guys sat and started to look worried from the tone she ordered them with.

'On Sunday morning, as I was leaving the station, I was attacked from behind and knocked out. The doctor at the local hospital reckoned they used chloroform.'

This had a jaw dropping effect on both the guys.

'No way,' Billy said.

'I was brought in here, sexually assaulted and locked in the cell there.'

McCallum shook his head whereas Lambie suddenly got animated.

'It's my fault, I shouldn't have left you,' he said.

'No Billy, it's not your fault. There is no way we knew somebody would resort to doing something as low and sickening as this.'

'It's not right,' McCallum started saying, then kept repeating it to himself.

'So, our number 1 priority is to catch the bastard that did this,' Denise added.

'Are you okay?' Billy asked.

'As well as can be expected.'

As she spoke she looked over at Andrew McCallum, who was still muttering away to himself.

'Andrew, are you okay?'

'What? No. I mean yes. Eh., I need to go a place.'

'What about your duties?' she asked, he was exasperating her to a new level, 'I need you both now.'

'This is more important, it is my duty,' he said, as he buttoned up his uniform jacket and walked past her and out of the station.

'What's that about Billy?'

'Search me.'

'Just me and you then Billy.'

'Right boss, what's the plan?'

'I think we need to come at this from another angle. I want you out making enquiries about cheap lamb. If they are stealing sheep then it must be to sell the meat. They can't be selling it legit, so it must be from the back of a van, if you know what I mean. Right?'

'Right,' Billy said, then thought about it. 'Who will I ask?'

'Billy, you are the local guy here. Money's tight everywhere. A lot of people like a bargain, no questions asked. Do you know what I mean?'

Billy nodded.

'This is where you need to start thinking for yourself.'

Billy started to look worried but with Denise's faith in him, he got up and rubbed his hands.

'I'm on it,' he said, heading out the station with a spring in his step.

Then he popped his head back in.

'Sorry if you think I let you down yesterday.'

'Billy, for the last time you didn't let me down. Don't mention it again. Now, go out there and help me catch the bastard that did this to me.'

Billy suddenly had the most determined look on his face then gave her a big thumbs up and left.

For once Denise was going to neglect her duty a bit, although she felt she was owed a bit of time off for the time and effort she had already put into her new career there already.

She checked the magazine rack in the corner of the office, looking for the latest local newspaper. Her priority, after her recent dealings in the boarding house, was to try and find new digs as soon as possible.

She was out of luck. Then it dawned on her where she had seen one, Anne, one of the other boarders, was reading it at the breakfast table this morning in the boarding house.

Slowly, she made her way back to the B and B. As she walked in she could hear vacuuming from somewhere up above.

The dining room was empty, so she checked the magazine rack and found the local rag.

Rather than sit there and read it, she headed back to the police station.

Denise hadn't held out much hope of finding decent digs, but her luck seemed to be in. Bedsit in the town, shared bathroom in converted house wasn't perfect but was better than the boarding house, which was too close to the cop shop for comfort.

Dialling the number, it was eventually answered by a posh sounding woman who told her the address and would be in all morning if she wished to view it right away as she had asked.

Denise noted the details and checked the street map on the wall. It seemed ideal, about 5 streets away, close enough for work and far enough away to not be on her front door.

She took the yellow peril and headed there right away. She got parked outside the door, there were only a few other cars in the street.

The area seemed nice. All sandstone terraced houses, many appeared like this one to have been converted to flats.

Marion Lewis answered the door at the first knock. Denise was surprised, she was a lot younger than she sounded on the phone.

Marion Lewis was a very stylish 40 something, and a looker for her age. She dressed in cargo pants and blue and white striped top and had curves in all the right places. Her make-up neatly applied, and her heady perfume smelled expensive.

'Denise, I take it.'

When she spoke, she sounded like she had on the phone, as if she had a plum in her mouth. It sounded a bit put on to Denise.

Denise nodded then followed her new landlady inside then

up the internal stairs. The place seemed too good to be true. Her apartment was on the first floor and the bathroom was only shared with one other tenant, although the other room wasn't let yet.

There were only 2 issues after Denise had been given the full tour. One was the décor that was bland. Magnolia with other shades of magnolia but she could live with it and put some soft furnishings to add a splash of colour here and there, the other, that she couldn't change, was her job.

Denise had heard that a lot of landlords shy away from members of the police force. Marion Lewis was keen to tell her about her hectic social life, golf in the afternoon, bridge club on Wednesdays, the endless dinner parties but hadn't thought to even ask anything about her potential tenant.

'Would you like a coffee,' Marion asked her. Denise had a feeling it certainly wouldn't be instant, something more exotic and obviously more expensive.

'Sorry, I am not a coffee fan. I haven't really the time, I am on duty.'

Marion looked her up and down, trying to guess her occupation. Then it seemed something clicked.

'You must be our new policewoman. I have heard about you.'

'Oh, all good I hope.'

'Yes, yes. We were at Marjorie Dunwoody's house on Friday, and somebody said you actually had our resident plods out on the beat. So funny.'

'So, me being in the police isn't a problem?'

'What? Of course not. In fact, it will carry a bit of kudos. My friends will be so jealous.'

'Good, well if everything is okay, when can I move in?'

'As soon as you like.'

'Is tomorrow okay?'

Next thing Denise had to do was tell Liz Wilson she was moving out. At the boarding house she found her having a cuppa in the kitchen.

'Hi. Is everything okay?' Liz asked, 'you know, after yesterday. I meant to pop up and see you were okay, but you know what it's like in here, everybody wants a bit of you.'

'I am okay. Well, as good as could be. The reason I am here is to tell you tell you that I am moving out tomorrow.'

'Oh. What's wrong?'

'With the digs? Absolutely nothing. The food's great. In fact, if I keep eating your food I will be the size of Hattie Jacques in a month. No, it's just too close to the station. I haven't been able to switch off since I got here.'

'Suppose so. Well, I will need to keep the money you paid for the rest of the month,' she added almost apologetically.

'No, you're fine. I paid for the month; you keep that. Take it as lieu of notice.'

Liz smiled, every penny was a prisoner to her, and it was good to have that wee bit extra.

While they were sitting in the kitchen a thought came to her at a tangent, they seemed to eat a lot of lamb. Sure, the Highlands were renowned for their lamb, but it wasn't cheaper than beef. Fact was, it was often a bit more expensive.

'Anyway, I know you are struggling. At least the cheap lamb helps.'

'Yes, it does.'

As soon as the words were out, Liz realised she had said the wrong thing.

'Liz.'

Liz looked down guiltily.

'Liz, do you know what that guy or guys that did this to me?'

'Yes. Robin told me you were knocked out and locked in your jail cell. It must have been terrible.'

'Oh yes, it was terrible. I was more than knocked unconscious, I was beaten and locked in the cell. More than that, before locking me in they raped me.'

Denise emphasised the word raped, as if it needed emphasising what terrible thing that had been done to her.

Liz's mouth dropped open as she looked up, utterly shocked.

'No way. Not Robert.'

'Robert. Robert who?' Denise asked, suddenly angry at Liz. Not just Liz, she was angry at herself for not thinking about the answer that was under her nose all the time.

'Robert McCallum. Andrew's son.'

'P.C. McCallum. His son!'

Liz nodded.

Denise got up and hurried out of the Band B, the adrenalin taking over and heading across to the police station as fast as she could go.

When she got there the door was unlocked. There was a bigger surprise inside. Andrew McCallum was standing behind the counter, waiting on her.

'We need to talk,' she said, angrily.

The P.C. handed her an envelope.

'What's this?'

'My resignation. My son is here, and he has a confession to make.'

Denise turned and saw Robert McCallum was sitting in the cell although the door was open. Suddenly her emotions were all over the place. Rage, disgust, the desire for revenge, everything her training taught her not to feel bubbled up within her. There was never training about what you do when you meet the person who raped you and there he was sitting in front of you.

Robert turned and had tears in his eyes. As her eyes were on him he started bubbling like a young lad.

'I'm sorry. I really am, but I never assaulted you. I butcher the sheep, that's what I do, I am a butcher, but I don't steal them, and I didn't even know Darren had done this to you.'

Denise turned and looked at the prisoner's father. He put his arms out and nodded.

'He is telling the truth. He could never attack a woman; I am sure of that. Anyway, he knows I would kill him if he did anything like that', the P.C. said.

The Detective Constable took a couple of deep breaths and calmed herself. She had to get her professional head on, and quick.

Denise walked up to the cell door and pulled it wide open. Robert cowered a bit in response.

'Okay, speak,' she said through gritted teeth.

'I am guilty of killing, butchering and selling the meat from the sheep stolen from the estate. I went in the car with Darren, but it was him who grabbed the sheep and put it in the back of the car. He dropped me and the sheep of at my house, that was the last I saw him on Saturday night.

I had no idea Darren came back later on Sunday morning and assaulted you.'

'Darren who?'

'Darren MacAllister.'

Denise turned to the police constable. 'Who is he?'

'Local low life. He has been on our radar for minor things but nothing on this scale.'

'But you must have known he was stealing the sheep for your son.'

'Stealing yes. The estate has so many sheep they haven't noticed for over a year.'

Denise shook her head.

Just then the door burst open and a red-faced P.C. Lambie burst in.

'I know who did it!' he said to Denise, triumphantly but baulked when he saw the other P.C. standing at the counter.

Then ushered his superior officer over.

'It's Andrew's son,' he whispered when she was close enough to hear the secret information he had without his colleague hearing.

'My mum said he is selling cheap lamb. Some of her neighbours bought it but she wouldn't.'

'Him sitting in the cells,' she said turning, allowing Billy to see past her.

'Yes. That's him. How did you know?'

'He just confessed. But you did well.'

P.C. Lambie was crestfallen that he hadn't solved it in time to be the hero of the hour, especially as he still felt guilty for leaving Denise to get attacked and hoped this would have made up for it.

'Right, before we do anything else, we need to pick up Darren MacAllister.'

Lambie stood with a puzzled look on his face. 'Why?'

'Because he did the actual assault, Robert only did the butchering and selling.'

'Do you know where this lowlife lives?' Denise asked Andrew.

'Sure. But I have resigned.'

'I know you have but before I can even think about accepting it, I need help apprehending this piece of shit MacAllister.'

'It will be a pleasure. Robert, you stay in there and don't move.'

KNOCK KNOCK

They took the yellow peril. Denise drove, McCallum sat beside her and Lambie was in the back. The old man looked tense, whereas the younger man was excited at the thought of there being at the arrest.

They drove past the house and parked a block away.

'I take it this is a normal council house, one front door, one back.'

Andrew nodded.

'Okay, Andrew, you cover the back, Billy and I will knock the front.'

They got out the car and gently closed the doors.

'Denise, can I borrow your truncheon. Don't want to be unarmed in case he thinks he is big enough to attack a man.'

Denise reached into the jacket of her suit. She knew a seamstress and had a special pocket sewn in all her work suits to take her truncheon.

Andrew hit it off the palm of his left hand.

'Nice weight to it,' he complimented.

'Yes, it's seen a bit of action too,' Denise said proudly.

At the house Denise watched until Andrew was right round at the back door before knocking loudly on the front door.

There was no immediate response, so she knocked again then bent and shouted in the letterbox- 'Police, come out or we are coming in.'

Suddenly there was shouting and what seemed like screaming from the rear of the building.

Denise told Billy to stay at the front and she went to the back. She couldn't run because of the stiffness she still had, but it was easing a bit and she managed to walk quickly round.

She found what must be the MacAllister lad, on the ground, writhing in agony, holding his groin with one hand, the other arm was round his back as P.C. McCallum was holding him down.

'Billy, you can come round now!' the D.C. called.

She could hear him approach as he ran round quickly to join them.

MacAllister was still squealing like a stuck pig.

Billy's face was a picture as he saw the captor on the ground and his mate holding him down.

'Quick, your handcuffs,' she beckoned.

'I haven't brought them.'

The Detective Constable blew in exasperation and went into her shoulder bag to retrieve her own.

Between them, the two P.C.'s got their collar on his feet while the D.C. snapped the cuffs on his wrists behind his back.

'He hit me in the balls with his truncheon,' the prisoner protested.

'I only put my arm out to stop you and you ran into the truncheon,' the wily old cop said, then added, 'three times.'

Denise read him his rights, only mentioning assault at the time, then ordered the guys to get him in the back of the car.

Both coppers sat with MacAllister between them. It meant Denise had to drive without looking in her inside mirror because the scumbag's face was staring straight back at her. She forgot and glimpsed in it once and he was smiling at her, which made it worse.

As he was led into the station the first thing the prisoner saw was Robert, sitting in the cell.

'You fucking grass!' MacAllister shouted and tried to break free from Robert's dad, who was holding him by the cuffs and simply pulled them up, stopping him in his tracks.

'You shouldn't have touched her; you went too far. Stealing's one thing but assault, no way man.'

'She saw us, I had to shut her up.'

Denise was standing behind them and heard it all.

'Sorry, but I didn't see you. I hadn't a clue who you were. All I saw was the sheep and I don't think I could have picked it out in an identity parade.'

McCallum took him into the second cell. Denise gave him the key to the cuffs so that he could loosen one end and secure him to the bracket on the cell wall designed for it.

The rest of the morning was taken with getting Robert's statement. When he was free to go, he left with his father. In the interim Denise had telephoned the Chief Inspector and told him Andrew was resigning forthwith. She said it was because of personal reasons and the Chief accepted it on the spot.

'Think we will go for lunch now Billy!' Denise said. She walked over to MacAllister's cell and started to pull her truncheon out from the special pocket in her jacket. She stepped into the cell and MacAllister flinched back, squealing and begging not to be hit. Denise then turned stepped out and locked the cell door behind her.

MacAllister turned as the door clanked shut, realising she was taking the piss.

'Fucking bitch!' he spat at her.

Denise smiled and walked away.

'See you after lunch,' she said as she made for the door.

'What about me?' the prisoner shouted after her.

Denise stepped back and looked into the cell.

'What about you? Are you hungry? Would you like me to bring you a bacon roll or two?'

'Yeah.'

'Tough. After what you did to me, you are getting nothing. That is a prison cell you are in, not a room at the Ritz.'

The prisoner gave her the bird with his free hand, making her laugh again.

'Do you know something, if I could get away with it I would come in there right now and beat the living daylights out of you. For what you did to me though, that wouldn't be good enough. Not by a long chalk.

You need to suffer like I did. No, more. Instead, you will go to prison. Prison officers are often ex-police and they like to protect their own. They will beat you every chance they get. As far as they are concerned, you are the lowest of the low.'

MacAllister's face dropped as he hadn't thought of anything like that.

'If you think that's bad, you will get a big butch cell mate who will do to you what you did to me, but you will be awake. They won't use a condom or lube either, your arse will be wasted by the time you get out.

Every time you cough you will shit yourself,' she continued, smiling as she finished.

Denise was quite proud that she kept her calm and hopefully put the fear of death, or something worse, into the wee shit, because that what he was, just a runt of a boy.

'Come on Billy, I am starving.'

With that they went out and locked the door behind them,

leaving their prisoner, who seemed to have recovered a bit of his cockiness, shouting and swearing after them.

Denise settled for a pie and sticky bun again, sitting on the bench opposite the shop. Lunchtime should have been downtime for her, but she couldn't help but think about the case.

During her lunch she suddenly realised that she was compromising police protocol. If she interviewed MacAllister she would have compromised the case because she was involved in it, indeed, she was the victim.

Throwing the uneaten bun in the nearest bin she hurried back to the station. As she hurried as fast as her injured body would let her, she was saying idiot, idiot, to herself. If she had gone any further with the case, the piece of human trash that abused her would probably, no, almost certainly, got off on a technicality if he had a good brief. Experience told her scum like him always got the best lawyers available.

Although it was lunchtime, the Chief Inspector was still at his desk and answered his phone on the first ring.

Denise quickly outlined the case. The Chief agreed somebody else would need to take over the case and they would be dispatched immediately.

He was angry that this was the first he had heard about the assault and everything else. The word unprofessional wasn't said but his tone clearly implied it. His other order was that when P.C. Lambie arrived back to watch the prisoner, she was to go to the hospital and get the Doctor who examined her to give her a detailed statement about her injuries.

DOCTOR'S APPOINTMENT

Denise swallowed as she reached out for the hospital door handle for the second time, although this time for a different reason. She wasn't scared now, it was, pure and simple, she realised she fancied the pants off the doctor.

Maybe if she saw him again she might find out her infatuation was just brought about because of the situation of the previous day, although she had to admit, she had fantasised about him several times since she left the hospital the previous day.

His lovely eyes, his caring smile and gentle hands she imagined running expertly all over her yielding body.

The receptionist was the same snooty cow from the day before.

Denise said she needed to see the doctor and was hit by a bit of attitude, not what she needed at that time.

Instead of giving it back, although she felt like it, she just showed the snooty bitch her warrant card.

'Police business, I need to see him now,' was all she said.

'I will see if he is available just now,' before adding, 'he is very busy you know.'

'So am I, and this is a very serious matter,' she said, emphasising the "very".

This brought a reaction that surprised Denise. She wondered for a second if maybe the doc had a reputation, and it wasn't a surprise, as if the receptionist expected the police to come looking for him one day.

Denise was asked to sit down in the empty waiting room and a minute later the doctor appeared.

'You wanted a word,' he said.

Denise's heart melted. She hadn't been wrong the first time she saw him, she still fancied the pants off him. She only hoped she didn't make it too obvious.

Denise got up. 'Can we go somewhere more private?' she said.

At that, he turned and took her back through to his office without saying anything else.

'How can I help you, Detective Inspector?' he asked when they were comfortably seated in his office.

'It's Detective Constable,' she corrected. For a minute she wondered if he was making a fool of her, like Urquart had, but he smiled at her, and she just melted.

She swallowed before speaking. Her mouth had suddenly got very dry and hoped she could speak when she opened her mouth again.

'What I need from you is a signed statement and a copy of your report from yesterday.'

She smiled as it came out the way she wanted to. Last thing she wanted was to look silly in front of him.

'Sure, no problem. But you could have just telephoned, you didn't need to come all the way out here.'

He smiled again and turned his head slightly again to look her straight in the eyes. His lovely, perfectly manicured hands were clasped together on his desk.

Denise looked at them and really struggled to contain her emotions at that moment and she sure she was getting wet as she again imagined the doctor's lovely hands roaming over her body.

Something told her he fancied her too, although it might just be his trained bedside manner.

'The thing is,' Denise said, turning on the charm, I need them today. In fact, I really need them as soon as you can do it.'

The doctor folded his arms.

'I could do it right now, but it will cost you.'

'I'm afraid I don't run to expenses.'

Grant laughed. God, she thought, even his laugh was bloody sexy.

'No, I don't mean money. I mean you will need to repay me by going out for dinner with me.'

'What? Sure, but I won't be able to for a few weeks.'

As soon as she said it, she regretted it. It sounded like she was offering her body to him for a quick 3 course meal. Not that she wouldn't, but she didn't want to sound cheap.

She felt the blood rush to her cheeks in embarrassment.

'What I mean is, I am so busy at the moment, I don't have much free time,' she said, trying to rectify the situation but not really doing so.

'I can understand that. That's fine, I am busy very just now too.'

He let that hang in the air while they just sat there while they just looked across the table at each other.

He broke the ice. 'Well, if you want to wait through at reception I will do your report post haste.'

The doctor returned 30 minutes later with a file for her and offered to show Denise out to her car. She felt like a schoolgirl with a crush as they walked across the gravel car park but tried not to show it.

They exchanged pleasantries and the doctor even opened her car door for her. It took Denise all her willpower not to lean forward and kiss him.

She squeezed past him and got comfy in her seat while the gorgeous Doctor leaned in to check she was all right.

Before he closed the door, Grant promised to be in touch soon to arrange the dinner she agreed to.

RE-INFORCMENTS ARRIVE

When Denise got back she had to park opposite the police station There was the Morris Minor, a large Police van, the Chief's car and another unmarked Granada in the car park, leaving no room for her.

Time to face the music she thought, she only hoped it wasn't a dirge.

As she reached the front door it opened and two big burly officers emerged, MacAllister dwarfed by them and shackled to one of them. The cocky smile missing replaced by a worried look. He ducked his head when he saw Denise avoiding eye contact.

She watched him put in the van but didn't wait to see it leave.

The welcoming committee inside consisted of Chief Inspector McKelvie, P.C. Lambie and another smartly dressed woman and man, obviously senior detectives. None of them were wearing smiles she noted.

'D.C. Kelly, this is Detective Inspector Bremner and Detective Sergeant Johnston. They are here to interview you,' McKelvie said abruptly by way of introductions.

There was an edge to his voice, one that hadn't been there previously, one that conveyed the seriousness of the incident they were there for, and probably his displeasure at her behaviour over the whole affair.

The two senior officers didn't proffer a handshake but merely nodded when they were introduced.

'Should we call you Denise?' the Inspector asked.

Denise merely nodded worriedly.

'I am afraid we only have the cells here to interview you in. If you would like to take a seat on the bunk and we can get started.'

Denise sat on the bunk in the second cell, she doubted she would ever be able to set foot in the first cell again. At least not for a while.

She spent the next hour going over everything that had happened, from the minute Urquart had walked in to make the complaint until she walked in the door minutes ago with the Doctor's report in her hand.

It had been done with little prompting and when she finished the Inspector hadn't any further questions to ask. The Sergeant had only one thing to ask, did she need counselling?

Denise shook her head. Apart from the twinges of pain she got when she had forgotten about the damage inflicted on her body and tried to move too quickly, she didn't feel affected by the incident at all.

The two officers looked at McKelvie who nodded, obviously a signal that they could go and taking the doctor's report with them, they left. Leaving behind an awkward silence.

All that could be heard was the ticking of the station clock.

Billy and the Chief had been sitting quietly through her interview and must have heard every word that Denise had spoken and now realised the seriousness of the assault and what a trauma she had been through.

After what seemed an age, but couldn't have been much more than 30 seconds , McKelvie got up from the fireside chair.

He ran a hand through his hair then said, 'We need to talk.

Let's go through to the office.'

He let Denise lead the way and invited her to sit on the only chair there, when they got there.

'You are a lucky girl. He could have killed you.'

Funnily enough, it wasn't what she expected to hear. Strangely it wasn't even something she had thought about.

The Chief shook his head. 'You haven't even been here a week and we have had more incidents that there have been in the past year.'

Denise didn't know how to take this so just sat silently.

'Are you sure you are all right?'

Denise smiled slightly. 'Yes.'

The Chief gave her a look.

'Really. I am fine. I have a bit of pain, but the Doctor gave me strong painkillers.'

'You do know you should have phoned this in straight away.'

She nodded. 'Yes, I know that now. I think yesterday I was in shock and not thinking straight. I t took me until lunchtime today to get it straight in my head, to realise the right thing to do.'

'Better late than never I suppose. I am not surprised, you have probably been in some form of shock the whole time because of the trauma you undoubtably suffered.'

The Chief waited before going on.

'Okay, what I am suggesting, no telling you, is you are taking the rest of the week off.'

'But we are understaffed here.'

'Denise, the station functioned before you came and will no doubt continue after you leave. I will get somebody else in.

Right now, work is the last thing you need to worry about.'

She went to speak again but nothing came to mind.

'Go. Now. Do not report back until next Monday. That is an order. Any problems, you have my number.'

HOLIDAY

Tuesday, after breakfast, Denise headed over to Cobblers Court and her new digs. Seemed a quirky name for a street, she would have to ask one of the locals why it got that name, but not now, she had bigger fish to fry.

Marion Lewis took a bit longer to answer the door this time. Probably doing her face because even at that early hour her hair and make-up were pristine.

Denise felt underdressed in her jeans and t-shirt, old trainers and anorak, next to her new landlady. Although she was dressed simply enough in a floral dress, that was low enough cut at the front to allow a glimpse of breast, and light pink patented heels, she just seemed to exude elegance in a sexy way.

Marion let her in and fetched her keys. Denise hurried up the stairs to her new digs. The room seemed larger than she remembered, and she had a nice, warm feeling that she was going to be happy there. Time would tell.

After that it was back to the Wilson's place to get her belongings.

When the last of her belongings were piled into the yellow peril, Denise returned and sought out Liz Wilson to give the keys.

Liz was in the kitchen, cooking up a stew. There always seemed to be a nice smell in the kitchen.

Liz said she was sad to see her go, especially as the two lads were leaving the following week too. Job finished, they were off to Crieff to another job, the week after.

Denise felt a bit guilty when she heard that, but deep in her heart she knew she had to move.

This time, moving her stuff to the peril had taken a lot longer as there were no big strong lads to help her with her worldly goods, and she had to carry them herself. The result being it was after lunchtime before the last box was carried up and emptied in her new digs.

Fortunately, as she didn't have a lot of stuff, the case and boxes could all go into a large walk-in cupboard she had, they would be needed for her next move, or when she headed back to Ayrshire. If she did, that was.

Job done, she sat on the couch for a 5-minute breather. She was well overdue it. Tiredness suddenly swept over her, and she lay down on the sofa for a quick 40 winks.

It was dark when Denise woke from her slumber. Obviously after the weekend's events her body must have needed it.

She checked her watch in the gloom. It looked like it was 10 o'clock. No, it couldn't be, she thought. That was when she remembered she didn't have a clock in the room, something she would need to get.

Putting the light on she found she was right, it was just after 10, no wonder it was dark outside.

Surprisingly, she wasn't hungry, even though she had eaten nothing since her hearty breakfast at the Wilson's. What she did need though, was a drink. She walked over to the fridge and pulled out the only thing she had in it, a pint of milk.

A big glass of milk was enough to fill her stomach and 10 minutes after drinking it she felt tired again, so she undressed and slipped into bed.

Waking up the next morning, she felt ready to take on anything. Her body seemed to have recovered from the effects of the assault. The other thing she felt was a rumbling in her stomach.

She groaned at it, because she had nothing in but half a pint of milk. A cup of tea would need to keep her going until the shop opened.

Later that day she headed into the nearest Woolworths, 15 miles away in Dingwall. She had written a list and managed to get everything she needed to brighten the bedsit up and all the other utensils the room didn't have. Mainly a bottle opener which she would need as she also bought a few bottles of vino in a wine store there. She was on holiday after all.

NEWER BEGINNINGS

Denise parked the yellow peril in the station car park, next to the Morris Minor. There was another car already there, a horrible browny coloured Morris Marina. Made her Avenger look better next to it. She wondered whose it was.

She found out as soon as she walked in, sitting at the fire drinking tea with Constable Lambie was a big bear of a man. The mug in his hand looked like he was drinking from a cup from a kid's toy tea-set.

He was as bald as a coot and wore an ill-fitting dark brown suit, but he had manners as he got up as soon as she walked in.

Billy, meantime, welcomed Denise back, beaming as he spoke.

Denise walked round to meet the stranger, who was obviously another policeman and put a handout for a handshake. She had always thought she had a decent sized mit, but it seemed to disappear in his hand that looked like a fleshy bunch of big bananas.

As usual she tried to show she was the match of any man with her firm handshake but this time her grip had absolutely no effect on the solid fingers.

'Detective Sergeant Allan Knowles. I have been looking after your wee place here. I just thought I would come in and get you up to speed.'

This puzzled Denise. For practically the last year, according to the day- book, nothing much happened in the town. Now her replacement saw fit to keep her updated.

They walked over to the book, and he went through all the entries since her last one on the previous Monday. Strangely, they were suddenly providing a service to the locals, something her previous incumbent only seemed to be doing in the bedroom department, before his sad demise.

Most of the issues were small and were already cleared up. The only one outstanding involved Rita Samson's car being covered in paint the day before.

Although she didn't know the circumstances apart from what was written. Denise could only imagine there were a lot of suspects, she got the feeling the locals shared her feelings about the shop owner and Rita wasn't liked in the village.

Allan then pointed to the first cell in front of them. 'That's the empty paint tin in there,' he said.

Denise walked round and leaned in, not wanting to cross the threshold, and lifted the tin up.

'Honeydew. Looks peachier,' she observed, from the paint that had spilled down the side of the tin and dried out.

'Anyway, that's you up to speed. I will leave you to it.'

Allan moved his large carcass through the gap in the counter and edged past Denise.

She nearly had to step back into the cell but resisted, she wasn't ready to go in there yet. Not that cell.

As the D.S. reached the front door, Denise stopped him with a question.

'Any news on the sheep stealers?' she asked.

'Yes. The copper's son is out on bail, but the other guy was remanded. Word is he will plead guilty but nothing definite yet.'

Denise felt relieved at the news as she watched through the glass in the door, as the big cop went over to his car. As he got in she smiled as she saw how far the car dropped to one side when he got sat in the driver's seat.

'That suspension won't last long,' she said, laughing to herself as she said it.

Then she clicked her fingers, it dawned on her why he made a special point of handing the job over to her, he was rubbernecking. Probably heard all week about the new policewoman who managed to get herself sexually assaulted in her own jail and wanted to take the opportunity to see her in person. She had more to get on with there, so let it go this time.

Ordinarily she would have chased after him and verbally ripped him a new arsehole. However, her weeks rest had mellowed her. For the moment.

Turning, she saw Billy was up from his chair.

'Are you ready to go to work?'

'Yes. I was busy last week, even found the dog that went missing on Thursday.'

Denise couldn't remember the full details, but somebody had phoned in to report her dog lost. The thing she found funny as she read it was that it was a retriever.

'Where did you find it?'

'I remembered what you said to me about thinking like a thief. Only in this case I thought, think like the dog and act like a dog. Be the dog. I thought.'

'Don't tell me you sniffed another dog's butt.'

'No,' he said ignoring her attempt at humour, 'I asked myself, what would you do if you were a dog? I found it standing outside the butchers. Seems he often throws out scraps, the dog remembered.'

'They say dogs are dumb mutts too. Good job Billy,' she added and genuinely meant it. Sure, it wasn't the crime of the century, but he got a positive result and used a bit of lateral thinking.

'Right, first job this week. The vandalism of Rita's car yesterday. What is the first thing we need?'

'We have the paint. We just need to find out who threw it.'

'Billy, that's the last thing we will find out. First thing we need is motive. We will need to speak to her again, ask her if anybody had threatened her recently, or anybody had been refused, what, cigarettes, something like that. Do you know what I mean?'

'Yes. I get it.'

'The other thing we need to know is where the paint came from.'

'There is only the 1 paint shop in the village.'

'Right, the plan of attack. First we speak to Rita, then we go to the paint shop which is further down the town. If they didn't supply it, they could point us in the right direction as to where it came from.'

Billy buttoned up his jacket and walked round to join her.

'Have you got all your equipment?'

'Yes.'

'Including your truncheon and handcuffs.'

He nodded.

'Good, let's go.'

As they walked down to the shops the streets were busy with people heading for work and kids heading for the local park. They were getting a few hellos and nods and friendly waves, more like what she expected from the country life. Although technically they were in a town, within a 5-minute walk they were in fields or woods.

They stopped and looked in the general store's window. There were a few customers, but the three servers were all there.

'Come on, let's go in. You do the talking and I will only step in if I think you are missing something. Okay with that?'

The P.C. nodded and went first.

Hugh stepped forward to greet them.

Denise looked at her assistant.

'It's your wife we need to speak too,' Billy he said, a little louder than Denise would have, and had the customers looking round, their nosiness piqued.

Hugh ushered them to the back store then left to be replaced by his wife, Rita, still sporting her horrible, dated skunk-like hairstyle.

Something had always bothered Denise about the hairstyle, and it was in that instant it dawned on her what it was, she reminded her of Cruella De Ville. Now that the thought was in her head, she would think it every time she saw her from that moment on.

'Have you got them already?' Rita asked, smiling and looking impressed.

'No. We just need a bit more information,' Billy said.

'Oh,' she said disappointedly, 'I thought that very nice Inspector had all the information he needed.'

Again, she smiled and looked straight at Denise, obviously mocking her.

'Do you know anybody with a grudge against you?' Billy asked, taking the lead.

She shook her head gently.

'No, sorry. I am well liked in the town.'

'No kids you have refused cigarettes, anybody like that?'

She shook her head again.

'No. We never sell cigarettes or alcohol to under 18's. We are very strict about that, the kids know not to even ask.'

There was a silence, it seemed Billy's line of questioning

had stalled. Denise stepped in to break the silence that was becoming awkward.

'It happened on Sunday morning, is that correct?' the D.C. asked.

'I think it must have been on Saturday night or the early hours of Sunday. When I went out to it late on Sunday morning the paint had dried in. You know they've ruined my pride and joy.'

'Where were you on Saturday night?'

'I went to the Pheasant Plucker for a few hours.'

'On you own. Was Hugh not with you?'

'No. He is back in the flat again, back on his own.'

The reconciliation didn't last long, Denise thought.

'Did anything happen in the pub?' Denise asked.

'What do you mean happen?'

'Any incident that might have prompted this?'

'No. It was a normal Saturday night; I had a few drinks then went home.'

'Alone?'

'That is none of your business,' Rita said quite abruptly.

Denise could have pursued it at that point but didn't, there was more than one way to get that information.

'What kind of car is it?' Denise asked. She knew it was a Mercedes as it was usually parked outside the shop but wanted to ask.

'It's a Mercedes cabriolet. That's a soft top if you didn't know, and it's ruined. Horrible cheap paint on my beautiful car,' she lamented.

'Could it not be somebody who had a grudge against your husband? What kind of car does he have?'

'He has the business van,' she said with almost disdain.

'He is not a car person, like me.'

Maybe because you are too fat and lazy to walk, Denise mused.

'Okay, we will continue our enquiries and get back to you as soon as we know anything,' Denise said before turning to go out, with Billy following.

The two police officers continued down the street heading for the paint shop.

'Sorry for jumping in Billy, I just thought you had run out of questions.'

'Yes. I dried up when she said that she didn't know anybody who had a grudge against her.'

'Sorry, I did spring it on you. First thing you need is a strategy. Tell you one thing, when I asked her about anything happening in the pub, she lied.'

'Really. How did you know?'

'Body language. Or rather her eyes gave it away. When she answered the other questions she looked us in the eye, but when I asked if anything happened in the pub, or if she took anyone home with her she looked up at the ceiling, away from us.'

'You're right, she did. I didn't know that meant she was lying.'

'You need to learn to read peoples body language, often it's not what we say but how we say it that matters. After we've been to the paint shop we will nip into the pub, see what did happen on Saturday night, if anything. How do you want to handle it in the paint shop? Do you want to take the lead this time?'

'No. I would rather watch the expert at work.'

Denise smiled; she had never been called an expert before.

The owner of the paint shop was sitting on a stool behind

the counter of the shop supping a coffee. There were rolls of wallpaper along one wall and stacks of paint behind him.

His eyes lit up when Denise walked in, but his attitude quickly changed when the P.C. walked in behind her.

'No trouble is there, Billy?' he asked.

Before Billy could answer, Denise jumped in.

'No. We are looking for honeydew paint. Do you stock it?' she said, getting straight to the point.

'No. I take it it's Crown matt emulsion honeydew you are after.'

'Yes, that's it.'

'I am afraid it's order only. I can have it here by Wednesday. Remember we close at 1 o'clock.'

'No, I don't actually want to buy some. I need to know if anybody bought it from you recently.'

'He shook his head.

'No. Last person, in fact the only person, if my memory serves me right, who had ordered that was Liz Wilson up at the Bed and Breakfast for her daughter's bedroom. Do you know it?'

'Yes. I know it quite well.'

'Of course, it's next door to the police station.'

'Yes, right next door. So, if nobody else bought it, where is the nearest place they could get it off the shelf?'

'You would need to go to Harpers Décor in Dingwall, they are the nearest Crown stockists.'

'Great, thanks for your help. Billy, have you anything to ask?'

'My bedroom is quite dark. Do you think using honeydew emulsion would help brighten it up? Or would it be too girly for me?'

Denise walked out of the shop, not wanting to hear the answer in case she burst out laughing. Billy was a nice guy but at times like this she wondered if he would ever be a real policeman. It seemed to be 2 steps forward and 3 back at times with him.

Billy caught up with her a few shops further up the street.

'Did that help? Denise asked.

'Yes. I think it's something to do with the Wilson's.'

She had meant about his own decorating dilemma but was glad he was switched on to the case.

'You might be onto something. Right, pub shouldn't be open, we will need to knock.'

When they got there a few minutes later both doors were closed.

'You knock,' Denise said.

Billy, with his usual enthusiasm, rattled the door, giving it a right loud policeman's knock.

Fergus opened the door a few minutes later and was exasperated at first when he saw them.

'Is this a raid?' he asked, putting his hands up as if in surrender.

'You are wasting your time, there's nobody in here yet, it's not 11 o'clock yet, you know.'

'Fergus, don't worry, it's nothing like that, just a wee enquiry you might help us with.'

He had lightened up a bit now and continued in his lighthearted vain, he straightened his tie and ran a hand through his hair.

'How can I help?'

'Saturday night. Rita Samson was in. There wasn't any trouble in the pub, was there?'

'She was actually quiet on Saturday night. She came in alone. Sat in the corner with a few of her friends. I would have said she was in good spirits and sank a few too,' he said, then laughed gently at his own joke.

'So, all in all, it was a quiet night. Nothing out of the ordinary,' he added.

'So, Rita left alone, did she?'

'No. She left with that young lad that's boarding with the Wilson's.'

'Colin or Andy?'

'The wee one, Chicko.'

'You mean Coco.' For a fleeting second she was glad it wasn't Andy. Why, she didn't know, but it was probably because her memory of him would have been sullied in a way, if she thought he had sex with Rita.

'So she left with Coco. Right. She must have forgot who she left with when I asked her.'

'Well, she looked like the cat that got the cream as she left. I actually felt sorry for the lad, I knew what he was in for.'

'Right, thanks Fergus. Sorry if we gave you a surprise.'

'It's fine. Guilty conscience,' he said before popping back into the pub and quickly locking the door behind him.

'Well, Billy, what do you think?' Denise asked, as they walked back towards the cop shop.

'Maybe she knocked that Coco boy back, he went back to the boarding house, got the paint and took his revenge.'

A big smile broke across Denise's face.

'You know Billy, there is a policeman in there after all. However, I don't think Rita would knock back any man.'

Billy smiled too, but he didn't know his boss had another theory that involved one of the Wilson's she didn't want to share with him.

'Right, back to the office and we will have a cuppa before speaking to Liz Wilson.

The kettle just started to boil when the bell on the front door clattered, announcing an arrival.

When Denise looked round all she saw was a bunch of flowers. The bouquet so big it hid the carrier. The delivery guy behind asked for Detective Sergeant Kelly.

Denise thought it was a wind-up. However, to provide a bunch of flowers that size would have been an expensive way to do it.

'Who are they from?' she asked.

'The card says, well done, from all at Drumbaggen Estate.'

'Urquart,' she said as she took them.

Billy walked over as the delivery guy left.

'Best put them in water?'

'What do I want with them? You could take them home and give them to your mum.'

'Oh no, mum won't have flowers in the house.'

'Why?' she asked, bemused. If there was some kind of allergy you got from cut flowers she had never heard of it.

'Mum says they didn't allow flowers in the wards when she was a nurse. Stole the air or something.'

'That's an old wife's tale,' she said.

'My mum is an old wife,' he said, shaking his head.

'No thanks, anyway. I know she won't have them in the house.'

'Tell you what I will do, I will give them to Liz Wilson, they will cheer her up. Always seems down to me.'

'No wonder, with Robin. Then Susan being pregnant. It takes a lot to run the guest house and she does it basically on her own.'

'Yes, I will take them over when I go to see her.'

'I will need to go home for lunch shortly,' Billy said, looking up at the clock.

Denise shook her head. It really did seem to be one step forward and two steps back with the constable.

'Do you really need to go home every day for your lunch.'

Billy got quiet and looked down.

'I need to make sure mum takes her medicine.'

'What?'

'She is getting really forgetful, and I need to check she takes her medication.'

'Billy, why have you not told me this before. Off you go just now. I will go over and see Liz just now and take her these flowers to her. Might cheer her up a bit'

BLACK MOOD

Denise rung the bell at the boarding house. From outside she could hear the dinging echoing through the building. Denise stood for ages and had to ring it another twice. Liz, it seemed was reluctant to answer it.

She persisted because she was sure Liz was in, she rarely went out, and but just as importantly, she didn't want to have to go to the trouble of carrying the big bunch of flowers back to the station.

Eventually Denise saw her former landlady approach through the glass door. She was walking quite slowly and was wearing glasses. As she got closer she saw they were dark glasses.

She unlocked the door and stood, stopping her from coming in.

'Hi Liz, thought you would appreciate these flowers. No good to me and if I fill the police station with them I would get talked about.'

Liz leaned out and took the bunch of blooms from her.

'I need to come in Liz. I am following a line of enquiry and need a word.'

Reluctantly, Liz walked away letting the policewoman follow her as she walked into the kitchen.'

'Like the shades,' Denise said.

'Oh these. I am just wearing them because I walked into a door yesterday, gave myself a bit of a black eye' she said as she prepared a vase for the flowers at the kitchen sink, with her back to the cop.

'What? I thought you were sunbathing out the back when you took so long to answer the door,' she said, trying to lighten the mood.

When Liz turned round after the flowers were sorted, Denise walked over and took the dark glasses off the older woman. She protested but didn't stop her.

'That's not a bit of a black eye. Oh, Liz, what has he done to you?'

Liz closed her eyes but never answered.

'I have seen plenty injuries like that and there were no doors involved. I worked in the domestic violence unit for a year. You do know it won't stop at this.

What I can tell you is you need to change things and now. Robin did this, I am right, aren't i?'

Liz still kept silent.

'Look, I am talking to you as a friend. Anything you tell me now will be strictly off the record.'

Liz didn't speak but nodded ever so slightly but enough to be affirmative.

'I can get you a number to phone. '

Liz shook her head and took the shades off Denise and put them back on.

'Even just talking can help. Where is Robin anyway?'

'At sea.'

'He will be when I catch up with him.'

Liz put the vase of flowers on the kitchen table and asked the cop if she wanted a coffee or a tea. Denise declined, she still had work to do.

'Liz, as I said earlier I am here on an enquiry. Where do you keep the paint you use to decorate the rooms?'

'Out in the hut.'

'Do you keep it locked?'

'Yes. The key is on the key rack.'

She pointed over and Denise walked over and checked. The keys were organised with the key for every room in the house having a tab. The hut key was in its place.

'Do you have a spare?'

'Not for the hut, no. It got lost years ago.'

'All the paint you have is kept in there?'

'Yes.'

'The honeydew paint you bought for Susan's room, is there any left?'

'I can't remember, I don't think so.'

'Do you mind if I go out and look in the shed.'

'Help yourself.'

Denise took the key and walked out to the hut. It was an old wooden hut that could have been doing with a coat of paint itself. The lock opened easily, and the door creaked very noisily as it swung open. If it was opened in the early hours, somebody surely would have heard it.

Surprisingly it was neat and tidy inside. The paint was stacked on a shelf. Now, if the honeydew paint the Wilson's bought was there, they were off the hook.

Denise had to pick up pots to check the contents of them all. Some had so little left in them she was surprised they kept them at all. If that was the case, why was there not a tin of honeydew with a drop in the bottom of it?

The search was unsurprisingly fruitless. With the Wilson's being the only people to buy the paint locally and the fact they kept pots that had very little left in them, Denise had to deduce the paint used to decorate Rita's German car came from there.

Liz was still sitting at the kitchen table when Denise returned.

'It looks to me like somebody took a tin of paint from your hut sometime between Saturday night and Sunday morning and splashed it over Rita Samson's car. Who do you think could have done it?'

'I suppose anybody from the house could have done it. The kitchen isn't locked so anybody could have walked in and took the key.'

'Who knew you kept your paint in the hut?'

Liz just shrugged.

'So, somebody came in here. Took the key, went out there in the dark, grabbed the paint then returned the key. Liz. Do you expect me to believe that?'

'Now you mention it, I found the key was missing on from the rack on Sunday morning. When I went out the hut door was closed but the key was in the padlock.'

'Liz come on. Tell you what, let's just say I am off duty. So, you can tell me, not as a policewoman but as a friend. I think we are friends. Honestly, I don't think the key was left in the lock, but I will put in my report the key was in the hut lock, but I want to know what you know.'

Liz walked over and closed the kitchen door.

The house was probably empty apart from the two of them, but Denise appreciated it was a gesture.

'Susan did it.' As she spoke her shoulders drooped, as if a large weight was taken off her.

'Rita has been giving her a sore time of it. She is all sweetness and light to the customers but there is another, nasty side to her. When they are alone in the shop she calls her a tramp, a trollop says she is carrying a bastard. She didn't tell me about it until I caught her sneaking back into the house at half past 2 in the morning. She had paint on her clothes where it had splashed back on her.'

Denise couldn't believe how much her attitude had changed in a week. It must be the surroundings she thought, giving her a different outlook to life. A couple of weeks ago she would be charging Susan with vandalism, open and shut case. Now, she was ready to throw her principles out the window again.

'Right, tell you what I will do. We stick with the story that it could be anyone in the house that did it unless there is a witness. If either somebody saw her doing it, which is very unlikely, or even walking through the streets at midnight carrying a tin of paint then she will need to be charged. If there are no witness, I go back to Rita and admit defeat.'

'Thanks Denise, you are a friend.'

Denise walked over and gave her friend a hug. She felt Liz wince under her touch, it was obviously more than her eye he hit.

'Liz, I am genuinely worried about you. It seems to me Robin's abuse is getting worse. I am not being over dramatic, but next thing you will end up hospitalised or,' she paused. 'Or dead.'

Denise walked out, leaving Liz sitting at the kitchen table, thinking on what she had said.

Denise and Billy were in the yellow peril heading for Rita's house. It was in the opposite side of town. Away from the old sandstone buildings, past the council estate to a newish private housing estate. The houses were probably only 10 years old. They all seemed the same, uniform houses and uniform gardens, a square of manicured lawn with flowers round the edges at the front. Driveway with a boring small car that was washed every Sunday, whether it was dirty or not. All inhabited by professional people or retired professionals, lawyers, bankers and the like.

At the end of the street was Rita's gaff. It was certainly different from the rest. The window frames and the wood round the eaves beneath the roof painted a garish purple, the grass replaced with a huge pampas grass surrounded by pebbles.

The driveway was empty, except for a patch showing the remnants of the honeydew paint that left a peachy coloured stain that had obviously been dumped on the car then washed off.

The wooden garage at the top of the drive was also painted the same horrible purple colour.

'Pampas grass in the front garden. Do you know what that is a signal for?' Denise asked her trainee.

'No. Should I?'

'Swingers,' she shrugged.

Billy's eyes opened to the size of saucers.

'Really. Wow. Like swapping partners for sex. Orgies and the like.'

'Yes, swapping and probably sex parties. She seems the type to me, what do you think Billy.'

'Yes, definitely. Imagine that, orgies in Glenfurny. Who would have thought? I wouldn't like to do that. You know, share. Not that that's likely that I will ever have a partner.'

'Come on, there's always someone. My father always said there's someone for everyone. Usually when another guy dumped me.'

Billy shrugged. 'Well, now we know why there was so many parties there.'

'Right Billy, to business. Have you ever done door-to-door enquiries?'

'Not since my training back at headquarters.'

Not for the first time, Denise wasn't surprised.

'Right, listen and learn.'

As they got out the car, they parked right outside Rita's gauche bungalow, they noticed her next-door neighbour was out checking his roses. Although he wasn't there until Denise parked the car. There was a neighbourhood watch area sign outside Rita's house. How apt, she thought, the neighbours were all watching her.

The two cops walked over to speak to him, while he pretended he didn't see them until they were walking up his drive.

He seemed engrossed in his roses and imaginary greenfly he was checking for. Nosey Parker had been in such a rush to get out and see what was happening he still had his slippers.

He was dressed just as Denise would have expected for a retired bungalow owner, corduroy trousers, white shirt without a tie and a brown cardigan. Oh, and leather slippers.

'No trouble officers, is there?'

'Your neighbour Rita Samson's car was covered in paint late on Saturday night or early yesterday morning. I don't suppose you saw or heard anything?'

'No, but if I catch the beggar that did it I will shake his hand.'

'Not a fan then?'

'That woman lowers the tone of the whole estate. Look at the state of that,' he said pointing towards her house.

'I mean purple paint. It's what I would imagine the colour they would paint a bordello.'

'Do you think one of the neighbours could have done this?'

'No. The neighbours around here are decent people, not like her. She lowers the tone of the whole neighbourhood. It shows the kind of person she is when this happens to her. Obviously she has enemies.'

With that he turned and walked away only to turn back.

'Another thing, the next time she has one of her so-called parties, I will be phoning you lot. Last time I complained directly to her. I told her my wife couldn't sleep because of the racket, do you know what she said?'

Before Denise or Billy could answer, he continued his rant.

'She, that disgusting woman, said tell your wife to get ear plugs. The bloody cheek of the woman. I tell you, next time, I will be on the phone to you straight away.'

Then he turned and walked back in the house, not willing to even waste any more breath on his neighbour from Hell.

They walked out of the drive past his brand-new Volvo.

'Right, Billy, you take this side of the road, and I will take the other. Concentrate on finding out if anybody heard or saw anything or anybody. No doubt you will get a lot of moaning about Rita and how she lowers the tone of the place but stick to asking if anybody saw anything.'

Denise had picked the right side of the road to knock. Most were out, the others were quick to dismiss her by saying they didn't see anything and were obviously not keen to get involved.

Billy on the other hand got another couple of curtain twitchers who, Denise could her from the other side of the street, were very vocal about their loathing of their tasteless neighbour and her want for gaudy décor and riotous undoubtably wanton sexual parties.

Back in the yellow peril they discussed their findings. The only thing all the neighbours agreed on was they had seen nothing. However, the consensus seemed to be if they had seen anything they wouldn't have told them.

'What now?' Billy asked, keen to know what his educator thought.

'Right the facts are this. The car was covered in honeydew paint. The only paint sold in the local shop, which is the nearest place to buy it, were the Wilson's. I checked and the paint they bought isn't in their hut. There are no witnesses, so really anybody who stayed in the Wilson's is a potential suspect. Then there is the fact Colin Carberry, who currently resides with them, was seen leaving the pub with Rita and was presumably escorting her back to her house.'

Billy sat nodding his head throughout. Denise thought he looked like the dog ornament her father had on the rear parcel shelf of a previous motor but didn't mention it.

'Agreed,' she eventually said.

'Now, the only person we need to talk to now is Colin Carberry. He went home with Rita the other night. Or maybe she changed her mind and knocked him back, so he decided to take his revenge.'

'The only thing wrong with your theory is that I don't think Rita would knock anyone back as you call it. Your theory might be right though, something could have happened between them.'

Denise loved the way Billy's eyes seemed to light up when he had an idea that he thought could help them, something that would prove he was a better cop.

'The other problem we have now is Colin will still be at work. I will need to go back to the Wilson's tonight and speak to him.'

'Do you want me to come along tonight?'

'No, it's okay, I want to see Liz anyway.' It was a white lie, he wanted to deal with the lads on her own because there was no

Colin without Andy.

She started her car and drove off.

Just as they opened the station's front door the station phone started ringing. Denise rushed round the counter and picked it up just as it rang off.

'If it's important they will ring back,' she said. She had hardly the words out of her breath when it rang again.

'Is that you D.C.Kelly?'

Denise recognised the dulcet tones of her boss, McKelvie.

'Yes sir.'

'I have some news and I think it will please you to hear it. Earlier today Darren MacAllister signed a statement pleading guilty to theft and serious assault. So, you will be spared the ignominy of having to go to court and give evidence or indeed have to face him again.'

'Not rape?' she said, the tone of her voice told of her disappointment.

'No. I am afraid we couldn't get that to stick. The fiscal was willing to accept serious assault.'

Her heart sank, she felt sick to the stomach. Ever the professional, she took a deep breath and put her feelings to one side before continuing.

'That is good news. Thank you for phoning, sir. I feel as if a big weight has been lifted off my shoulders.'

'It does mean you won't have to go to court and face him again.'

He paused before continuing. 'I know you must be gutted.'

'To be honest, I don't think it's right he should get off with a lesser charge.'

'You know as well as me how these things work. The prosecutor knows what they can get to stick, and the defence lawyer will be looking for some kind of bargain to get their client to plead guilty. The problem the fiscal would have is that if we went after a rape conviction and lost, the guy would be out in a few months.

Don't worry, the judge will be given all the facts. He won't get off lightly.'

'Yes. I know you are right,' she said but it still left a bitter taste in her mouth.

'Have you got a pen handy?'

'Yes.'

'Right, take a note, D.S. McCall's funeral is next Monday at Balgay Parish Church in Dundee at 2:30 pm. You would not be expected to attend but obviously the two P.C.s who worked with him will be expected there.'

'I think I would like to go sir.'

'Fine. I will arrange cover at the station for the Monday. As ever, I am at the end of the line if you need me for anything. I will see you on Monday then.'

Denise put the receiver down and turned to Billy, who had been waiting on the call ending so that he could put the kettle on.

'Good news and sort of bad news. MacAllister has pleaded guilty to theft and serious assault.'

'Not rape?' Billy said, bemused.

'No, prosecutor thinks it might not stick.'

'Is that the good news and the bad news?'

'No. The bad news is D.S. McCall's funeral is on Monday and the boss expects you and McCallum to be there.'

The constable face dropped a bit.

'It's in Dundee.'

'Well, I won't be going to it. No way.'

'The Chief says you are expected.'

When the Chief says expected to be there, it means you will be there.

Billy shook his head. 'No way. I haven't got a car. If I took the Morris do you know how long it would take me to get to Dundee in it?'

Denise didn't answer. Having witnessed his driving first hand, she could realistically have said about 8 hours, although she would expect to get there in less than half that time.

'We can go in the yellow peril.'

'Your car. Do you mean you are going too?'

'Yes, well, I only met him the once, but we seemed to get on.'

Billy, as ever, missed the attempt at humour.

'Do you think Andrew will go?'

'Billy, the Chief settled it that Andrew didn't lose his pension or the police house for a few years anyway, when he left. He could have, very easily have lost both. After all, McKelvie must have known Andrew's son was stealing the sheep and butchering them to sell when he got the reports through.'

'Oh, I didn't know that McKelvie helped him out.'

'Yes, McKelvie seems a straight up kind of guy, especially after what he did for McCall. So, are you still not going?'

'What, of course I will go if it's your car. We could take turns driving if you like?'

'No, you won't be insured,' she said, panicking at the thought of him driving her precious peril.

'That wouldn't look good, if you are charged with driving with no insurance after a fellow copper's funeral.'

Really, she couldn't stand for anyone, even Billy, driving the yellow peril.

It felt strange ringing the doorbell at the Wilson's boarding house. A week before she was living there and had her own key. Now, standing there, she felt like a bit of a stranger.

Susan answered it.

'Is this about Saturday night?' she asked coyly.

'Yes, I need to speak to Colin. Do you know if he is in?'

Susan just nodded and moved back to let her in.

'You know where his room is.'

Denise started for the stairs when Susan spoke again.

'I couldn't help it. On Saturday she called me for everything. I got so angry I nearly told her who the father of my baby is. She would really have cracked up if I had said.'

Denise looked round to see if anyone was around. Just at that moment there was a creaking from above as someone was coming down the stairs.

One of the old spinsters appeared at the landing above.

'I am here to try and clear you. Don't say anything else,' Denise said, putting a finger to her lips afterwards.

Denise walked past the old woman and up the middle of the stairs, deliberately making them creak as she went. All the time she was wondering what the big secret about the baby's father could be. Still, she had Coco to see, the other thing could wait.

Denise rapped on the door to room number 1.

Coco answered it wearing just a pair of y-fronts, a t-shirt and white sports socks.

'I'm not ready yet mate,' he said, opening the door without

looking round, then realised it wasn't Andy when he didn't follow him in.

'Oh, sorry it's you. Wait until I get my trousers on,' he said when he turned round, then he quickly closed the door over again.

A minute later the door re-opened, and Colin stood there with his jeans on and sporting a big beamer of a red face.

'Sorry, I thought it was Andy. Were you looking for him?'

'No. It's you I need to see.'

'Ow.'

'Yes. Saturday night. I believe you left the pub in the company of Rita Samson. Is that correct?'

'Yes. How, what has she said?'

'Nothing. Why?'

'Well, because I didn't stay the night like she wanted.'

'No. Why not?'

'Because she is sick.'

'Sick?'

'Yes. First of all, she wanted Andy to come with us. Wanted a threesome.'

Denise just shrugged. There was nothing against the law in it as far as she knew, and it wasn't the most sordid thing she could think of.

'She got angry when he said no to her. Then, on the way back to hers, she said she wanted me to do her every way.'

Denise looked puzzled, although she knew exactly what she meant. Anal wasn't exactly perverted by any stretch of the imagination.

'She meant I was to do her up the bum as well. I wasn't going to do that, that's what poofs do and I ain't one of them.'

Denise herself had never participated in the act herself but only because it never appealed to her. Plus, nobody had ever asked her if she was up for it.

'So, that was it?'

'No. It's worse than that. We went back to hers and she stripped off. Do you know she had no hair on her.' He paused as he thought about what to call it. He settled on, 'her fanny.'

Denise stifled a laugh. Obviously it was the first time he had encountered a shaven haven. Still, nothing yet that she thought was weird.

She was still wondered how bad it could be for Coco not to do the business. Especially after bedding bendy Wendy.

'Then she said come through to the wet room.'

The redness from earlier was staring to creep into the lad's cheeks again as he was getting embarrassed about what he was going to tell her.

'Back at hers after we stripped off in the bedroom she led me into the bathroom. She told me to lie on the floor and said she would pee on me. It's called a golden shower. It feels hot and you will love it.'

'I said I don't care what it's called, you aren't pissing on me, no way. Then she said after that you can do it to me, then we can shower together and soap each other all over.'

There was a silence and Denise was trying to work out what happened next. Did he do the disgusting deed?'

'That was when I grabbed my clothes, ran out and left. She came running after me and stood at the front door naked and screaming for me to come back.'

'Then what?'

'I had to stop round the corner and get dressed. Then I went to Wendy's and stayed the night there.'

'You didn't come back here to the boarding house?'

'Not until about 8 o'clock in the morning. Why?'

'Somebody took a tin of paint from the shed here and poured it on Rita Samson's Mercedes.'

'What, is that the lying bitch said, that I did it?

A rage boiled inside him at the thought of the previous Saturday night, something he wanted to forget, put right to the back of his mind. Now, it seemed, the cow was trying to get her revenge for running out on her.

'Wow, wow, calm down. Nobody is accusing you. I am only investigating the facts as I know them. Now, I am sure bendy, I mean this Wendy woman will say you spent the night with her.'

'Too right, she would be proud that a young stud like me would spend the night with her,' he said quite loudly, as his cockiness had suddenly returned.

'Do you know her address?'

'No. But I can take you to the house if you want.'

'No, it's okay Colin, I will take your word for it.'

Just at that the other room door opened and Andy came out.

'What's going on? Are you looking for me?'

Denise smiled at the cockiness that he had too. As he walked toward her the heavy smell of Brut reached her before he did.

'No. Just investigating a wee incident from Saturday night.'

'Colin was with me all night.'

Denise laughed. 'No, it's okay, he has an alibi. Unless of course you were with Wendy too.'

'No chance, not me. Did you know we are leaving this week?,' he said. She thought he was hinting at what was in his mind, the unfinished business from their last night out.

'Yes. Liz told me the job was finished here and you are off to Crieff next.'

'We are leaving straight after work on the Friday. We are having a farewell drink down the pub on Thursday night if you fancy it?'

'No, sorry. I have a big day on Friday, can't afford to get drunk the night before.'

'You could nip in for one.'

'Yes, like the last time. I went in for a couple and ended up still there at last orders.'

'Yes, I still think about that night,' he said with a twinkle in his eye as he thought again about what might have been.

'Anyway, I am finished for the night. Time to go back to my bedsit.'

'We are off down the pub, why not join us?'

'No. Not during the week. Anyway, I might see you before you leave.'

Denise walked away, wondering to herself if she hadn't been assaulted would she have given Andy a going away present. He was kinda cute after all and it was nice to know she was still fanciable to a young man a lot younger than her.

RILING RITA

Denise had one thing she needed to do after she had her tea the next morning and that was to visit Rita.

After what Coco had told her the previous night and what her neighbour had said, she saw her in a different light. Certainly not any nicer. She had never liked her from the first time she stepped into the shop on the day she arrived.

Indeed, Cruella De Ville, Denise thought, who she would think of her from now on whenever she saw Rita, would probably have been a nicer person if she was real.

She was in the middle of filling her P.C. in on what she found out the previous night when the phone rang.

The call was quite short and sweet. When Denise turned to face her colleague, she had a surprised look on her face.

'Well, well. Billy, I am afraid you can't take the Morris when you go home for lunch today.'

'Oh,' he said. 'It's okay, I will walk. Good to get out and about, get noticed. Meet the locals, let them know we are there for them if they need us.'

'Do you not want to know why?'

Suddenly his interest was piqued.

'Why? Was it something to do with that phone call?'

'Yes. The Morris needs to be here, they are taking the Morris because they are delivering a new squad car, a Ford Escort. It's coming at around 1 o'clock they said.'

'Will I get to drive it?'

'Of course. It's just a squad car, the same as the Morris.'

Billy laughed. 'It's certainly not the same as the Morris.'

'We are getting a new squad car. It will be treated the same as before and we will drive it as and when required. Now, before they take it, is there anything we need to take out of it? Any personnel stuff.'

'No, I don't think so, but I will check.'

Then he looked at her before adding, 'I would like to say goodbye to her before she goes. It has been with us for over 10 years.'

Denise was surprised, she would have guessed at 20 years, not 10.

'Of course, you can,' she said. 'You can do that when I go and have a word with Crue, I mean Rita.'

'Do you want another cup before you go. Good news always makes me thirsty.'

'Go on then, you've twisted my arm.'

As Denise walked down the street she smiled to herself. Although the weather up to know had been okay, today it just seemed nicer.

The early morning sun was bright although the last chills of winter still hang in the air, the signs were that spring was just around the corner.

Bright yellow daffodils had suddenly sprouted and seemed to be littering gardens and waste ground alike. It was hard not to smile along with them.

Denise looked in Samson's general store window. Only Rita and Susan were working, no sign of Hugh. She watched as the single customer in the shop at the time was served and made her way out.

She pretended to closely study the strange display of cleaning products in the window display but was actually watching the events unfolding in the shop.

Even through the thick plate-glass she was sure the owner was berating the shopgirl again. Time to make her entrance.

The bell clanged to signal her arrival and an awkward silence fell between the other two followed.

'Good morning Detective Constable,' Rita said in her most charming voice.

Denise wasn't sure, but it sounded more like cuntstable than constable, not that anything the shopkeeper did could make her like her less.

'I take it you found the culprit who vandalised my beautiful car.'

'I think we need to talk in the back. Just in case any customers come in. We wouldn't want to be washing our underwear in public,' the D.C. said, although she now doubted she ever wore any.

Rita beringed past her with attitude. In the back shop she sat at the large table that sat in the middle of the room. Denise kept standing.

'Mrs. Samson, P.C.Lambie and myself have made extensive enquiries into the vandalism of your car. We found out the paint was stolen from a shed in the town, but nobody witnessed either the theft, anybody walking through the town in the wee small hours carrying the paint or the actual vandalism itself.'

Rita had folded her arms as the policewoman spoke. Then she balled her fists and put her arms out before she spoke.

'So that's it then. Whoever did this gets off with it Scot-free. Able to attack my belongings whenever they want.'

'My enquiries were not helped by you with-holding information when I interviewed you.'

'That was nothing to do with what happened to my car?'

'Oh. How do you know?'

Rita looked at her, suddenly thinking it might have been Colin, who did it. Obviously somebody she hadn't figured to be the guilty party.

Although probably wrong ethically, Denise wanted to deflect Rita's suspicion away from Susan although she probably wasn't even a suspect in her eyes, or she wouldn't still be serving in the shop.

'What has really surprised me is I saw signs up that yours is a Neighbourhood watch area but none of your neighbours seemed willing to help. Indeed, some were quite willing to complain about you and your anti-social behaviour.'

'My anti-social behaviour!' she said, raising her voice.

'There words, not mine.'

For once Rita had nothing to say just sat raging to herself.

'Well, if anything changes I will be back in touch.'

Denise turned and walked out the back room. Susan was staring straight at her, and she winked conspiritually at her.

The young girl smiled then turned away before Rita could see her.

Billy had, unsurprisingly, taken an early lunch and was with Denise when the transporter arrived with their new car.

The Ford Escort, resplendent in the blue and white panda colours, wasn't brand new but only 2 years old, decades younger than the car it was replacing.

Denise and Billy stood outside the station watching the delivery guy get the new car ready to be unloaded. The phone rang inside so Denise handed the keys to Billy and went in to answer it.

Sylvia Morton, the local headmistress was calling. She

wondered if they could supply 2 police to assist with crossings on the Friday morning as the children were going from the school to the church for their Easter service.

Denise suddenly thought back to her own schooldays. She never attended church as a regular thing but loved going with the school. There was a certain reverence about the inside of a church when you are little. The grandeur of the fittings, the reverential air the organ music seemed to supply and most importantly, after the service they were on holiday.

At the back of her mind something niggled, she had something she wanted to do that day but as she spoke to the headmistress it wouldn't come to mind.

Fact was, she was looking forward to it. All the happy kids, excitedly looking forward to church, holidays and Easter eggs on the following Sunday.

Maybe a few kids would look up to her and think they might want to join the police too. That was why she decided she would wear her uniform on the Friday. That and the fact she wanted to see it still fitted okay before Monday's funeral.

FRIDAY SERVICE

Friday morning and Denise walked into the station wearing her dress uniform. She hadn't told P.C. Lambie, and he looked stunned.

When she walked round the counter to the office he looked her up and down.

'What's wrong, have you never seen a woman in uniform before?'

'No. It's just you always wear trousers; I've never seen your legs.'

'Oh, are you a leg man?'

Billy got a bit embarrassed and said nothing in response.

Denise laughed. The dress skirt went down to her knees, so hardly any of her legs were showing. Especially as she was wearing tan tights and black Doc Marten shoes.

The uniform fitted her better than she thought. The main reason for that was she had left the Wilson's place just in time. Her healthier eating now stopped her putting on any more weight than she wanted.

'I wanted to make a good impression on the kids. Plant a small kernel in their minds and when they grow up, who knows?' she told the P.C.

'They grow up nuts. Like MacAllister,' he replied.

As soon as he said it, the constable realised he had said the wrong thing and deeply regretted it.

'I'm sorry, I didn't mean,' he spluttered. 'Not like that.'

Denise put her hand up to shut him up. She swallowed hard and tried not to think about the little rapist scumbag for a second longer than she needed.

'So, have you ever helped take the kids to church service before?' she said, quickly changing the subject, hoping she could get him back feeling at ease.

'No. We have never been asked.'

Why was that not a surprise, she thought. She walked over the street map on the wall.

'Right, I walked the route yesterday. The main road we need to stop traffic at is Melbourne Road. You can take the car and park it here.'

Billy smiled. He liked driving the new car.

'Then when the kids are all past you walk behind us to the church. I will walk along beside them, that way they should stay on the pavement.'

The church service parade went perfectly, and the teachers seemed very pleased that the police presence had helped, and the kids felt more important with their uniformed escort.

Back in her room, Denise was just happy to get her uniform off. Although it wasn't girded on her, after 9 hours it was starting to pinch some bits that had obviously expanded since she was measured and fitted for it some time ago.

As she ate her tea, beans on toast, she decided she deserved a drink. She had a couple of bottles of white wine in the fridge but fancied going to the pub for an hour. After all, Andy should have left the town so there wouldn't be any awkwardness that she felt whenever she met him.

There was slight drizzle in the air as she walked up the

street towards the pub. Her brolly sheltered her, however it meant she was nearly at the pub before she realised there was a bright light flashing further up the street.

'That's the boarding house,' she said to herself, before realising it was in fact a blue light, an ambulance. Picking up the pace she ran the rest of the way. Liz. It was then she realised what she had to do today, pick up Robin and warn him within an inch of his life what would happen if he raised a hand to his wife again. Now, it seemed, she was too late.

The fact she had warned her on Monday that it would end like this didn't make her feel any better.

Just as she reached the ambulance they were carrying the stretcher into the back. She was shocked to see it was Robin getting carried in.

'What happened?' she asked.

The medic looked at her but wasn't forthcoming.

'Police,' she said, encouraging him to speak.

'Plain clothes, is it?'

Seeing as she was dressed in jeans, t-shirt and denim jacket, he couldn't have been more right.

'Officially I should be off duty, but these are friends of mine.'

'Guys been given a going over. Pretty bad, we think he might have some internal injuries.'

Just at that, Liz Wilson appeared. She had her jacket on and was ready to go with her husband in the ambulance.

'Any idea who did it?'

There were tears in Liz's eyes. 'No. Somebody knocked my door and told me. Said they just found him on the ground outside. I didn't want him lifted in case he was injured more.'

'No, you did the right thing. These guys are professionals.'

As ever, there were a few nosey neighbours hanging around watching.

After the ambulance left, with blue lights flashing and siren blaring, the nosy folk stayed out, talking about it.

Denise quickly crossed over before they went back inside.

'Did anybody see anything?' she asked loudly enough for everybody to have heard.

Like Rita's neighbours earlier in the week, nobody wanted to speak to her, knowing she was in the police. In fact, the questioning resulting in them all disappearing back inside out of the drizzle, as there was nothing left to see or talk about.

The notion of a drink was off her now and she looked down the street, wondering who else might have seen somebody getting assaulted at 6 o'clock on a bright evening and on a busy street.

Just at that Susan came out of the house.

'I'm sorry about your dad,' she offered.

'I'm not. He deserved it for what he did.'

For a minute Denise thought he might be the father of her child.

'What's that?'

'He would come home every weekend and abuse mum. He thought nothing about hitting her. I hope he dies.'

'Do you know who beat him up?'

'Yes, but I won't tell you. Anyway, it's too late, they have left the town now.'

Denise knew straight away she meant it was Andy and Coco. But, if she didn't know for sure, she couldn't do anything about it.

She walked back down towards the pub and realised she was wrong to think like that. Giving somebody a clout to warn them off was one thing, however it looked as if they had gone too far. Hospitalising him was going way too far.

After she interviewed Robin, she would pass on their details to their home station, or even Crieff Police because they were heading there next.

Reaching the pub door, she could hear things were pretty rowdy. The events at the Wilson's had put her off socialising. Instead, she turned and headed back down the hill, to the bedsit and her own company and a bottle of wine.

D.S. LESLEY MCCALL, REST IN PEACE

P.C. Lambie and Andrew McCallum were sitting waiting for D.C. Kelly when she arrived at the station at 08:30 precisely. She wasn't even sure McCallum would have turned up. She had personally told him about the arrangements and McKelvie's request but, as ever, being a man of few words, he hadn't said one way or another if he was going.

'My, my, you two are keen.'

'It's a duty we have to do. Even though I feel a bit of a fraud wearing this uniform again,' Andrew said.

'Remember, Andrew, Chief Inspector McKelvie went out of his way to approve your retirement on full pension.'

Andrew looked to the floor.

'I think you owe him this.'

'Yes, well I'm here, aren't I.'

'Are we having a cup of tea first?' Billy asked.

'No!' Andrew quickly said. 'We will be stopping at the first bus stop and every public convenience so that you can pee if you have a drink just now,' he added.

Denise stifled a laugh. It was a sad day, after all.

'Right then, let's go,' Billy said, keen now there was no tea on offer.

Billy had commandeered the passenger seat while the ex-cop sat in the back. The reason he had was that if he wasn't in the front of a car for any distance he was car sick. That was enough to convince Denise. She didn't want any technicolour yawns decorating the inside of her pride and joy.

She put on her latest cassette, Rod Stewart's Never a dull moment. She bought it at Woolworths the week before. Until then she hadn't had a chance to hear it.

It played softly in the background as she drove. Denise liked the blond rocker's music and although it wasn't too loud, she hoped the other two were enjoying the music.

About half-way through the first half of the tape, the music critic in the back seat spoke up.

'I don't want to sound cheeky hen, but that sounds shite to me. Have you no country music?'

Denise tried not to be perturbed but she was. Rod Stewart was brilliant, she thought. His husky voice sent shivers through her body to parts the other two occupants could never dream about reaching.

To prove a point, she switched from cassette to radio and told Billy to try to find any country music. Something she was sure he couldn't find.

The sound varied from heavy rock to the spoken word to pop with much crackling in-between as he tried to do as his boss asked, twiddling the station knob as he tried to comply with her wishes.

Eventually, as he was unable to find country music as asked, he asked what he should do.

'Ask Hughie Green in the back. He knows more about music than me, obviously,' Denise said.

'Andrew. What will I put on?'

'I don't mind,' he said. 'As long as it's not that shit she had on earlier.'

Denise knew then it was going to be a long journey and a

longer day.

Outside the church it was more like a police convention than a funeral. Waiting to go in were hundreds of uniformed officers resplendent in their best dress uniforms. Chief Inspector McKelvie, approached the group of 3 and informed them they were to be in the guard of honour, the group that stood outside the church in two lines while the coffin and the chief mourners walked in. Denise felt a fraud. If it had been up to her the deviant in the box would have been exposed for the pervert that he was. Instead, she had to pay tribute.

However, as the coffin was slowly carried past, behind him a woman who must have been his grieving sister walked with her distraught family, it was only then Denise realised the Chief had been right. The family that was left behind were suffering enough thinking McCall had died a good guy. How hard would their lives be if they knew the sordid truth?

Once again, Denise thought how hard it would have been for her if she found out something like that about her father. She would have been absolutely devastated.

They arrived back at Glengurly that evening just after 8 o'clock. Denise felt that she needed a drink but the other 2 wanted home. Billy Lambie got dropped off first.

After he got out the car, the retired cop was quiet, as he had been all day, although Denise thought he had a look on him that made her think he was desperate to say something. She thought Billy was going to be the subject of his bombasting. Instead, he only offered her some advice.

As he was leaving the car, he leaned back in. 'A word of advice. The Mac Allister's are telling everyone they are out to get you. They are a nasty lot, watch yourself.'

Before she could say or even ask him anything else, the door was slammed, and he was off. Denise drove back to her digs and hoped the wee MacAllister runt wasn't in her dreams that night.

Denise arrived first the next morning. Before she had even got the front door open the phone was ringing. She rushed round to answer it.

'Good morning, Glenfurny,' was all she managed to get out.

'I want my neighbour charged with breach of the peace.'

Denise could tell by the excited voice and heavy breathing that followed; the caller was really worked up. Her first job was to slow him down and calm him.

'Okay sir, and you are?'.

'Stephen Brown.'

'Who is your neighbour you are calling about?'

'Surely you know. Rita Samson.'

Straight away she thought she didn't need an identikit picture or police artist's impression to picture the caller, it was the obviously the first neighbour, the nosey one, she spoke to the previous day. Mister Brown, she would have called him Mister Beige, she wasn't far off the mark, just a few shades darker.

'Okay sir. I will be round to see you in 10 minutes.'

She hung up just as Billy arrived.

'What's up?'

'It would appear Rita Samson has annoyed her neighbours again. Or at least one of them.'

'Right. Are we going round there just now?'

'No, it's okay, I will go. You have your cuppa and man the phones.'

'Okay,' he said, not needing much encouragement.

As she drove the yellow peril through the quiet town, she hoped the nosey old guy had the sense to get somebody to witness Rita's tirade. She would have loved to arrest the old pervert and charge her, even if it was only for a breach of the peace.

Rita parked the yellow peril at the same place as the last time, right outside Rita's gaff.

Before she was even halfway up his drive, the front door was opened, and Mister Brown was standing at the front door impatiently waiting.

Behind him his wife looked round him, she hadn't appeared out the previous day. She looked a right wee nippy sweety, Denise guessed this would be a two-pronged attack.

'Thank you for coming so quickly. I want her charged,' he said, pointing towards the house that was the blot on the neighbourhood. The "her" was also said with utter contempt.

Denise took out her notebook. Although she only used it as an aide memoir, writing only relevant notes, it assured people that they were being listened to and taken seriously.

'From the beginning, if you don't mind.'

'Right. Last night at about 9 O'clock,' Stephen started, only to be interrupted by his wife, leaning round so she could be seen.

'It was quarter to 9. I was just doing the cocoa.'

Long live the rock and roll lifestyle, Denise thought.

The wife's interruption had annoyed Stephen and he took a moment to compose himself before starting again.

'Last night at approximately a quarter to 9 our doorbell rang. I wasn't expecting anyone, especially at that time of night. When I opened it, she was standing there where you are. Her hand came up and she pointed her finger straight at me. She said, you complained to the police about me. She said it was because I was jealous of her lifestyle because we were boring old sods.

Then she followed that with a terrifying tirade. At one point I thought she was going to hit me.

Her language was disgusting, that of a guttersnipe. She said all I had to look forward to was being six foot under in a box in a hole in the ground. The sooner the better, she said.'

While he was talking he was getting agitated and there were flecks of white matter forming at the side of his lips.

Denise gradually moved back, out of range of his phlegm.

When he stopped to regain his composure, his wife butted in.

'Don't forget she called you a pompous prick.'

He gave her a sideways glance, obviously, he had decided to omit that fact.

All this was hardly a breach of the peace Denise thought. Still, she had to pacify him.

'Were there any witnesses?'

'My wife was at the living room window the whole time.'

She was rather coy now. 'I didn't want to get involved or I might have said or done something I would have regretted. Then you might have been arresting me.'

Denise smiled; she knew the wifie was talking utter crap.

'Did anyone else witness her tirade?'

'No. Just the two of us. Although some of the neighbours must have heard her. They would know I don't speak to my wife like that.'

'I take it you are retired?'

Mr Brown nodded.

'What was your occupation?'

'I was the local bank manager for over 30 years,' he said, his chest raising a bit with pride at his career accomplishment.

Denise thought she could have scripted it, he looked like the stereotypical retired bank manager.

'The thing people don't realise is your spouse cannot give evidence against you in court and by the same reasoning they cannot be a witness for you. Without an independent witness, we cannot proceed any further. It's your word against them, I am afraid.'

The retired bank manager's brow furrowed. Realising what she was saying, he started blustering.

'You what. You mean she can come over here and call me everything under the sun and get away with it. You could take the word of that trollop against mine, who have been an upstanding citizen all my working life serving the community.'

'I am afraid so; at times the law can be an ass. Unfortunately, that's the way it is. If you don't have independent witnesses we cannot take it any further. I sympathise with you, but I don't make the laws. I fully believe she came over here and abused you. However, in the eyes of the law if you don't have another witness out-with your family there is nothing much I can do.'

The couple looked at each other. Stunned. Bemused. Angry.

'What I can do is have a word with her. An official word saying we will be taking no action this time but if she repeats it she will be charged.'

'That's it.'

She thought that would have pacified them, obviously not.

'Well, the other advice I can give you is if she turns up at your door again phone a neighbour to witness what she says.'

The couple looked at each other again, furrowed brows showing.

'You do have neighbours you could call,' Denise said, trying not to be cheeky but also not being too surprised if they said no.

'Yes, The Wayman's next door are good people, they would help. Colin and Jenny across the road would help too.'

'You should pre-empt them by telling them what happened and that you will phone them if she turns up at your door again.'

Realising this was the best they could get, they turned and smiled at Denise.

'Right, I am off to the shop to read her the riot act. I am afraid that's as much as I do,' Denise said, relishing the prospect.

'Thank you very much,' Mrs Brown said.

'Yes. I am sure you will do your best,' he added reluctantly.

'Oh, don't worry on that score,' she said, before turning to leave.

Denise scribbled something in her notebook and left them to return to their retirement.

Denise headed the peril back towards the station. As she drove past the local square she saw a familiar figure heading down the street towards her. P.C. Lambie was out on the beat, without even being prompted.

She drew up beside him and told him to get in.

'What's up?'

She told him what had happened and what she was going to do about it. He was going to drive her in the squad car down to the shop.

'I thought you would just walk down.'

'Billy, remember that first day I arrived. You drove us next door to the Wilson's.'

He nodded although looked puzzled.

'There is an incident, we are showing there is a police presence, that was your words. You taught me that.'

Billy smiled. He couldn't believe he had actually taught his new mentor something. Boy, his mum would be proud, he thought, it was his father that told him the same thing many years ago.

Billy parked the squad car right outside the Samson's shop.

'Want me to wait in the car?'

'No. You come in the shop with me and just wait inside the front door.'

Rita and Susan were serving and there were a couple of customers getting served. The two police officers went in and waited just inside the shop, standing silently until the customers left.

Ideal, Denise thought, the gossip and rumours would be out before they were.

'Is this about my car?' the Cruella De Ville lookalike asked when they were alone.

'No. I have received a complaint about you.'

Rita looked puzzled. Denise thought the Oscar for best puzzled look goes to Rita Samson.

'Do you want to speak in the back or do you want to air your dirty laundry here.'

Rita walked brusquely from behind the counter towards the back shop without saying a word. Denise and Billy followed.

The shopkeeper stood, turning with her arms crossed.

'Well, what did the Brown's say now?'

'I didn't say it was the Brown's.'

'It's always the Brown's. They complain about everything.'

'Not to us they don't. Do they P.C. Lambie?'

He shook his head.

'You are right, it was the Brown's. So, you aren't denying

you went to their house last night?'

'No. I had a drink or two last night. Then I decided to tell them what I thought of them.'

'You called him a pompous prick.'

Rita laughed. 'That's right. You have met him, he is.'

'That's as maybe but you cannot do that. Now, they have agreed you should be let off with just a warning this time.'

'They agreed!' she said, losing her temper that had clearly been sizzling under the surface about her neighbour's complaint since they walked in the shop.

'Look, if they had said you would have been charged with a breach of the peace. I managed to talk them down to a warning. I have 2 options. Either you accept a verbal warning her about your behaviour or we go down the station and do it officially and in writing.

If it is a written warning it will go down on your record and that could, of course, affect your licence to sell alcohol and tobacco. The local licensing board at the council will find out.'

Rita banged a fist down on the table then looked at the policewoman with utter distain.

'Are you threatening me?' Rita asked.

'No. Just pointing out the possibilities your actions could have.'

'Okay, let's get it over with now.'

'Rita Samson, I am officially warning you that if you confront any of your neighbours and threaten or abuse them you will be charged.'

Rita surprisingly hung her head in shame.

'That includes customers or staff.'

Her head shot up.

'No way. Not in the shop. Never. My customers are my living.'

She beringed past, back into the shop with Denise following.

The only other person in the shop was Susan.

'Susan dear, have you ever heard me being abusive to any of our customers?'

'No.'

'Have I ever been abusive to you?'

Susan's head went down slightly. 'No.'

Rita turned with her arms out to face Denise.

'Whoever is spreading such vicious things about me should be being investigated by you.'

Denise nodded gently. 'Well, if you keep yourself to yourself then this will be the end to the matter.'

P.C. Lambie walked ahead and opened the door for the D.C., and they walked out together.

As they got back in the car they could see the 2 customers were now standing down the street pretending not to watch what was going on at the shop.

'Well, that went well,' she said, smiling.

'Do you know something Billy, if it wasn't for the Wilson's and the Samson's we wouldn't have anything to do.'

Billy laughed.

'It's given those 2 busybodies something new to talk about,' he said as he drove slowly past them, waving to them as he did.

Back at the station a large delivery lorry was filling the car park, waiting for them to get back. There was no room for anybody else to park there and Billy had to park the police car out in the street.

The driver got out as they approached.

'I was just about to dial 999,' he said. joking.

'What have you got for us?' Denise asked.

He checked his clipboard.

'Electronic typewriter, radio station, 4 radios and various stationary items.'

The two cops looked like each other. It was like Christmas to both, but for different reasons. Denise desperate for a new machine for her reports whereas Billy looked forward to the street cred he would have while talking into a walkie talkie. He had seen them on TV cop shows and always wanted 1 for himself.

Once taken in, Denise disappeared into the office to unwrap and set up the typewriter, while Billy busied himself setting up the radio station.

By the time they were both done it was almost lunchtime.

'Can I take my radio home with me. We can test how far our reception is.'

'Sure. Well, I am heading back to the flat to do some ironing. What about we do a soundcheck at 12:30 exactly.'

Denise had her ironing board ready to start when she noticed the time. It was one minute before the half hour and just then her radio cracked into life.

'P.C. Lambie calling Detective Constable Kelly.'

'You forgot to say over, over,' she corrected him.

Denise could imagine him standing proudly in the living room at home, showing off to his old mum. He wouldn't be happy his first attempt wasn't quite right.

'Roger, Detective Constable Kelly, sound check. Over.'

'Roger P.C. Lambie. Message received and understood. Coming through loud and clear. Over.'

'Radio check, over. Over,' Billy said, now familiar with the correct procedure.

She sat the radio down and started ironing. Boy, she thought, she laughed at the Brown's earlier, she wasn't living the rock and roll lifestyle either.

NIGHT OUT

Having survived another week Denise decided another bottle of wine would be drunk that night.

After having her dinner, she opened the fridge to get her wine out. As she reached in the fridge something Andy said came into her head. Nobody should be sitting in on a Friday night. Sod it, she thought, the pub it was. The loclas were used to her being about now, surely she would get a better reception than the last time.

Before going out, she decided to get warmed up with a big glass of wine, get her cheery and in the mood for a good night out, something she thought she deserved.

She dressed all in black, a colour than dominated her wardrobe and stepped out, ready for fun. It was a lovely bright evening and she headed for the pub with a spring in her step.

As she got to the main drag she could hear music in the distance. It was coming from the opposite direction she was heading, must be from the caravan park she guessed.

From where she was it was probably the same distance to the park as it was to the pub. There must be a disco on, she thought.

If there was a disco, she could see if there was under-age drinking as Andy and Coco said. Chance to investigate for herself and she for herself if the lad's allegations were true.

Decision made, she headed towards the music.

There was a doorman just inside the caravan park's clubhouse.

'Have you got a ticket?' he asked, putting his hand out to accept it.

'No. I thought it would be pay at the door. Is it a disco?'

'No, it's a stand-up comedian.'

Denise wasn't sure if she fancied it and her face was telling the doorman the same thing.

'It's Happy Harvey Hood. He is very good.'

'The thing is, I am a policewoman. I heard you were selling drink to under-agers, and I thought this was a disco. Came down to see for myself'

'No way. Definitely not. We would lose our licence if we did that. My staff all know that and know they would lose their jobs if we caught them doing that. They might come here after drinking their own drink, but they will not be served at the bar in there.'

'So, who are you?'

'Colin MacGregor, I am the joint owner here.'

Denise smiled. 'You know back where I come from a joint owner would be a man with a spliff.'

Colin was not impressed in the least.

'The comedian is in there. Now, do you want a ticket. He has just about to get started.'

Standing in the foyer they could tell the noise had changed from music to mirth.

'How much is it?'

'A pound or one -fifty with a pie after the comedian.'

Denise got a pound note out of her purse and headed for the entrance door.

Just before she opened the door there was a huge laugh from the audience. As it went quiet she walked in. From her experience anybody going to the toilet or like her walking in late, were fair game for the stand-up to take the rip taken out of them, so she was ready.

She waited until he was mid-joke then made her way through the tables and headed for the bar. The comic clocked her and wasn't letting her off.

'What's wrong love? Have trouble parking your broomstick.'

She didn't expect to be called a witch, but she was dressed all in black after all. Instead of answering back she waved gently and continued towards the bar. She knew the worst thing she could do was answer back, then he would really ridicule her, she was sure.

'Do you know witches don't wear knickers, it lets them get a better grip on the broomstick,' he continued, getting a bigger laugh than the last one.

'I am wearing knickers,' she called back.

'Yes, but the night is young,' he went on cheekily.

Every eye in the hall seemed to be on her, some concentrating more than others. Denise tried not to be embarrassed by the attention.

'What's your name love?' he then called after her.

She stopped and turned toward him.

'Denise,' she called back.

'Don't tell me, your uncle got the job of naming you and your brother's called de-nephew.'

This seemed to be his biggest laugh of the night so far, she guessed and smiled back at him.

Somebody said something to the comedian, she guessed telling him of her occupation.

'You are a police officer?' he called out next.

She waved in acknowledgment.

'Did you know the police horse is unique. It's the only animal with a prick on its back and another beneath,' he said. This was met by hysterical laughing, much of it probably aimed at her and her employers.

She got her drink, her usual vodka and coke, and managed to get an empty table at the back. As the show went on, she actually enjoyed it. She even the jokes slagging off the police, which he seemed to have an ample supply of.

His jokes were laugh a minute. Even Denise, who always thought she was sharp-witted struggled to keep up at times.

Much of his act involved slagging off his wife. If she was in the audience she must have some sense of humour, Denise thought.

The joke she liked most about his wife was: did you know the word wife is actually an acrostic, it stands for washing, ironing, fucking etcetera.

As the audience howled with laughter Denise couldn't help but think most of them were so dumb they wouldn't even know what an acrostic was.

Her favourite joke ribbing the police was: I watched a policeman in Glasgow went into the back of a panda. He was barred from the Calderpark zoo. She liked that one especially because she hadn't heard it before.

The truth was there weren't any panda's at Calderpark but jokes aren't about the truth.

It also took her back to her childhood when a trip to Calderpark, less than 20 miles from her home, seemed a great adventure then. Quick half hours car journey now.

The other joke that got a huge laugh was about when you are getting arrested and being read your rights, when they say anything can be used in evidence, say- stop hitting me officer.

That was an old one, but even she joined in laughing. Must have been the way he told it.

From where Denise was sitting, she could see the whole room. It was good to watch the way the comedian worked the crowd. He picked on 1 or 2 people and constantly referred to them in a funny way. Lucky for her, she seemed to be too far away to pick on again, apart from the constant japes slagging the force off.

She admired the comedian. It was one thing that really scared her, public speaking. She couldn't stand up in front of a crowd like him.

Harvey looked about 30 to 40 years old and quite good looking. He had a happy go lucky attitude, or so it seemed. Could be a total prick off stage she mused.

Then Denise noticed a woman was staring at her. Oh, a lot of them would take a drink and move their eyes to see her, the new cop in the town, but one just constantly stared straight at her and it was starting to spook her. She wanted to know who she was and headed to the bar for another vodka.

When the guy in front of her staggered off with a tray of drinks she asked the barmaid for another vodka and coke.

When the barmaid brought the drink to her, she asked who the woman with the home dyed hair job was. The barmaid said she would need to narrow it down, most of the women there couldn't afford a decent hairdresser.

She added she was staring straight at her, she could feel her eyes burning into her back, and was wearing a leopard-print shirt.

The barmaid scanned the audience and saw the woman, who was , as Denise guessed, staring straight at them.

'That's Ivy MacAllister.'

A cold shiver ran down Denise's spine. Andrew McCallum

had warned her the MacAllisters were out to get her. Now she was in there beside her and no doubt the rest of her clan, leaving her a sitting duck.

She imagined it being like a bird of prey staring down its quarry, waiting for the chance to pounce on its defenceless target and right now she was the target.

Denise sat back down and wondered how she could sneak out safely. Ivy MacAllister was still staring straight at her. Also at the table were no doubt the rest of her family. Ugly looking Neanderthals, dropped into jeans and t-shirt, covered in Indian ink tatts and filled with lager, and that was just the womenfolk. The men were worse.

The first thing she could think of doing was phoning 999 and getting a crew out from Dingwall to save her, but by the time they got here it would be too late, it was over 30 minutes' drive away.

Then she thought if she got a chance to call the joint owner over he could help her out by calling her a taxi. There again, on their first meeting she accused him of supplying drink to under 18's so there was no guarantee he would help.

Just then the comedian finished his act to thunderous applause. As he left the stage pop music blared, signalling the disco had started.

The dance floor was starting to fill up then the DJ announced the food was being served. Suddenly, the dancers and the rest of the drinkers, rushed to line up to get their pies.

A chance to go, Denise thought, as the MacAllisters would no doubt be desperate for their pies. The queue for food snaked through the tables right across the dance floor. Most of the crowd were in it with one obvious exception, Ivy MacAllister, who still sat staring in her direction.

Denise got a fright as a set of keys clattered down on the table, almost in front of her. This was followed by a vodka and coke.

'Mind if I join you?'

Denise looked up and saw the perpetrator was Harvey Hood, who was smiling down at her.

'Why, do I look as if I am falling apart?'

'Oh, beautiful and funny. You should be on the stage, a right cop-median.'

'Ha ha. So, why do I get the pleasure of your company?'

'I felt sorry for you for all the police jokes I aimed at you.'

'Yes, you gave me plenty. You read the audience all right, they were desperate to laugh at me and the force. An easy target, not many people like the police. But what about the others you picked on, why not buy them a drink?'

'What others?'

'The wee dirty looking guy you called Columbo?'

Harvey just shrugged.

'What about the big hairy guy you kept calling Bungle? You gave him it tight.'

'Well, he does look like a man in a bear suit.'

'You seem to have an answer for everything. So, why me?'

'Okay, keys on the table. You were on your own and looked like you were looking for a bit of company.'

'I need more than company.'

Harvey's eyes lit up.

'Not like that. There are people in here would like to do me damage.'

'Why?'

'Because I am a policewoman. And because I arrested their son for assaulting me.'

'That sounds like a pretty good reason.'

Denise took a sip from the drink Harvey had bought her.

'God, that's strong.'

'It's a double.'

'If I drink all that I will be flat on my back.'

'Drink up.'

Denise laughed. 'You are so full of it.'

'I may be, but you haven't told me to go yet.'

'What about your wife? She wouldn't be happy to know you are chatting up a poor defenceless woman.'

'She wouldn't care. We split up, I'm about to get divorced. She said I loved stand-up more than her. I said I love opera more than her and I hate opera.'

Denise laughed then showed him her ring finger and the bit that wasn't tanned where her rings had been.

'Snap.'

Denise took another drink and looked over to see Ivy still looking straight at her while shoving a meat pie in her mouth. That was a horrible image she didn't want to see again.

'I really need to get out of here,' she said. 'Could you call me a taxi?'

'You are a taxi.'

'I'm not being funny now. That woman over there that's staring at me.'

Harvey looked round the room as casually as he could then looked back at Denise.

'Yip, you aren't imagining it, she is staring at you. She is like a tampax, she wants your blood.'

Harvey picked his caravan keys up and showed Denise the tag. It had the number 14 on it.

'You could shelter with in my caravan. I could make you a coffee.'

'I don't drink coffee.'

'That's okay, I don't have any coffee anyway.'

Just at that Ivy was off her seat. She was being dragged up to dance, much to her annoyance.

As soon as she disappeared from view, Denise snatched the keys from Harvey's hand.

'Right, let's go.'

Denise hurried out of the hall. Going as fast as she could she was out of the building and running towards the caravans, although struggling to go very quickly in her wedges. Why hadn't she worn flats, she wondered as she struggled to run flat out across the gravel road?

Quick as she could, she opened the van door to No.14 and slipped in. Harvey followed and he quickly locked the door behind them.

Harvey switched the light on, but Denise spat 'No,' and it went out again just as quickly.

In the dark, the silence was only broken by the heavy breathing from both.

Denise could sense Harvey getting closer then felt his lips meet hers. Gently at first, but when she responded it got more heated.

It was interrupted by shouting outside. The MacAllister clan appeared to be out hunting as a pack, chasing round the park looking for her.

In the caravan, their eyes quickly acclimatised to the dark, there was enough dappled light from the roof vents, to let Denise make out Harvey's silhouette. She put a finger to his lips then took him by the hand and led him through to the bedroom.

For some reason the drama, the adrenalin, the alcohol and the need for sex, took over her senses.

'Do you have condoms?'

'Yes,' he whispered, his breathing slightly laboured again.

'Let's do it.'

Denise felt her way round the bed and sitting on the opposite side, started to strip off.

Suddenly there was a banging on the caravan door, the thumping a copper would have been proud of, demanding to be answered.

'Don't answer it,' Denise hissed.

The thumping got louder; they weren't going to go away.

Harvey, dressed only in his trousers, pulled his vest back on then walked through, leaving Denise alone and slightly panicking. She was stripped down to her bra and pants and trapped in the bedroom with no way out.

She moved over the bed and looked and felt around in the near pitch dark, straining for something to defend herself with.

The front door must have been opened because Denise could hear the shouting getting louder. There was more than one person shouting but she couldn't hear what they were saying.

'She is through in my bedroom naked,' she heard Harvey say, quite loudly.

The only thing was a small metal stool to sit at the dressing table, for doing make-up. If anyone barged passed Harvey, Denise was armed with the stool, they were going to get crowned with it.

'Wow, wow, wow,' she heard him say although her heart was thumping so hard she struggled to concentrate.

'Wow, cool your jets, I am only kidding wee man. I walked

her out the hall and there was a taxi waiting. I thought I was going with her but when I walked round to the other side to get in, the bitch shot off without me.'

Whatever the human detritus from the MacAllister clan said, Harvey added, 'I will fuck her too if I get the chance.'

Then the door slammed shut and firmly locked.

When Harvey made it through to the bedroom, Denise was still pissed at him.

'What was that wee charade all about?' she said, a bit louder than she should have.

'Shoosh, they might still be about,' he whispered.

'Look, we had to get rid of them. If I just said you weren't here they wouldn't have believed me, they would probably have waited all night for you to come out. With my wee story they will be off looking elsewhere.'

'What about your final line? Going to fuck me.'

'Surely I deserve something after that performance.'

Harvey moved forward and kissed her again. This time, with the adrenalin still coursing through both, it was hot and steamy, culminating with them both on top of the bed, what little clothes they had left on being discarded.

'You will have to be gentle,' Denise whispered. This was the first time she had even contemplated having sex since her assault.

'If I say stop, you stop. Okay.'

'Yes, sure,' Harvey whispered back.

'I mean it, I have had self-defence training.'

'Relax, I am allergic to pain.'

Denise tried to relax as Harvey slid off the bed and rolled the condom on. She knew if she wasn't relaxed her vaginal muscles could contract and not let him enter easily, making the whole encounter even worse.

Harvey was obviously experienced and went on top of her, gently guiding himself to the entrance of her sex. The condom was obviously well lubricated because the penetration was painless although she could feel he was in.

'Slowly and gently,' she mouthed just loudly enough for him to hear, his ear just above her as she spoke.

Harvey did as he was told. Slowly and gently, he started and continued until he increased the speed bit by bit finishing at a crescendo. He felt her shudder beneath him as she orgasmed before he filled the condom with a load of his seed.

After pulling out, he lay on his side, for the second time that night trying to get his breath back.

Denise lay beside him and sobbed gently.

'Come on', he said, 'I wasn't that bad, was I.'

Her sobbing stopped and turned to a gentle laugh.

'No. I think you were great,' she said as she patted his chest.

She slipped off the bed and went to the cramped shower room.

Firstly, she sat and peed. It was a relief for her in a couple of ways. She breathed out in relief, her bladder must have been the size of a beach ball after all the coke and vodka it held. The second relief was it ran from her painlessly. Since her assault she had a few nippy, stingy moments but not this time.

She got up and looked in the mirror. Not being a fan of too much make-up, she cleaned off the bit of foundation and lippy she had on.

Next she got a wad of the cheap, crappy toilet paper and wet it before douching lightly. It was hard to imagine the relief she felt but it seemed clear no permanent damage was done by the missing MacAllister, who was currently in jail, awaiting sentencing for his crime.

Denise was almost sure there would be a welcoming committee back at her bedsit so she hoped she could stay there in the caravan that night.

Harvey was still lying on the bed in the darkened room when she went through. Still naked, he had a hand over his flaccid manhood as he held on the dishevelled rubber.

'Is it okay if I stay the night,' she asked.

There was only the light shining down through the corridor from the toilet, but she saw his eyes light up, thinking of the prospect of a repeat performance.

'Only for protection,' she added, before he got above himself.

'Of course, you can. As long as you don't snore.'

'Well, there is only one way to find out.'

Denise woke when the cold crept through her left arm that had slipped out from under the blanket. Like a wick drawing combustible, her arm seemed to have drawn the cold through her alcohol infused body, enough to make her shiver uncontrollably.

It was still dark, and she struggled to see the time on her watch.

It looked like 4:04. No, it couldn't be. Leaning up she flicked on the bedside lamp and checked again. It had been 4:04 but just flicked over to 5 past.

Harvey stirred beside her. 'What time is it?'

'It's 5 past 4. Go back to sleep.'

She slipped her legs round to get up.

'Where are you going?'

'I am going to head back to my bedsit.'

She gathered her discarded clothes and headed back through to the shower room.

When she got dressed she went out and found Harvey, up out of bed and fully dressed.

It was her turn to ask; 'Where are you going?'

'I am going with you. If those loonies are hanging about you will need a big strong man to help you.'

'Are you a big, strong man?'

'No,' he said, 'but I can run and get one.'

Denise laughed. 'Ever the comedian. Look, you don't need to. They will have given up waiting.'

'What if they haven't?'

Denise leaned forward and kissed him. 'Thanks.'

'Okay,' he said, 'wait until I have a piss.'

And they say romance is dead, she thought.

The walk back up to the town was bracing as a light frost was starting to paint the town white. Harvey leaned in and pulled her towards him.

'You can't come in,' she warned him, 'my landlady is a right dragon.'

'Look, we have had a lovely night. If I found out you were assaulted after you left me I wouldn't forgive myself.'

'That's lovely, but you were expecting an invite in. Weren't you?'

'Well, if you invited me I wouldn't say no.'

'Look, I haven't moved in here long. I wouldn't want my landlady to think I was a strumpet.'

Harvey collapsed into a laughing fit.

'A strumpet? Are you a Victorian lady?' he said, when he managed to control himself.

'Well, that was what my gran would call a lady who was, well, easy. What would they be called in your family?'

'My mum would call them slappers and my dad called them new slabs.'

Denise was perplexed.

'New slabs?'

'Yeah. He calls them that because they are easily laid.'

Now Denise lost it, laughing noisily before the comic joined in. Then she calmed herself and shooshed him.

'Be quiet, it's not even 5 o'clock yet.'

'You made me laugh,' he whispered.

They stopped next door to her digs.

'I'm just up here, next door' she said pointing up to the house.

'Well, at least there is no sign of anybody waiting to do you in.'

He was right, it was as quiet as a graveyard, which is probably where she was heading if the mob got to her earlier.

'Thanks for saving me,' she said, then leaned in and kissed him.

He responded and she tasted mint, he had obviously brushed his teeth when he nipped in for a pee. She too had given hers a rub with her finger, just so she didn't smell like an old winey.

'You sure you don't want me to see you up to your room?'

'Nice try Romeo. Look, I told you, I don't want the wrong kind of reputation.'

This time Harvey leaned in and kissed her. Denise melted into him and squeezed his bum with her right hand.

'All right, lover boy but you need to be quiet,' she whispered in his ear.

'I will be quiet as a mouse, but you might find out I am a rat.'

Denise woke up for the second time after 9 o'clock that morning. She got up and quietly went through to the toilet. Next she made tea and sat watching Harvey as he slept soundly in her bed.

She was just finishing her cuppa when he stirred.

'Morning,' he croaked as he struggled to open his eyes in the bright morning light, as Denise had opened the curtains in the hope of rousing him.

'Morning. Not much wakens you.'

'After our session, no wonder I conked out after it.'

He got up and she admired his naked body. He wasn't exactly trim, too much drink and the wrong kind of foods on the road had seen to that. He wasn't toned but he was big where it mattered.

'I will need to go to the toilet.'

'You can't. You will need to do it in the sink.'

'What? Why?'

'Downstairs, they will hear everything. I have already been to the loo. If you go they will know I have somebody up here.'

Shaking his head, he padded over to the sink and stood on his tiptoes while he held his impressive manhood in, relieved himself, sighing as he did so. Then, he shook it and rinsed it away, shaking it as he did so.

'Listen, I need to get to the caravan park,' he said, turning to face her. 'I need to check out, I am doing a show in Dingwall tonight.'

'Could you cover that up when you are talking to me,' she said, smiling.

He was standing proudly naked in front of her.

'We can't go just now; we need to wait an hour. They will be off to the shop's dead on 10 o'clock,' she said pointing downstairs.

'They are creatures of habit, every week they go out at exactly the same time. Get ready and I will make you a bit of toast while we are waiting.'

Harvey was seriously miffed but couldn't complain too much, not after the fun they had the previous night.

'Okay, but as soon as they are off we are out of here.'

Denise and Harvey sat on the sofa, ready to go, as they waited for her landlords to go and get their weekly shop.

As soon as they heard the front door close, they were up on their feet. They stood at the front door and heard their car start and drive off.

Harvey rushed down the stairs and Denise followed after, pulling the door closed and locked behind her.

Outside, just as Denise and Harvey stood on the front step a car passed and Marion looked out, shocked to see her lodger with a strange man leaving her house.

Denise hadn't realised that Marion's car was facing the wrong way and they had to go to the end of the street to turn around.

'Shit, busted.'

'Is that your landlady?'

'Yes.'

'You mean I crept about all that time, peed in the sink and sat for ages waiting for them to leave and it was all for nothing.'

'Yes.'

'Well, that's a bummer,' he said, then they both burst out laughing.

DINGWALL OR BUST

Denise drove into the entrance of the caravan park and turned in a big circle, leaving her ready to leave when Harvey got out. She offered to take him to his caravan, but he wanted dropped there.

As she hit the brakes they felt a bit soft as she drew to a halt to let Harvey out but thought little of it and imagined it was due to the gravel surface.

'Well, thanks for a lovely evening,' Harvey said. 'I take it this is goodbye.'

'Ships that pass in the night,' she said.

Harvey leaned in to kiss her and she turned and offered her cheek.

'See you then,' he said, getting out.

'Bye,' she said softly then Denise drove off and didn't look back. She glimpsed in her wing mirror and saw him waving. She didn't respond.

Denise drove up the road from the caravan park and took a left, the opposite direction from her flat. She was headed for the nearest big police station, it happened to be in Dingwall. The MacAllisters were more than she could handle on her own she realised.

A bit further down the road she had to stop at a junction. This time she noticed her brakes were definitely soft, or spongy as her father would have described them.

'Well, peril, seems like you need a service too,' she said to her wee car, thinking that was the reason the brakes were not as strong as usual.

Once out in the country the views let her forget all her troubles. After seeing the detectives, she fancied eating in a nice restaurant. Surely there would be a nice Italian in the town.

As her mind drifted to thought of some tasty pasta, her concentration lapsed, and she headed over the brow of a hill too quickly, only to find there was a very steep drop beyond. She tapped on the brakes just to get her speed under control but got no response. Putting her foot harder, it went down to the floor. The speedo showed she was already going at over 60 miles an hour and gaining as the incline caused her to speed up even more.

She took a deep breath to relax, her Advanced Driving had prepared her for this. Although not for what she suddenly realised what waited at the bottom of the hill.

There was a Rover parked on her side of the road and the driver was busy changing a tyre. That wasn't mentioned on the course.

After putting on her hazards she pulled the on the handbrake and leaned on the horn, desperate for the guy below to notice and get clear off the road. If she hit the car that was bad enough but killing him would make it a million times worse.

Dropping down a gear and continually pulling and realising the handbrake slowed her slightly but there was no way she was stopping before the bottom of the hill- she was heading straight for the Rover.

What made it worse, opposite the stopped car the road was lined with trees. Big pine trees at that. There was no gap in them she could aim for as a run-off on that side of the road, she could only hope she managed to steer past the Rover and run up the opposite carriageway until the yellow peril ran out of momentum.

The Rover owner, who she could now see was old and white

haired, continued working at his car, oblivious to the impending danger. The blaring horn warning was being ignored.

After continuing to work the handbrake, she slowed a good bit but still whooshed past the broken-down car safely.

In order to be as safe as possible, she steered as far from the other car as possible. She thought she was safe as she sped past the other car, but her front tyre caught the grass verge, instantly pulling the car onto the grass.

She battled with the steering, pulling as hard left as she could. Beneath the car, the wheels were churning up the grass, throwing dirt and stones into the wheel arches, the noise unbearable.

The inevitable happened and she thudded into the first tree. The cars momentum was slowed but it ploughed on, hitting another huge pine before drawing to a sudden stop.

The force of it stopping suddenly threw her forward, then her seat belt jerked her back quite violently, jolting her neck and left her sitting there shaking.

When the reality of what happened sank in she screamed.

'Oh my God. The peril!' she cried out. 'I am sorry dad, I've killed her.'

Her hands shook uncontrollably as she struggled to unclasp her seatbelt.

She tried to get out the driver's door, but it was wedged against a tree, and she couldn't open more than a few inches before it hit pine.

Panicking, she got over the centre console, past the gearstick and handbrake and got out the passenger door. Her legs were shaky, but she ran round the front of the car to see the damage.

She burst out crying as her father's pride and joy, which was really bought with her in mind, was stuck and undoubtable wrecked, probably a write off.

The old guy started to walk up to see if she was okay and if she needed help. Although it wasn't his fault, she couldn't face talking to him, she'd probably tear a strip off him.

Just then, the next passing car stopped, and the driver and his wife quickly got out to assist her.

'What happened,' the woman asked.

'My brakes failed,' she said through sobs.

'John is a mechanic,' the woman passenger said, as an introduction to her hubby.

'Surprised that happened in a car as new as this, certainly won't be corrosion,' he said and immediately went round to have a look at the car for himself.

'Don't get your trousers dirty. We are going to my mothers to visit,' the woman called after him.

'Are you okay?' she asked, concerned as Denise had manged to stop crying but looked as if she wasn't quite with it.

The white-haired Rover owner who had been changing his tyre went back to the task, glad somebody else had taken the caring task away from him.

'I'm fine,' Denise said, then burst into tears again.

'It's my car. My dad bought it for me,' she blabbed.

The woman cuddled her before her husband, John, appeared back. Just at that moment another car stopped to see if they could help.

'Have you hit a rock or anything? Driven over a pavement?' John asked.

Denise shook her head. She drove her car carefully, very carefully.

'Then I think somebody must have damaged your brake pipes.'

'Deliberately?' she asked, surprised then angry at the thought somebody would do this deliberately.

'Well, I would say there are signs of mechanical damage.'

'How do you mean mechanical damage?' she asked, now bemused as to how it could have been damaged.

'I just mean there are scratch marks on the brake pipes, looks like they could be slightly pierced. If it was only one side you would still have some braking. Not having any at all would point to both being tampered with. That would rule out it being accidental.'

'Fucking MacAllisters,' she said to herself through gritted teeth.

John's wife turned to the other car's occupants. 'We will wait here; you go and call the Police and an ambulance.'

'I don't need an ambulance,' Denise called after them, but they had shot off up the hill by then, keen to do their civic duty.

'Would you like to sit in our car while we wait. It could be a wee while, it is a Saturday afternoon after all.'

'Yes, you are lucky the road isn't busier,' John added.

It was then Denise realised how lucky she and the other guy was. If a car had been on the other side of the road it could have been carnage. For a few minutes she forgot she had been asked a question and stood looking back down the road where she could have been in a serious crash and could have been badly injured, or worse.

The old guy with the Rover was now putting his jack and tools back in the boot of his car. He might not have been doing that if she had smacked into him, she thought.

As these thoughts went through her head, she had to think hard what John's wife had asked her before she could reply.

'Sorry. No. I prefer to stay out here. What's your name, you never said? I am Denise.'

'I am Caroline. You are in shock I am sure; don't you want to take a seat?'

'No, I feel fine.' She went round to the front of her car, looking again at the damage. The front headlight was smashed and the front wing dented in. The whole driver's side was also bashed in, although she couldn't see how bad it was but was the reason why she couldn't open the door.

John followed her round.

'Is my car bad?' she asked John, wanting his professional opinion.

'No, I don't really think so. There doesn't appear to be any structural damage and the roof is intact. I would be surprised if it was a write-off, it looks worse because it's stuck there.'

She turned to Caroline. 'I am more upset because the car is the only thing that reminds me every day of my dad. He passed away recently and left the car to me.'

'Ow, that's a shame. Would you like a drink? We have some Lucozade in the car. It's for my mother, we always take her a bottle but I'm sure she won't mind when we tell her what happened to you.'

'No, really, just waiting with me has been great.'

The wailing of sirens could be heard in the distance, getting closer. Why they had the blues and two's on was anyone's guess, the road was quiet. Save for a few rubberneckers who slowed as they drove past to stare at them and the smashed car.

The ambulance arrived first. They stopped 10 feet in front of the scene. There were 2 medics, both men. The first walked quickly over to them while the other busied himself noisily opening the back doors of the ambulance.

'Who was the driver?'

Caroline motioned with a hand to Denise, who by then had wiped her face and seemed fine.

'Look, I am okay. I had my seatbelt on and wasn't going too fast when I hit the trees.'

'Come on into the back of the ambulance and we will have a wee look.'

'Was there anybody else in the car?' the other medic asked as he joined them.

'No, I was driving alone.'

The medic then took her arm gently and led her up towards the ambulance. As they were walking the Rover drove past, the driver intent on not looking round, as if none of this was anything to do with him.

As he disappeared from sight, Denise realised she hadn't taken a note of his registration number. How unprofessional, she chided herself. Just because she had been in an accident wasn't an excuse for shoddy police work she told herself.

The 2 medics were very professional, checking her over, blood pressure and other vitals, as well as checking there were no bones broken or other injuries she was denying herself were there.

By the time they had finished they agreed she didn't need to go to hospital, but they were still advising it, just to be sure. She steadfastly refused and the medics left to attend to their next call.

The police arrived as the ambulance was driving off.

The two officers got out and went over and the car and the crash site.

'Funny place to crash,' was the first thing the first 1 said to her. 'Straight bit of road and you ended across the carriageway and into the trees there.'

The guy was, what Denise would call a total dick. Was he talking like that because she was a woman? That would make him a chauvinist dick.

She took a breath before starting.

'My brakes failed. I managed to slow down as I came down the hill but there was a car in the dip. The driver was changing a trye and I swerved over to this side to avoid him.'

The copper looked down but obviously there was no sign of the car now and frowning as if he thought she had imagined it as an excuse.

Caroline and John were talking to the other cop so couldn't corroborate her story at this time.

'Ask John, he is a mechanic,' she said, pointing to the guy that was being spoken to by his mate.

'Friend of yours is he?'

'No. He and his good wife were good enough to stop and help me. More than you seem to be doing.'

The cop ignored her dig.

'Of course, you will need to be breathalysed.'

'Yes, I know the procedure.'

'Oh, have you been breathalysed before,' he said, almost smirking, thinking he had a serial traffic offender.

'No. I am a police officer.'

He looked at her as if this was another ploy of hers.

Angry at his attitude she reached into her shoulder bag then realised she had taken it out before going out the previous night, not wanting to lose it when out socially.

'Oh shit,' she said when she realised she had left home without it.

This had the guy smirking even more.

'Right, let's start with your name.'

'Detective Constable Denise Kelly.'

The P.C. wrote it down while looking at her sceptically.

'Denise Kelly, and you say you are a Detective Constable,' he said in the same tone.

'Yes. I am stationed at Glenfurny Police station, and I was on my way to the Dingwall Police station to report that I am being targeted by a local family there. Obviously they must have done this to my car.'

'Right,' he said, gently nodding as he spoke.

Just at that the other policeman signalled him, pointing to the sticker on her windscreen. It was the logo of the police training college that officers used as an unofficial way of letting other cops know they were also old bill.

Policeman one made a face, dismissing the suggestion that it proved nothing.

The second cop then gestured his mate over towards him. They weren't very good at subterfuge because Denise clearly heard him ask her name. After he said something, and a lot more discussion, the first cop changed his attitude completely.

'Sorry about all this D.C. Kelly. What I suggest is my colleague P.C. Burns will drive you into the station. I will wait here with your car. We will need to get it towed back to our garage to have forensics look at it.'

Denise thanked the couple who stopped to help then joined P.C. Burns in the Ford Granada Police car.

He radioed ahead then drove off. They went past the peril and turned at the first field entrance before heading back that way.

Denise didn't really want to look at the crash scene but realised it might be the last time she clapped eyes on her car and stole a look.

'So, you can't be from here with that accent. Where is it you are from?'

Denise thought it was funny. Compared to the locals, with

their heavy Highland twang, she didn't think she had an accent at all. Suppose if you are different you stick out, she thought.

'I'm from Irvine in North Ayrshire. I am up on a years secondment, seems there is a lack of detectives up here.'

'You are based at Glenfurny. That's a quiet wee town, isn't it?'

'You would think so but it's anything but. I've already been assaulted, and I am quite sure it was the same family that sabotaged my car.'

'Assaulted.'

'Yes, knocked out. When I was unconscious I was locked in my own cell.'

'No way.'

'You mean you never heard about it?'

P.C. Burns had obviously heard about the rookie cop from down south who was attacked and locked in her own cell. Well, now he had met her. It must have been what he was whispering to his mate earlier.

'No.'

The cop waited too long to answer, Denise knew he was lying.

They reached the station shortly after. Burns got out and escorted her in, opening the doors before her.

Inside, behind the desk, the sergeant's attention was piqued at the arrival of one of his bobbies with a pretty woman with him. Burns had radio'd ahead and explained why they were coming in. Before the sergeant could speak Denise jumped in.

'I am Detective Constable Denise Kelly. I am here to see the duty Inspector. I believe it's Detective Inspector Cook.'

She knew who was on duty because she was warned on the drive in that the Inspector had wandering eyes. Not that he had defective vision but had an eye for anything female.

The desk sergeant nodded, recognising her from the stories circulating, before calling up to the senior policeman.

Denise stood quite embarrassedly waiting, in her head it seemed to her that all the cops in the Highland division knew her, by reputation at least, as the rookie D.C. from down south who got assaulted and locked in her own cell. That would stick with her probably until something worse happened to her, she guessed.

The door to the stairs opened and D.I. Cook appeared. He was a big man, tall and heavy with an almost bald head he was trying to ignore by having a comb-over. He stuck a big, chubby hand out. Denise gave her trademark strong handshake, but her hand seemed to sink into the flabby fingers.

'Let's go up to my office.'

As they walked up the stairs, the echoing acoustics amplified the sound of their footsteps meaning any attempt at conversation was worthless.

As they reached the top landing the senior officer opened the door and let his minor through. Far from being polite, Denise was sure he just wanted to eye up her bum. She kind of wished she had been left to make up her mind about him and she wouldn't have felt so self-conscious.

She was led through the detective's room, a large room with a collection of zoned off computers, to what must have been Cook's office.

There was only 1 other officer there in the detective's room and Cook called him to join them.

Cook got behind his desk and waited until Denise was comfy and the other D.C. had arrived with a large pad to take notes before he started.

'Now, Denise, is it okay if I call you Denise?'

Denise nodded.

'That's a lovely name,' he said smarmily. 'Now, you believe somebody tampered with your car's brakes.'

'Yes, sir,' she answered.

'Please, it's Charles. We are all fellow cops. This is Brian,' he said, pointing to his scribe.

'It's Ryan,' the young cop corrected but the boss ignored it, not for the first time.

As Denise listened to Charles, she couldn't help but notice that although there wasn't much hair on his head, there was plenty growing down his nostrils and out of his ears. Nothing like any womaniser she had ever come across.

'Right, tell me what happened, from the beginning.'

Denise started her story from the moment Urquart walked in the door, through the chase and getting knocked out. For a moment she thought about missing out the sexual aspect, but she was sure the old pervert, because she had decided by now that was what the Inspector was, had read the report of the full incident.

As she recalled waking up in pain, the Inspector started licking his lips. Denise started to feel queasy and continued without looking at him.

As she told him about seeking sanctuary from the baying mob and having sex with Harvey she sensed him moving awkwardly in his chair. She wondered if he was getting turned on even more.

The story ended when she got in the car with P.C. Burns to get to the station that morning.

The Inspector went quiet. He clasped his hands together and put them up to his face, the second finger touching his lips and the third finger resting on his nose as he thought.

'Would you like a coffee?' he asked.

'I wouldn't mind a cup of tea.'

'Right, Brian, take Denise up to the canteen and get her some tea.' He looked at his large gold watch. 'Back here in 15, no make it 20 minutes.'

As the 2 cops made their way to the canteen, Ryan muttered to Denise, that the Inspector's problem, well his biggest one, was that he didn't listen.

Denise didn't agree with him, it was obvious to her his wandering eyes and sexual innuendo were worse.

When they returned the Inspector was reading a file that seemed about 20 pages thick.

'Interesting family these MacAllisters. Petty theft, car theft, assault and ow, a bit of drug use.'

His hands went back together, as if in prayer mode. When his hands came down he beamed a smile.

'We cannot let an attack on one of our officers to be treated lightly. This lot will feel the full force we can come down on them with. This drug use gives us what I would call our in, as it were. It's too late to arrange anything for tomorrow but first thing on Tuesday morning we will raid their house. They will all be arrested and brought here. While that is going on we will search the house and have an incident room set up in Glenfurny for door-to-door enquiries and get the evidence we need. If there was a mob running through the streets in the early hours of the morning there will surely be witnesses and we will find them.'

He looked at Denise, who didn't look impressed.

'Oh, by the way, what is the name of this stand-up fellow again?'

'Harvey Hood.'

'Never heard of him. He can't be very good. Do you know where this comedian chappy is preforming tonight?'

'I don't know, he just said he was in Dingwall tonight.'

The Inspector smiled at Denise then turned to the other young D.C.

'Tonight Brian, we are going out. We are going to see this Harvey Hood chappy. Do you like comedy?'

'It's Ryan,' he corrected again. 'Where is he on again?' he asked.

'You are the detective, go and find out.'

The young D.C. looked puzzled.

'Now. Go,' he was ordered with a dismissing hand.

Denise got up to leave but the Inspector told her to close the door and take a seat again.

'You could go with us tonight if you want. It would be a pleasure.'

'No thanks. I really need to get back to Glenfurny.'

RECOVERY

Sunday and Denise hoped for nothing but a quiet day, something that had deserted her since the day she rocked up to Glenfurny.

She lay in bed wondering how different her life had changed so much in 6 months. Before, she was happily married, living in a new house and working in, not exactly state of the art but modern police station in Irvine.

The most she had to deal with was a breaking and entering or shoplifting at one of the high street stores.

Now she lived in a bedsit in a small town in the Highlands, in a Victorian style cop shop and so far most of the crime in the area centred around her.

Still, at least the people here seemed genuine, almost a product of a bygone age, the way they were when she was growing up, where people didn't lock their doors, and everybody knew everyone else's business.

Maybe life wasn't so bad up here, if she could just stop being the focus of all crime. Or at least just be investigating it.

Sod it, she thought, pyjama day. Lounge about reading, watching rubbish on the telly and eating junk food.

Denise struggled to get out of bed the next morning. The pain in her back and shoulders was unbearable. She couldn't understand why she hadn't felt it the day before but now it was pure agony.

Whiplash, she was sure. Anyone else would have called in sick and went back to bed, but not her, this just made her more determined to get to work.

When she was ready to get dressed, she went downstairs and knocked Marion's door. It was Marion herself who answered and was surprised to see her, especially in a dressing gown.

'I need a big favour. Could you help me get my bra and blouse on?'

Marion pulled a face. After all, it wasn't a request she had ever had from anybody and certainly didn't expect it from a lodger.

'What did that guy do to you?' she asked, concerned and angry in equal amounts.

'What? Oh, no, I have got whiplash. I was in a wee car crash yesterday. Think I need a good massage.'

'Have you got heat rub?'

'No.'

'Right, you go up and I will bring some up.'

Denise kneeled on her sofa as her landlady requested and jerked at first when she felt the cold heat rub hit her battered body even though her landlady was gentle about it. Marion had a magic touch as she massaged the rub in, and Denise felt her muscles being relaxed. Then she felt the heat kick in.

When the massage was finished she found she could get her clothes on by herself with just a bit of bother and some discomfort. The relief, though, was palpable.

When she was dressed she asked Marion if she heard any commotion outside the house on the Friday night. She hadn't but she would ask Johnny, her hubby, if he heard anything.

Denise walked up to the police station that day. She had

to, being carless. Her main priority that day was contacting her insurance and arranging a replacement car from them, she couldn't do much without a car. Especially in a backwater like Glenfurny.

Billy was already at a morning cuppa when Denise walked in. He went to get up to make her cuppa, but she told him to keep sitting, she had a lot to tell him.

Billy was staggered at her tale. Surprise turned to anger when she told him about the mechanic saying he reckoned her brakes were deliberately fractured.

'Do you think this is the work of the MacAllisters?'

'Almost certainly.'

'Are we going down there?' he offered. The MacAllisters were local worthies, but this was a new level for them.

'It will be Kelvin. Right wee ruffian. We have had a few reports about him. Vandalism and petty theft but nothing like this.'

'Just hold your horses. That lot are out of our hands just now. Tomorrow morning, they are going to get raided. Drugs bust.'

'Drugs. I know the father Paul smokes a bit, but they don't sell it.'

'Well, I have a feeling they will find drugs tomorrow.'

Billy thought about it for a moment before it dawned on him what it was she was getting at.

'Why don't they just arrest them for what they did to your car. You could have been killed.'

'Okay, question for you. Say it is Kelvin and he admits it. What can you charge him with?'

'Attempted murder.'

Denise shook her head.

'Assault,' was his next guess.

Still wrong, she signalled.

'Surely it's not just something like wilful damage,' he guessed again.

'Yes, you are probably closer to the truth,' she said and left it at that.

'What would you think then?' he asked.

'If he pleads guilty and he hasn't got a record as long as your arm he might get away with being charged with a lesser charge like vandalism. Let off with a warning and a fine.'

'Are you sure?'

'Yip. I discussed it with Inspector Cook. He says they need to pay for their treatment of a fellow officer. That was me he was talking about. A fine and a warning isn't punishment enough.'

Billy started shaking his head.

'What's wrong with you?' she said.

'Sounds to me like they are going to plant drugs in the house? That's not right.'

'Not right. Not right!'

Denise moved with a speed her beaten body defied, she jumped towards Billy where he sat, grabbed a handful of shirt and tie and pulled him up while she got down and right into his face.

'I will tell you what's not right. Ivy MacAllister spawned the progeny of the Devil. One of her scum knocked me unconscious and raped over there in that cell. Sexually assaulted me. That means he raped me against my will.

One of her other sprogs sabotaged my car and I could very easily have been killed. Not right, you say, trying to get them to pay for those crimes. What they did to me wasn't right! Nobody should treat a dog the way they treated me.'

Beneath her grip, Billy started crying. Denise let go of her grip but continued her tirade.

'You were quite happy to turn a blind eye for your pervert boss McCall who wanked himself to death. Oh, no, he was one of your own. What about me? Am I not one of your own?'

Denise had to stop to get her breath back. As she looked down at Billy, still blubbering like a baby, she realised that all the pent-up loathing she had for the MacAllisters had suddenly been unleashed on the last person in the town she would want to hurt.

'I'm sorry Billy.'

'No, I am sorry', he blubbed. 'You are right, they shouldn't get away with it. If anything had happened to you, I would have killed them.'

'No, you wouldn't.'

Billy dried his eyes with his fingers.

'I'm sorry, I speak without thinking.'

'Yes, Billy, sometimes you do. But you need to stop that. You need to start thinking for yourself. You know, I think you feel you are a bit of a fraud in that uniform. Your father was a pillar in the community. You wanted to follow in his footsteps, but I think you feel his footprints were too big for you to fill.

I haven't been here long, but I know one thing, you are a good policeman. What you need is to start believing it yourself and when you do, you will be an even better one.'

Billy looked at her but said nothing.

'Think you need another cuppa. I need one.'

After her tea, Denise sent Billy out on the beat with instruction that if anyone mentioned anything about the disturbance on Saturday night he had to take note what they knew but to say nothing about what he knew about it. Play dumb, she instructed. He would be a natural, she thought.

Meantime, Denise busied herself with getting her insurance sorted. It took a while to get anywhere because hers was quite a unique situation. Eventually they reached an agreement and was promised a call back later about a replacement car.

As she was at a loose end after that, something came to mind after talking about McCall: she still had his wee black book to look through.

As she unlocked the safe she felt anxious as to what it would tell her, if anything. It might, as she hoped, dish the dirt on the villagers or could just be a list of the woman he had slept with.

She started at the back of the book, as the most recent could have the most relevance.

"Lorna Dawson, blank, Myra Burns 3 stars, Celia Ball 4 stars."

Damn, she thought, it was just a list of his conquests and scores. She wondered for a moment how his sliding scale worked. Quickly forgetting that, she wondered if there were any of the women she knew getting mentions. Rita and Liz specifically.

Liz was actually given a page of her own with 5 entries, 4 stars, 4, 5 and 3 and finally a 2. What caught her attention was at the bottom after her ratings it said "Liz is worried about Susan and HiS baby."

His baby. No, Susan had denied it to her. There again, would a young girl like her be bragging about lying in bed with an old womaniser 2 or 3 times her age. Pushing a pram saying the dad- he is the old pervert policeman. No way, she thought.

 Denise kept thumbing through looking to see if there was an entry for Susan. Nothing, but she did find an entry for Rita Samson. A single star and the word perve beneath it written in capitals. Denise was surprised, she thought the two would have been ideal bedfellows.

There wasn't a mention of Susan or anything else that interested her, so the book was put back in the safe in case she needed it later. What kept coming back to her though was the entry that said "HiS baby".

Later in the day she got a call from her insurance, she could pick up her replacement car anytime from the Vauxhall garage in Dingwall. She was pleased because she was keen to get mobile again, but she realised it meant getting a lift over there from Billy.

Billy, on the other hand, was pleased at the thought of a long drive in the new Escort.

As they headed off Denise didn't know whether to be pleased or not because Billy definitely drove a bit quicker in the new car than he did in the Morris. However, now he knew her better, he wanted to talk to her, and he had the annoying habit of turning to face her, even when he was cruising along on a country road at 60 miles per hour.

As they got near her crash site, he told him to pull over in a lay-by. She told him off for his bad driving and warned him they were approaching a big dip on the road.

Pulling away, the warning had the desired effect. He wasn't facing her now because he stopped talking to her.

As they went over the hill towards the section where the yellow peril met its possible demise, she looked down at her hands, that were in her lap.

Heading back up the hill, Billy slowed the squad car and said, 'Looks like somebody has crashed here too. There is police tape across the trees there.'

'Drive on Billy!' she ordered, still refusing to look round.

As they reached the outskirts of Dingwall Denise opened up to him.

'Billy, the crash site earlier, that was where I crashed.'

'Oh, I never thought.'

No, you never do, she thought herself, but never said.

Her replacement car was a Vauxhall Viva. Funnily it was the same light blue the Police Escort was. The only difference being it wasn't blue and white halves and didn't have flashing lights across the top. She only hoped this wouldn't make it a target for the MacAllister clan.

Denise drove to the Police station the next morning but couldn't get parked near it. The Incident room had appeared overnight and there were unmarked police cars all around the place.

As she passed the Incident room she could see inside and there was a briefing going on. She really wanted to go in and see what they were being ordered to do but knew she couldn't or shouldn't.

Half an hour later the station door opened, and Inspector Cook walked in. She thought he would have been back in Dingwall spearheading the enquiries from there.

'Detective Constable Kelly, Detective Inspector Cook. Pleased to meet you again.'

She was surprised at the formality, it had only been 2 days since they last saw each other.

She shook the hand he pushed forward firmly, but with the same result as before and his squidgy fingers. This time they were damp, she hoped it was with sweat and not any of his other body fluids.

'This is P.C. Lambie,' she said by way of introducing her sidekick.

Billy walked over to the counter and proffered a hand that the senior officer completely ignored.

'Just thought I would keep you up to date with what is happening. At 6 o'clock this morning we raided the MacAllister's house, and the whole motley crew are currently all down in Dingwall, helping us with our enquiries.'

'Did you find drugs?' P.C. Lambie asked.

Behind the counter Denise kicked him gently on the shin.

D.I. Cook looked at the constable with distain.

'What do you know about the MacAllister and drugs?'

'It's well known in the town the father, Peter, smokes cannabis for medicinal reasons.'

'What are these medical reasons?'

Billy's mouth opened and shut like a goldfish as he tried to think of an answer.

'The only thing I could discover from his medical records is that he has a heart problem.'

Billy smiled, thinking he had been right to speak up, until the Inspector spoke again.

'That being is that the man is heart lazy.'

'Oh.'

'Yes, P.C. Lamont, he has been smoking banned substances practically under your noses and all this time you have done nothing about it.'

Denise glanced across at Billy, who was seething at the Inspector. It was bad enough ignoring his offer of a handshake but then accusing him of neglecting his duty had added to his ire.

She suddenly saw another side to her sidekick and hoped it spurred him on in his career.

The Inspector, on the other hand, seemed to relish showing off how clever he was. Maybe she would get a verbal roasting like Billy just did.

When she looked at Cook again she saw he was back to staring at her again, eyeing her up and down lasciviously and licking his lips before speaking.

'My men are heading for Cobbler's Court where they will start to do door-to-door inquiries before heading towards the caravan park and knocking doors on the way there. If this mob were running through the streets hunting after you there will be witnesses. I can guarantee we will find witnesses and these louts will not be getting away with what they have done to you.'

'Thank you sir.'

'Oh, by the way, your Harvey chap was very funny. I spoke to him after his act when he was chatting up some loose woman. He confirmed what you told me about the other evening but in greater detail.'

Denise felt her skin crawl at the thought of the 2 of them discussing her sex life.

'I will keep you updated,' he said, before having a final lip lick towards her, then giving Billy a disdainful look and leaving to return to the mobile incident room outside.

When he left Denise turned and looked at her subordinate without speaking.

'He is a pompous prick,' Billy said with venom in his words.

'Never mind that. You said earlier that you speak without thinking then put your big size 9 in it. Did you find drugs, that was a stupid thing to say?'

'Well, you are wrong, they aren't size 9's, they are size 10's.'

'Size in this case doesn't matter, it was what you said that counted. Always remember, first impressions count for a lot. The Inspector's first impression of you is that you are an idiot. No matter what police work you do now, you can't change that impression.'

'I don't care what he thinks about me.'

'Maybe not Billy, but you need to get into practice of treating all your superiors nicely, even if they are pompous pricks.'

'You are right. I am sorry. I will think before I speak in the future.'

Denise almost ventured to look out the window in case any pigs were flying past.

By 5 o'clock, there was no sign the rest of the coppers on the case finishing. Denise knew she had to stay late, to find out how the enquiry was going. Billy wanted to stay and Denise appreciated the gesture.

As usual, Billy had to go home for his tea and brought Denise a bowl of mince and tatties that she wolfed down with a can of Irn Bru.

When she finished it she was full to the ginnels, she realised why Billy was growing out of his uniform, if he was eating food like that on a daily basis.

There had been traffic outside all day, going back and forth, all the while she waited eagerly for news. From about 6:30 onwards the traffic seemed to lessen, and the number of cars dwindled. Soon after, Detective Inspector Cook appeared.

'Well, D.C. Kelly, good news. One of your neighbours was returning from the public bar at about 12:30 on Saturday morning when he saw somebody under your car. At first he thought he had fallen and asked him if he was okay. He said his mate had thrown his wallet under the car as a joke.'

'Really?'

'Yes. The good news he gave a very clear description of this Kelvin MacAllister lad.'

'Bingo.'

'Bingo indeed. So,' he said, turning to face Billy, 'we also found an amount of drugs which was sufficient for it to be classed as more than for personal use. You will know that means we can continue to hold them until the morning. That gives us time to bring the case together and I am sure charges will be brought by the morning.'

'Thank you sir,' Denise said while Billy just nodded. He was scared to say anything else for fear of another dressing down.

The Inspector proffered his hand again which Denise shook. For the last time she hoped because it made her skin crawl.

As the door closed behind him she turned to Billy.

'If I never see that man again, it will be too soon.'

Billy was quiet for a moment, then said, 'I would say the same but I don't know what it means.'

On that light moment, they both laughed.

Next morning the incident unit was still there but empty now, job over. Denise parked the Vauxhall next to the Escort in the street. She had lain awake half the night, wondering what was happening in Dingwall. Would they be charged and with what?

If Kelvin was charged, could she stay in the town? Surely the MacAllisters would hate her more, she would be the reason two of her progeny were locked up and set to do time.

Billy arrived later than usual and looked as if he hadn't slept. He seemed back to his old quiet self.

'Is your mother okay?' Denise asked.

'She's fine. I couldn't sleep. I kept thinking about what I said yesterday.'

'Look, Billy, I'm sorry about my outburst yesterday. I must

have been festering those thoughts about the MacAllisters, and unfortunately for you bore the brunt of it.'

'No. I should have given you my full support. You have done that to me since you first walked through that door. I let you down and I am sorry.'

'Okay, if you feel sorry, you make the tea.'

Denise sent Billy out on the beat after his tea. She then spent the morning either watching out the front window for a visitor from Dingwall or staring at the phone, willing for it to ring with the news she craved. She thought about phoning the Dingwall station but couldn't bear to talk to D.I. Cook, imagining him on the other end of the phone slavering at the thought of her body that he had been staring at salaciously and doing God knows what beneath his desk.

Billy arrived back just after half past 10. While he filled in the daybook, Denise helped by encouraging him to write as much detail in it as he could, while they talked about who he had spoken to and what about. While her attention was focussed on helping Billy she never saw the car draw out in the street.

So she was surprised when the front door opened and D.I. Cook and the other cop from Saturday Ryan, walked in.

'D.C. Kelly,' Cook said, licking his lips. It was probably an involuntary action now as he had probably been lusting after women for so long.

'Good news, I think.'

The "think" made her heart sink a bit.

'This dreadful boy Kevin,' he said before being interrupted by his junior.

'Kelvin, sir,' he said.

Cook continued as if he hadn't been interrupted. 'Has been charged with wilful destruction for the damage he did to your car's brakes. He will also be charged with breach of the peace.'

All the time he spoke to her, his eyes seemed to stare at her lips then move down to her chest area. Although her breasts were well hidden, she was sure he was checking the size of them by following the contours of her clothes.

Bust inspection over, he went back to staring in her eyes, something that was just as stomach churning.

'I can see you are disappointed with this, not the result you hoped for.'

She nodded gently. 'Not at all.'

Although she spoke quietly, she felt like screaming at him and the whole establishment for letting her down again.

'Well, I can assure you he will be dealt with severely. The judges here in the Highlands use the full weight of the Law, not like the namby pamby types you have down south. They will be told about the accident and damage to your car, and indeed the fact you could have been seriously injured or even killed and I can assure you he will be eating prison food for a long time.'

Denise swallowed hard before speaking.

'What about the rest of the clan?'

'As you know this Ivy woman is very much the matriarch and what she says goes. She has been warned that if as much as a hair in your head is harmed she and her kin will be blighted by us. As there is past history of drugs at her address we can also raid their hovel as often as we want.'

Denise thought this might seem a good deal to him, but he didn't have to live here. Straight away she thought she should contact the Chief Inspector and ask for a move away from Glenfurny. He could hardly disagree; he knew her time there had been Hellish. Plus, she played ball by keeping quiet about the McCall incident.

'What about the drugs?' Billy asked. Then he moved his leg away out of Denise's range in case he had spoken out of turn again.

Charles Cook turned and looked straight at Billy, initially with contempt but then broke into a smile.

'To be honest with you young man, there was not enough cannabis to charge them for dealing although if we were going down that route we would have found some more. The funny thing is when they were being released, the father asked if he could get his grass back. Bloody cheek of him.'

This brought a release, and everybody laughed.

'Honestly, dear, you will have nothing more to worry about with that family. Now, I have my card here with my business and home numbers on it, if you need anything, day or night, just call me.'

He stared at Denise as he spoke, emphasised the anything, that made her skin crawl and stomach turn at the thought of the man even thinking about her.

With that, he turned and left with his D.C. trailing after.

Denise looked at his fancy personal card that must have cost him a pretty penny to have printed. Admiring the calligraphy, she then ripped it in half and tossed it straight into the wastepaper bin.

A CHIEF INSPECTOR CALLS

Friday again. One thing Denise knew for certain; she wouldn't be going near the caravan park that evening. Or the pub. A night in front of the telly sounded just great, she thought.

She hoped to hear from the police garage that morning. She still didn't know whether her pride and joy, the yellow peril, could be saved. She also worried if it was repaired, would it be the same car? People had told her their cars were never the same after a bash and the peril had been given a right good thump.

First call that morning wasn't about the car at all. It was Chief Inspector McKelvie's secretary asking her to attend a meeting at the Inverness headquarters at 2 p.m. Asking meaning- be there.

Straight away she had the sinking feeling that the bosses at the Highland police force had decided that she and they were not working out. Surely they couldn't say the things that had befallen her were her fault. Relations between the local Police and the residents of Glenfurny hadn't been as good for years, the MacAllisters and Rita Samson being the exceptions.

Maybe they would offer her another post in the Highlands. It would be better than having to return south, returning with her tail between her legs having failed. Or at least she thought that would be how it would be viewed down there.

'Something wrong?' Billy asked. 'It's not the yellow peril, is it?'

'No. I have just been summoned to headquarters this afternoon. I have a feeling I might be heading back down the road to Ayrshire.'

'No way. Do you want me to phone McKelvie, put a word in?'

Denise smiled; it was the last thing she probably needed.

'Que sera sera sera, Billy.'

'What?'

'Que sera sera means whatever will be will be. It's a bit like what's for you will not go by you.'

'Oh, right. I mum says that a lot. Well, if you go I for one will miss you.'

'Oh, come on. You will get a new boss.'

'Sure, but I don't want a new boss. I am happy with the one I have.'

'Me too, but unfortunately I am only a Detective Constable, there should be a Detective Sergeant here in charge anyway. We don't make decisions like that. That's way above our pay grade, as you once said.'

They were disturbed by the phone ringing. It was the Sergeant in charge of the police garage in Dingwall. The C.I.D. were finished with her car, they had fixed the brakes and it was being transported, as they spoke, to her insurance company to repair. The insurance assessors had checked it while it was there and said it was repairable.

Denise put down the phone and said a loud "yes," her car was going to be fixed, it wouldn't be written off.

'Meeting cancelled?' Billy asked.

'No. Good news, the peril is on it's way to my insurers body builders. She is going to ride again.'

'That's good. You love that car.'

'Yes, Billy, I do.'

The doorbell clanged and they looked round to see who had entered. It was a blood chilling moment for both when they saw their visitor was probably the last person they wanted to see, Ivy MacAllister.

If Denise was going to be leaving, she would tell this woman what she thought of her and her nasty, vulgar, shower of human detritus she called her family.

'Detective, I am Ivy MacAllister.'

'Denise folded her arms and was literally biting her tongue, controlling her wrath until she was ready to unleash it.

'I just want to apologise; say I am sorry,' she continued.

Denise was astounded, those were the last words she expected from the woman's mouth.

'Sorry!'

'I know it doesn't sound much but I don't want you to think my family are a bad lot.'

On the evidence Denise had, she seemed way off the mark with that.

'Look, I didn't know Darren raped you. Honestly I didn't. He told me Robert McCallum knocked you out and locked you in your cell. We all thought it was funny. After he was arrested, he told us he was set up by you because Robert was a policeman's son.

You can see why we were angry when he was arrested. We thought he was innocent and was getting set up and wrongly, we blamed you.

If I had known he raped you, I would have dragged him in here myself.'

The woman stopped talking and tears filled her eyes. 'I was abused by an uncle when I was young. I know it's not right,' she said, then left it at that.

Denise suddenly felt sorry for her but couldn't let her guard down fully.

'What about Kelvin then?'

Ivy sniffed hard before continuing.

'Look, I just said you needed taught a lesson, brought down a peg or two. Let her know she was dealing with the wrong family if you messed with us again. That was all, I just wanted you to be warned off. The idiot shouldn't have touched your car. First I knew anything about it was when we were at Dingwall police station.'

Then Ivy put her hand out to shake in friendship.

'Fresh start.'

Denise was reluctant at first. After all, it wasn't minor things here horrible progeny had made her suffer. Then she relented, maybe it wasn't her fault her kids were wicked. After all, it took some guts to come and face her.

'Fresh start,' Denise agreed.

Denise leaned her hand over the counter and shook. For once she gave a normal handshake instead of her usual knuckle-crusher, only for her adversary to turn the tables on her, almost breaking a few of her fingers.

Denise smiled; this was a woman after her heart. She felt sorry she had mis-read the woman.

With that Ivy left. After she was gone, Denise turned to find a beaming Billy.

'Well, that's good news. If Ivy is on your side in the town, you will get no more trouble.'

'Oh, how's that?'

'Most of the folk in the town are scared of her. Right dragon, she is. Seems you have tamed the dragon.'

'You just tell me this now.'

'Sorry.'

'Billy, you need to stop apologising. Or rather, you better start thinking so that you don't have anything to apologise for.'

Billy went coy. 'It's not my fault. For years I have been a policeman here and have been left on my own most of the time. Les didn't help, he just wanted to chase women all the time. People before him were just the same.

Andrew McCallum didn't bother either. He was just passing time as he was waiting for his retirement. All we did was sit in here while he told me tales about the old days and the things he and my dad got up to in the so called good old days.'

Denise looked and saw he had tears in his eyes.

'None of the bosses wanted to help, then you came along. Now I am finally starting to feel like a real policeman.'

'Well, P.C. Lambie, I am happy I have helped but as I said earlier, that decision is out of our hands now.'

THE MEETING

Denise had meant to be parked up long before her meeting was due, and left Glenfurny in plenty of time, but it seemed all the farmers between their and Inverness wanted to move their sheep down country roads that day.

She arrived at the headquarters in Inverness with only 5 minutes to spare and she still needed to get parked up and get to the meeting room. Luckily there was a space behind the station and after hurrying round she managed to get in the front door dead on 1 0'clock.

The desk sergeant phoned through, and she was directed upstairs to one the conference rooms.

Denise knocked gently and heard McKelvie call "come" authoratively from inside.

Walking in, she was greeted by a large table with three Inspectors behind it, a secretary taking minutes and a chair in front, obviously for her.

McKelvie was in the middle, obviously chairing the meeting. Invited her to sit before he introduced the other 2 gents sitting either side of him. The secretary, the only other woman in the room, wasn't included in the introductions.

Chief Inspector Roddie was first. He looked about 20 years over the retirement age and his large, hooded eyes gave him the appearance of being asleep, which half the time he probably was.

Chief Inspector Cowan looked too small to be a policeman and had more braid and medals than a banana republic tinpot dictator.

'Gents, this is Detective Constable Denise Kelly. She has been seconded here from U Division in Ayrshire for the next year.'

The other cops muttered something unintelligible and McKelvie continued.

'I think we can safely say you haven't had the easiest start to your time here and we asked you over to tell you what we have planned going forward.'

McKelvie smiled and Denise started to feel a bit more at ease but was still on her guard.

'Firstly, we have looked at your actions since you came here and also your record from U division. Almost everything is exemplary, and I understand you have passed your sergeants exams last year.'

Denise nodded.

'I have spoken to my counterpart in Ayrshire, and we have agreed that your actions and work here has been first class. The result being we agreed you should be promoted.'

This took the wind from her sails, the last thing she expected.

'It is my pleasure to tell you that from today you will be promoted to the rank of Detective Sergeant.'

Denise gasped. This was the last thing she thought was going to happen at this meeting, she thought she was heading back down south.

'Are you happy to accept the post?'

'Yes, sir.'

'As far as your career goes, there are 2 options we have available to you. There is a currently an opening here in Inverness in the serious crime department for a Detective Sergeant.'

Denise felt her heart beat a bit faster, her dream job. The job she naively thought she was coming up to the Highlands to do. Now that, and the whole lifestyle she dreamed of, was hers for the taking.

The Chief waited for that to sink in.

'We also realise that I personally and we, as a force, have let things slip at some of our satellite stations, like Glenfurny. Going forward we realise we need to man up there and that would mean a crew of 4, a Detective Sergeant, a Detective Constable and 2 Police Constables, one of which will be a cadet.'

'The Detective Constable would be fresh out of Police college and would need a strong Sergeant to mentor them. That could also be your role, if you chose to stay there.'

Denise rubbed at her brow. Why give her a choice, she thought. If she was told she was going to work in Inverness she would have been overjoyed. Now, putting it up against staying in Glenfurny, it left her with a big choice to make. After the time she had since arriving, nobody would blame her for high tailing it out of there but what had happened had probably made her love the place and the people, well some of them, even more.

'Have you any questions, Detective Kelly?'

'If I decide not to come here to Inverness to work just now, will the chance be there in the future?'

'To be honest with you, I don't think it would be. In my opinion, at this stage in your career, it would be a feather in your cap to be working in the serious crime department.'

'Can I have a minute,' she asked.

'Oh, of course Denise, this is a big decision. If you want to have a breather, step out and take 5.'

Denise did as she was offered and walked out. This was where it was happening, where she would be stationed if she chose to work here. Walking down the corridor, it hadn't any nice feeling to it. She found the ladies toilet and went in and looked in the mirror.

'It's up to you kid,' she said, 'Inverness or Glenfurny.'

Her reflection didn't have the answer either.

Instead of heading straight back to the conference room, she went in the other direction. The serious crime department must be down that way.

At the end of the corridor was a large open plan room with partitioned off desks, each with a computer. A computer each, Glenfurny didn't even have 1 yet.

As she looked in through the glass on the door it was opened, and a sombre looking Detective walked past, not even acknowledging she was there.

The door closed and a moment later the same thing happened again, another plain clothes policeman came out and ignored her as he passed.

Decision made.

Denise returned to the conference room confidently.

'Gentlemen, I would like to stay on at Glenfurny.'

Chief Inspector McKelvie looked surprised.

'Right, well if that's your decision I wish you all the luck. The new recruits, if you want to call them that, will be joining you on a week on Tuesday. Unless there is an ongoing incident when you have your new crew, I will want 7-day cover with at least 1 person on duty at any time during the day. That will now be your job to manage that. Do you think it's do-able?'

'Yes, sir. I am not going to say it will be easy, but I will give it my best. Thank you gentlemen.'

'Your new contract will be mailed out to you, and it just leaves us to wish you all the best in the rest of your career here in the Highland Police force.'

'Thank you again gentlemen, I won't let you down.'

Denise sat in her replacement car in the car park and let out a roar.

'You beauty!' she called out. Her struggle since arriving in Glenfurny now seemed all worth it now as it had earned her 3 stripes on her arm.

'Shit, I should have asked him for a car,' she said before starting the loan car and heading back home.

That was what she thought of Glenfurny as now, home.

Driving through the countryside, the green had never been greener, the views nicer and the Highland countryside never been prettier.

She smiled to herself as she thought Billy would be so pleased she wouldn't be leaving. Getting more cops to work with should also please him.

As she arrived back at Glenfurny before 4 o'clock, she decided to head back to the Police station to tell him the good news. She stopped in her tracks before the Samson's general store. There was an ambulance with it's blue lights flashing. Billy must have been in the vicinity as the Ford Escort squad car was there parked beside it, and also had its blue lights on. Not needed, obviously, but that was just P.C. Lambie being super-efficient.

Denise parked her car and hurried up towards the shop just as they brought out a stretcher.

'Oh my God.' She uttered as she saw it was Susan Wilson that was strapped on. She was lifeless and her head was swathed in bandages.

As the medics put her into the ambulance, and Billy not being in sight, got out her warrant card.

'How is she?' she asked worriedly.

The ambulanceman glanced at her i.d. then shook his head

gravely.

'We are taking her to the hospital to deliver the baby. We hope we can save the baby, but it doesn't look like we will be able to save the girl.'

Denise was shocked to the core, but she still had a job to do.

'Which hospital are you taking her to?' she asked, sure that Lawson didn't have the facilities like an emergency room.

The medic turned to his mate who was obviously the senior man.

'She has to go to Dingwall.'

Just at that there was a noise behind as Liz Wilson burst through the small crowd of onlookers gathered on the pavement. She was still wearing her apron.

'Is she okay?' she asked before stepping up beside Denise.

One look at her daughter, deathly pale and lifeless beneath the oxygen mask, told her what she wanted to know.

'No. No. no, no, not my wee lassie,' she cried.

'Liz. They are taking her to hospital to deliver the baby.'

As Liz took this in, the medic urged urgency.

'We need to go. Every second counts.'

'I'm going with her,' Liz said.

'Sure,' he said, 'but you will need to sit up the front.'

She took off her apron and thrust it at Denise. Denise stepped back and the driver followed.

'Come on, we need to go, now!' the driver said, realising every second counted for the unborn baby.

In a flurry the back doors were shut, the driver jumped in the front and the ambulance sped off lights on and sirens blaring.

Denise feared for Susan and the baby, Dingwall was more

than half an hour away, even racing there.

As the ambulance was speeding off as Billy walked out from the shop.

'How did you get on?' he asked.

'Billy, that's not important now. What the Hell happened here?'

'Susan slipped out the back on some oil and fell down the back steps. Rita was alone in the shop with her, she had to try and help her before phoning the ambulance.'

'What? I want a word with her.'

Just then Robin Wilson emerged through the crowd. He was walking slowly with the aid of a stick, the reason why he only just got there. She realised she hadn't managed to visit him, or Liz, since he got out of hospital, but other things got in the way of that. Before he could ask what was happening, Denise handed him the apron then pulled him away from the rubberneckers who were keen to hear any snippet to feed their gossiping frenzy.

'Robin, I am sorry to tell you, your daughter is in a bad way. She might not make it.'

For some reason Denise didn't expect emotion from him and was surprised when he burst into tears.

'Not my Susan,' he said through the tears. 'It was her last day too.'

'Robin, they are off to hospital, that's the best place for them.'

'Billy, you see to Robin,' she urged quietly before marching into the shop.

She found Rita sitting alone, through the back shop, crying. Her sobbing sounded false to her she wondered if the tears were from a bit of fresh onion in her handkerchief.

'What happened?'

'Susan went to take the rubbish down to the bins. Somebody must have dropped cooking oil on the top step, and she slipped. She must have landed head-first on the stone step. She looked terrible; I think she is dead.'

'No, she isn't dead. They are keeping her alive long enough to deliver the baby.'

Suddenly Rita stopped crying and gave Denise a stunned look.

'The baby isn't dead?'

'No. Not yet anyway. Can I use your phone? I need to get a forensic squad here.'

'Forensics. Why?'

'Why? There has been a serious incident here. I need to follow the protocol. It looks like we could have a sudden death. Forensics will need to do check everything here. Where is Hugh?'

'He left a few hours ago to go Edinburgh with his mates to watch the rugby. Won't be back till some time on Sunday. Will I be able to re-open tomorrow?'

'Is that it? That young girl could die, her unborn baby's life is hanging by a thread and all you are interested in is your bloody shop?'

'Life goes on, girl. People still need to eat.'

Right at that moment Denise felt like pulling the disgusting fat cow up by the collar of her horrible nylon overall and throwing her down the back steps.

Come on girl, be professional, she urged herself.

'I need you to leave the shop now. Whether you open or not will depend on the forensics team on what they find, if anything, and if they are finished by tomorrow or not.'

Rita got up and headed out, not before emptying the till.

While she was doing that, Denise was phoning the Dingwall police station. She was good at remembering numbers and dialled it right first time.

After giving the details she took the keys off Rita then ushered her out of the shop.

Billy was over at the crowd talking away to them when Denise and Rita emerged from the shop.

'Billy, would you drive Mrs. Samson home.'

'No, it's okay, I have the car.'

'Rita, you must be in shock, I don't think you are in a fit condition to drive.'

Rita thought about it before saying, 'you are right. I don't feel well at all.'

Rita tottered off and got in the squad car, suddenly not too sure on her feet.

'Billy, when you come back come round to the back shop. It isn't locked because it's a crime scene. I will need to stand guard until you get back. We are waiting for forensics.'

It suddenly dawned on P.C. Lambie what his superior was thinking.

'You mean.'

'Keep it under your hat. Say nothing to Rita, let her do the talking.'

Billy signalled silently with a wink that he understood then left.

There were only a quite a few folk still waiting for something else to happen. How empty your life must be to have to witness somebody else's misfortune to give you something to enrich yours, Denise thought.

'Shows over, folks, nothing left to see here,' she said, before turning down the alley at the side of the shop to go round the back to secure it.

Denise walked round to the back of the shop. The back door was unlocked. She opened the door and looked in. There was a bloodstain at the bottom of the internal staircase, obviously where Susan had landed.

Denise closed the door and locked it then went back round to ensure the ghouls had left the vicinity of the shop.

Billy joined her 10 minutes later.

'Have you locked the back door?' he asked.

'Of course. Billy, I have dealt with hundreds of big incidents, I know what I am doing?'

'Sorry. I just want to make sure we get this right.'

'Well?' Denise asked.

'Well, what?'

'What did she say?'

'She was quite quiet. Then she said, am I in trouble? I said why? She said because I might have dropped the cooking oil on the floor. The container I was carrying might have been leaking. She meant to get Susan to clean it, but a customer came in and it went out of her head.

I reassured her that the forensic team were so good they could build a picture of exactly what happened. She was quiet after that.'

Denise nodded her head. 'Well done Billy. I'll bet she was quiet.'

'What does that tell you?' she went on.

'That she suddenly realised she wouldn't get away with it, if she did it of course.'

'No, Billy, she must have thought she was clever enough to get away with it then realised she wasn't so smart. Modern detective work is more advanced than people realise.'

'You really think she pushed Susan?' he asked, surprised.

'My female intuition is screaming to me that she did it. We are just waiting for the proof then we nail her.'

'You are lucky, I don't have female intuition.'

Denise smiled when she realised he was just joking.

'Look, Billy, this looks as if it could be a late one again. Do you want to nip home and see your mother's all right?'

'No. I could phone my aunty Renee. She can go in and see she is all right. I can nip up to the station and call her. It's about time I made my career the most important thing in my life.'

'Nice to know. Off you go, I will wait here until you get back.'

Billy stood quiet, waiting for something.

'What?' Denise asked.

'Are you going back to Ayrshire?'

'I said earlier, with this going on, it's not important just now.'

He looked at her, waiting for even a hint at what lay ahead for her.

'Okay Billy, I am afraid you are stuck with me for a bit longer.'

Billy smiled, the biggest smile imaginable, then hurried up to the station to phone for his aunty to see to his mum.

The forensic crew arrived at just before 6 o'clock. After ascertaining what had happened, they took control, as was their role. Denise waited out front of the shop while they did their work and offered Billy the chance to sign off for the night.

Billy, buoyed by the earlier news that his next in line was staying on, volunteered to stay with her for as long as it took that evening. Maybe the thought of what happened the last time he left her on her own prayed on his mind.

Colin Boyd, the guy in charge of the forensic team, came out of the shop and joined them at around 8 o'clock. As he peeled off his surgical gloves, he shook his head. 'I am not 100% sure what happened here, but it doesn't seem natural.'

'What do you mean?' Denise asked.

'The blood spatter is not consistent with somebody falling forward. Even if she twisted in air as she tried to save herself. What I heard was the injury was at the back of her skull, how could that be.'

This was along the lines of what Denise thought but wanted it confirmed. She held her hands up. 'What does that mean in English?'

'Basically, if you are asking me did she fall forward or backward, I would say she fell backwards down the stairs. Now if you are also asking did she fall or was she pushed, without all the information to hand now, I would have to side with her being pushed.'

Denise nodded; her instinct was right. She felt it in her bones Rita had something, no more than something, to do with the young girls "accident".

Within a few minutes his crew dispersed, and Denise and Billy were alone at the shop. They locked it securely and headed back for the Police station for a quick debrief.

'Do you want the kettle on?' Billy asked.

Denise would have killed for a drink right now, she thought, although her choice of thought was so wrong, but she wanted to get back to her flat asap.

'No, Billy, let's get this over with. So, with what you have heard so far, what do you think?'

Billy looked at the clock, then said, 'I think Rita pushed her.'

'So do I Billy. The question is why?'

'I think it's something to do with, who the baby's father is.'

'I think you are right. Are you 100% sure it couldn't be Les?'

Billy looked at her as his mind computed who she thought of as Les, until he realised she meant Les McCall.'

'Les McCall the father? No. No way. Les would always brag about who he bedded and how he had, you know, did it. Sleeping with a young girl like Susan would have been top of his accomplishments. We would certainly have known all about it, every sordid detail.'

This threw Denise's theory out the window. She was sure Les McCall was the daddy. If it wasn't him, who was it, she wondered.

'Right, Billy, time for home. I will need to be here first thing. Unlike you, I need my beauty sleep.'

Billy, missing the joke completely, nodded and left for home.

Denise did likewise. Rita, who would be desperate to open the shop in the morning, would need to wait until she deemed the time was right to hand over the shop keys.

RILING RITA AGAIN

Just after 9 o'clock the next morning, Denise headed for the Police station. She saw there was already a queue outside Samson's general store as she drove past. Denise could have stopped at the shop and handed over the keys as she saw Rita waiting impatiently with her customers but, like the old saying, why should Mohammed go to the mountain, she could come to her.

Plus, she knew Rita would be pissed off by having to walk up to get the keys.

Rita followed her Denise's car as she saw it headed for the station's car park, just as the policewoman expected her to do. When Denise walked in, the kettle was on the boil. Billy was there already although it was his day off and Denise hadn't asked him to come in. He was there bright and early even though they were on duty until nearly 9 o'clock the previous night.

'What are you doing here?' Denise asked.

'Thought I might be needed. Oh, Rita Samson had been up here 3 times already, looking for the keys of the shop. Quite narky she was.'

'She better not be narky with me; I am just in the mood for her.

On cue, the door opened, and Rita barged in.

'Mrs. Samson,' Denise greeted her with mock pleasance.

'Detective Constable Kelly. I would have thought you could have brought the shop keys to me last night or early this morning,' she said with the false joviality she thought she had perfected.

'I am still waiting for the okay from the forensics team to release the premises back to you. They haven't phoned, have they Billy?'

He shook his head. Denise wasn't surprised, the forensics guy told her she could release the shop back to the keyholder, she was just ignoring the fact to rile Rita even more.

'I will give them another phone for you.'

Colin Boyd had given her his card which she left next to the phone. The call was answered almost instantly.

Denise had a conversation with one of the workers although she knew all along it was okay. The person on the other end didn't know the details of the case and needed to speak to Colin Boyd.

She turned to Rita. 'They are just checking.'

Rita said nothing but stood at the counter fizzing mad at all the hanging about, she had a business to run.

The minutes ticked on, and Rita started drumming on the counter with her big, pink nails.

Denise kept the phone to her ear, smiling as she did so.

'That's great, I will give her them back, Bye.'

She turned to Rita.

'The forensic team say they are finished with your premises for the moment. They think they have all the evidence they need. Once the autopsy and everything is complete, we will have a better picture of what went on yesterday. However, to keep your business going, I am allowed to give you the back your keys.'

Denise said they were in the safe and left to get them. In reality, they were in her handbag. In the office she took them then out then waited for another few minutes before she took them back through.

Denise handed the keys over. Rita snatched them out of her hand then, without speaking, scurried out to get back down to her shop.

'Well, Billy, no remorse today, is there?' Denise said when they were alone again.

'No, definitely not. The more I think about it, the more I am sure she did it. She had no remorse, just wanted the shop open. What I want to know is why did she do it?'

'Billy, I think you have hit the nail on the head. If we find that out it would answer a lot of questions. You know Billy we could make a good policeman out of you yet.'

Billy beamed proudly.

'Now we are alone, I can tell you what I was told yesterday at headquarters.'

'Last night you said you aren't going back to work in Ayrshire.'

'That's right. Actually, I was offered the chance to work in the serious crime squad in Inverness, but I preferred to stay here.'

'Why? Surely it would have been better for your career.'

'Yes, it probably would. However, from what I saw yesterday they are a load of stuffed shirts. In all my career I have been fighting prejudice because I am a woman trying to be a success in a man's world.

I didn't need to be as good as a man, I had to be better. Down in Inverness I am sure I would be back in that position again, whereas here you take me for what I am. You listen to what I say because I am more experienced, and you can learn from me and don't resent the fact I am a woman.'

'The other reason I listen because you treat me as a person as well. Not some dumb yokel, that's the attitude I always get from the other senior officers. I think they resent being sent to a backwater like Glenfurny.'

'Then there is the other news, I have been promoted to Detective Sergeant.'

'Wow. Well done. That's brilliant. I haven't known you too long, but I know you deserve it.'

'Thanks. They are also increasing this station to a 4-person team.'

She said person, not because of her, but because she had a feeling any females from the police academy would be placed with her. That was never said, more implied.

'What do you think of that Bill?'

'I'm glad you aren't going but I am sad we won't be a team anymore.'

'We will be a team, just a bigger one.'

'I like it the way it is. But, if it means they are taking this station seriously, I suppose that's a bonus.'

Denise, although she had known Billy for too long either, was pleasantly surprised at that reply.

They were interrupted by the station door opening.

A tall guy, who looked like a double wardrobe with a suit on walked in. Denise's friend Jan, from back in Irvine, had a saying she often used when a fit guy appeared. It was "she wouldn't kick him out of the bed if he farted" and Denise would have agreed with her about this guy. Then she thought he must be a cop. After John Kelly, her rat bag husband, she vowed to herself never to date in the job again.

It looked to her this guy must have been assigned to take over the case. At least it wasn't creepy Cook, as she had now decided to call him.

'Detective Sergeant Kelly, I presume.'

Denise stuck a hand out.

'Not yet. I haven't got the new contract yet. Still constable Kelly.'

'A mere formality that. I am Detective Inspector Harry Golder. I have heard a lot about you.'

Denise wondered exactly how much and hoped the bad bits didn't sway his opinion before he got to know her.

'I have been assigned to take over the Wilson case, but I see it as rather joint investigation we will be working on it together.'

Denise nodded. As he looked into her hazel eyes with his piercing green eyes, she was worried she might have to break her vow of fellow officer chastity. Her only hope now was that he was married, then it would be a definite no-go for her. After the hurt she got from her hubby's infidelity, she could never inflict that on another woman.

'I have read all the notes we have on the case, what is your take on it, from the local point of view.'

'Susan Wilson worked at Samson's general store for the past 3 years. Rita Samson openly wanted her husband to sack her but he refused because she was pregnant and it would look bad for them as a business.'

'How do you know that?' Golder asked, impressed.

'Local knowledge. Susan was over 8 months pregnant and, according to her father, she was working her last day in the shop before stopping for maternity leave.'

Golder nodded as she spoke. Christ, he even nodded sexily, she thought.

'Supposedly, she slipped from the top stair at the back of the shop while taking out the rubbish. According to the shop owner, who was the only other person in the shop, she was in the front shop when she heard a scream.'

'What did she slip on?'

'The owner reckoned there had been cooking oil dropped

on the top step. How convenient.'

'She reckoned?'

'Sorry, she said she spilled it. Wrong word.'

She felt stupid, after getting brownie points before.

'There was no love lost between the two, Rita and Susan. Susan recently vandalised Rita's Mercedes by pouring paint over it.'

'What?' Billy said. Denise realised this was news to him, she hadn't divulged she knew who was guilty of the paint throwing.

'I will tell you later', she said to him, before continuing.

'We now need to wait on the forensics, but I reckon she was pushed. Hopefully they managed to deliver the baby last night and it seems to be doing well. The next thing I was going to do was phone the hospital and see what the latest was.'

As if on cue, Robin Wilson walked up to the front door. The Inspector opened the door for him, and he walked slowly in, leaning even more heavily on his stick.

He looked a broken man. Dishevelled, he was wearing the same clothes Denise saw him in the previous day.

'Hi Robin.'

His eyes filled with tears.

'Susan died last night in the hospital.'

The Inspector, realising this must be the father, put a consoling hand on his shoulder.

Robin started crying again.

Denise managed to control her emotions and stifled her tears. Although she knew the girl was almost certainly going to die when she left in the ambulance, but seeing her father break down like that made it almost impossible not to feel his pain.

'Is Liz still at the hospital?'

Robin wiped his eyes. 'Yes, she stayed all night. Morag is doing the cooking here,' he answered. Morag was one of the women, Denise assumed were spinsters, that stayed there permanently.

'Liz just wanted you to know,' he added, before turning to leave.

'What about the baby?' Denise asked. There must have been news by then she thought.

Robin turned back.

'She said about the baby. I can't remember. It's a boy or a girl,' he said then turned again and shambled off.

When the Inspector closed the door behind him he turned and put his hands up.

'Is it a murder investigation now?' Denise asked, certain she knew the answer. The reply though surprised her.

'No. It's got to stay as a suspicious death at the moment. We will need the forensics to get a better picture. First thing I think we should do is go and see the scene for ourselves.'

'We can walk from here. It's just down the street.'

Although the Inspector must have had a big stride, he obviously slowed and walked at Denise's pace. They started talking about each other after he broached the subject. She told him about her impending divorce, he said he was single and had recently broken up a long-term relationship.

This put Denise's heart and head in turmoil, it would have been easier if he was married, she thought. Business first, she thought. Afterwards, who knows.

The shop was busy, after all it was a Saturday morning.

Rita was manning the food counter and another young girl stood beside her, obviously Susan's replacement who was learning the ropes.

Denise led her superior through the shoppers, heading for the door to the back shop. Rita stopped serving and moved across towards them.

'It's okay Mrs. Samson, we just need a look at the back shop.'

She opened the door and let them through before going back to serve.

As they got near the back step the strong, sharp smell of bleach met them. The place had been scrubbed clean; all traces of the incident removed.

'Bit different from yesterday,' Denise said.

'What was it like?' Harry asked.

'There was oil on the top step here and a blood spill down the bottom of the stairs. I knew Susan quite well, so could I only gave it a cursory glance, left it to the professionals. There was something about the whole scenario just didn't feel right.'

Harry looked at his watch.

'The autopsy is at 1 o'clock in Dingwall. I take it you will be coming with me to it.'

'Yes. Of course,' she said, it was her job after all.

However, the thought of watching Susan's body being cut up was probably the worst thing she wanted to see that day, or any day for that, but duty calls. As ever, she had to put personal feelings to one side.

'We will take my car,' the Inspector offered.

'I don't have a pool car yet. Maybe I will get one as part of our expansion.'

'Expansion?'

'Yes, we are going to a 4-man team. Sorry, 4-person team.'

As they made their way out of the shop the Inspector informed Rita they were finished in the back shop, for the time being.

'We might see you later,' Denise added, having a dig and putting a seed of doubt in her head. Denise was certain she was guilty of something; she just needed the proof.

HEADING TO THE AUTOPSY

Denise enjoyed Harry's driving, a welcome relief from Billy's, as they headed into the country. It was only the thought of what lay at the end of the journey that lay heavy on her mind as they passed through the beautiful countryside.

'I saw your car in the garage before it went to the insurer's place.'

'Was it bad?' she asked, dreading the answer.

'No. Cosmetic really. Both near-side door panels and the driver's side windows are busted, and the headlight cluster smashed but apart from that and a respray, it wasn't as bad as it could have been.

She realised then how shocked she must have been after the crash because she never even noticed her window was busted.

'I can't wait to get it back; I call it the yellow peril.'

'You gave your car a name,' Harry said, chuckling.

'Why not? Fits really because my life seems to have been in peril since I got here.'

'Quite the statement car, bright yellow with the black vinyl roof. Your choice of car says a lot about you, you know.'

'Oh, and what kind of car do you drive, Harry?'

'I have a red sports car in a lock-up in Dingwall.'

Denise nodded, impressed, although she hadn't seen it, she

couldn't imagine him driving about in an old banger.

'Okay, what do I think the sports car say about you. Is it a soft top?'

'Yes.'

'Right. So, you have a car with the folding down roof. You wouldn't drive about town like that, that's for plonkers. No, you would prefer driving in the countryside. Am I right?'

'Go on.'

'Yes, you like to look cool. Aviator sunglasses, driving gloves, tall model-like beside you, her hair streaming behind her as you speed through narrow country lanes. You stop at a country pub, miles from home for a late lunch. You have a meal and a drink. Then she says let's have another drink, one drink leads to another then you have drunk too much to drive and need to book a room and stay the night.'

'Is this about my car or is it a Mills and Boon story?'

'Just having a bit of fun with you.'

'Right then, my turn. Bright yellow eye-catching car, attention seeker. Not run of the mill, likes to be different.'

Harry was glancing across at Denise as he spoke, looking for a reaction. She just smiled but was letting nothing away.

'In my mind the owner of this car is flamboyant and is the type who would have an affair with a colleague and would not be averse to open air sex, on a blanket on the ground in the countryside somewhere.

Denise laughed and laughed. The guy was clearly flirting, maybe he thought she was too. Maybe she was.

'What. Am I way off the mark?'

'Way, way off the mark. This was my father's car. When he died last year I inherited it. My car before getting the Avenger was a 5-year-old, dark green Morris 1100. What does that say about me? I'm an old banger.'

They laughed together but as they went over the brow of the next hill Denise went silent. This was where the peril almost had its demise.

As they drove past the crash site, Denise looked away while Harry sneaked a glance.

'Still sore,' he asked.

'Yes. I think I will be until I get her back.'

They drove the rest of the way in silence.

AUTOPSY

When they arrived at the mortuary, Harry asked Denise if she was sure she wanted to go through with witnessing the autopsy as she knew the girl personally. It would be bad enough witnessing a young, otherwise fit young lady who was a stranger to him, he couldn't imagine how he would feel if it was somebody he knew well.

Denise simply shook her head.

'Let's go,' she said, with steely resolute.

As soon as they walked in the front door, the cloying smell, a mixture of all the chemicals and disinfectants, caught the back of her throat. Then the cold hit her. Every mortuary she had ever been in was the same, as if warning your other senses that what you were about to see would be even more repulsive.

The mortuary theatre was quite dark except for the main light at the front centred on the gurney where Susan Wilson's body lay. Her lily-white body looked almost ethereal. In fact, Denise thought she looked so peaceful it was as if she was just sleeping. The bandages had been removed from her head darkness showing the damage the fall had inflicted and her belly still bloated, the only evidence the baby had been removed was a caesarean scar.

Her thoughts were interrupted by a crackling from a speaker above as the pathologist started his commentary, describing to the two of them what he was doing.

'Subject is a female Caucasian, 18 years old. Blood samples have already been analysed and there were no sign of drugs or other stimulants in her system.'

As he spoke he checked he had all the relevant equipment necessary to dismember the body. The body. That was all it was to him and the policeman next to her.

The pathologist picked up an electric saw, needed for cutting into the skull and other bony structures, and pressed the start button sending the cutting wheel spinning with a screeching noise.

No, Denise realised she was wrong, she couldn't watch.

'Sorry, Sir, I can't watch.'

The Inspector didn't object and sat back to let her out. She brushed past him and left, just as the pathologist said he would start with assessing the trauma to the head. Before he could do anything else Denise was running for the exit door.

Outside, she found a bench and plonked down on it. Why did she ever think she could sit and watch a post-mortem being carried out on Susan? Had her job made her into some kind of monster? Or did the fact she ran out prove she was human after all?

She looked at her watch. It was just after 1 o'clock. Harry would be inside for best part of 2 hours, what was she going to do now, she wondered.

The hospital was in the same grounds as the morgue, she could walk round and see how the baby was doing she thought. Maybe see Liz as well. Poor thing, what a state she would be in. Not only would she be grandmother to the baby but now she would be its mother too.

Denise didn't think Harry would leave without her, but she left a note on the windscreen of the car anyway, telling him where she was going.

As she walked through the grounds, she thought about Harry. Should she abandon her principles and make a play for him? Surely all cops couldn't be the same as John. Or maybe she should just ask him if he had a name for his todger. If he did, she thought she would run a mile from him and maybe give men up for a while?

Inside, the hospital was well signposted, and she quickly found her way to the entrance to the maternity unit. Before she opened the doors to look for the reception area a matronly figure appeared before her.

'You are far too early, visiting is from 2 until 3 o'clock, young lady,' she said snootily.

Denise had her warrant card in her pocket. She had hoped saying who she was would have granted her access to where she needed to be without having to use it. Although everywhere seemed to have a jobsworth nowadays, it seemed she found the maternity department's one, the matron.

She flashed the card.

'Police. I am here to see the Wilson baby.'

'Oh, right. Poor thing, losing her mother like that. She is in the special baby care unit. Follow me.'

Denise had wanted to ask how the baby was but didn't get the chance. The matron was an absolute force of nature and zipped through the ward leaving Denise, who was no slouch, in her wake for the most part.

They stopped outside the entrance door to the special care unit and the matron stopped and spoke quietly.

'Normally, you would need to gown up but as we will not be touching anything we don't need to. So, remember, no touching anything.'

The poker up her arse wasn't as hard as Denise first thought.

As she peaked through the door, Denise saw Liz cuddling her new little granddaughter. She smiled at the touching picture until the matron, who was standing just in front of her, spoke.

'Oh no,' she said, then turned to Denise, her sadness telling her something was very badly wrong.

'Oh no,' Denise echoed. She knew what it meant; it looked like Liz would be facing a double funeral soon.

Surprisingly, Liz wasn't crying. She just rocked gently with the baby in her arms.

The matron walked over and spoke quietly to Liz, while looking in Denise's direction. Obviously telling her there was somebody there to see her.

Liz never moved, never even looked over.

The matronly one walked back over to Denise.

'Think it's best you leave. Leave her alone with her thoughts and her granddaughter.'

'I was just wondering if she wanted a lift back to Glenfurny. I won't be leaving for a few hours, but I could wait if she was going to be a wee bit later.'

The matron went back to Liz and obviously passed the message on. Liz just shook her head, still not acknowledging Denise. The matron looked back and shrugged.

Denise left the special baby unit, in a daze, wondering what to do next. It was nice outside; she decided she would just go back to the mortuary and wait for Harry. As she walked, all she could think of Liz and how she had lost both her daughter and granddaughter in barely the blink of an eye.

Poor Liz, she thought, her hard life had just got a whole lot harder to bear.

Denise waited on a bench outside the mortuary.

Harry approached about 2 hours later, looking very down.

Denise looked at him questionably.

'Looks like you were right. Almost certainly murdered. We

just need the evidence that it was the shop owner that did it. The forensics should back up what the pathologist said.'

'What else could have happened if she wasn't pushed?'

'We both are sure we know what happened, but as I said, we just need to prove it now.'

'It just got worse; the baby was born last night but died a short while ago. Now there could be 2 murder charges pending.'

'Oh no. You must be cut up.'

'Yes, but not as much as Liz. Losing both your daughter and the granddaughter you were looking forward to within a day of each other. She is devastated.'

'How do you know she died?'

'I went a walk over to the special baby unit. Liz was cuddling the poor wee thing. Didn't even look in my direction.'

'Everybody mourns differently' he said, before adding, 'right, let's get back and get the bitch nailed.'

LIZ TOO

Harry was pacing up and down in the front office of the police station.

'Pacing isn't going to make the report come through quicker,' Denise said. She was also on tenterhooks and his annoying actions weren't helping her nerves, in fact they were making her feel worse.

'They promised it this morning,' he replied.

They were there alone on the Sunday morning, waiting for a fax with the final forensic report.

The phone rang, making them both jump, as it wasn't what they were expecting.

Harry, being closest, picked up.

'Hello. Yes Charlie. No.'

Denise wanted to know the other half of the conversation, especially when Harry looked over to her with a concerned look on his face.

What, she mouthed.

He just shook his head gently.

'Yes, we will tell him.'

Harry didn't even have the phone in its cradle and Denise was on his case.

'Tell who?'

Harry looked to his feet before speaking.

'A woman jumped in front of a train on the outskirts of

Dingwall last night. She had no identification on her except a hospital name band that said baby Wilson.'

'No. Oh no. Not Liz too.'

'Definitely seems so. Dingwall are sending a car for Robin to go and identify her, but they want us to break the news to him first.'

Denise never spoke.

'It's okay, I know it's personal to you. If you want I will go and tell him, but I think it would sound better from somebody he knows.'

'Will it?' she said with a nip in her voice. Would it matter who told you your whole family had been wiped out within 2 days of each other?

Harry knew she was right. What did it matter who told you your wife committed suicide to get away from you and your life together?

They walked across to the boarding house sombrely.

'Do you want me to do the talking then?' Harry offered, after his dressing down.

'No. As you say, it might be better coming from me, somebody he knows.'

She knocked on the door and rang the bell. Quietly at first, but with increasing intensity as they were being ignored.

Eventually one of the boarders, one of the spinsters, stomped down the stairs and across the landing. Obviously angry because her Sunday rest was being disturbed. She opened the door with a face that would turn milk sour but didn't even ask why they were there, just turned and headed back up the stairs to her room.

'Is Robin in?' Denis called after her.

She shrugged, not even turning around, then continued on

her way, just glad the noise had stopped.

Harry knocked the owner's flat door. On the third knocking the door opened a bit and a drunk looking Robin appeared through a crack in the door. His eyes were bloodshot, he was unkempt and stank of booze.

He walked away, leaving the door open, for the two cops to follow him in.

Robin plonked himself back on the couch where it looked like he had been sleeping. He lifted a glass of whisky with from the side table with a shaky hand and drank greedily.

'It's bad news Robin, I am afraid.'

'Not my granddaughter too?' he said, looking pleadingly at her.

Liz obviously hadn't spoken to him before she decided to take her own life.

'I am afraid it's not just her?'

Robin looked but struggled to focus on what she was saying, not comprehending what she meant either.

'Last night, Liz died as well.'

'Liz. Dead. Liz is dead. Are you saying my Liz is dead?'

'I am afraid so, Robin. It would appear she fell in front of a train.'

'You mean she jumped. She couldn't face living with me anymore. I killed her.'

He crumpled into a ball, crying uncontrollably at his guilt.

Looking at the sorry excuse of a man before her, she could understand why Liz did it.

'You will need to identify her. There is a car coming from Dingwall to take you to the mortuary. I suggest you sober up a bit.'

She nodded over to Harry, and they left him and his bottle on their own.

NOISY NEIGHBOURS

The phone was ringing when they walked back into the station. Denise hurried round and answered it.

'Hello. Yes. Okay, we will be right round.'

It was Harry's turn to try to guess the other half of the conversation.

'Let's go. That was Rita's neighbour, Hugh has turned up and is causing a disturbance.'

With the skill of a rally crew, Harry drove speedily while Denise navigated through the quiet streets, getting to Rita's in what must have been record time.

The shop van was parked outside, and a raised voice could be heard from somewhere round the rear of the house.

'Hugh's back from the rugby then,' Denise explained as they hurried round.

'He should be happy, we won,' Harry added.

'I know you did it! Open up! You had no right to change the locks, it's still my house! Let me in you murdering bitch!'

'Fuck off! If you don't I will phone the police and get you arrested. Just go!'

Denise walked round to see Hugh. He was wearing a kilt and Scotland rugby shirt. He had temporarily stopped shouting and was looking around the ground obviously looking for something to throw at her while Rita was hanging out one of the upstairs windows.

She was naked, at least from the waist up that they could

see, and her hair was sticking out in all directions like an ugly Medusa. The disturbance obviously dragged her from her bed.

'Right, let's just settle down!' Denise shouted, her head going between them like a Wimbledon umpire as she tried to keep a check on both.

Hugh though, wasn't for calming down.

He gave up looking for a missile and resumed his shouting.

'She did it! That murdering bitch killed my daughter!' he said, pointing his finger accusingly up at his wife. 'Murderer!'

Denise was perplexed. Susan was his daughter? That was news to her. Maybe that was why he gave her a job in the shop.

'Susan slipped and fell. It was an accident,' Rita shouted back at him. 'Get over it.'

'You fucking liar! When I get my hands on you I am going to kill you!'

'Hugh!' Denise screamed at him from only 3 feet away to get his attention.

This finally snapped him out of his almost trance like state, so concentrated on shouting at his wife he was oblivious to everything else.

'Come round the front with us, we need to talk to you,' he ordered him.

Harry stood in front of Hugh, towering over him as he did so, he realised he better do as he was asked.

'I want him charged, you heard him, he said he would murder me!' Rita called after them.

Denise stared back as she walked away. Rita looked an absolute state, with her pale naked body, her pendulous tits swinging as she pointed an accusing finger down towards her husband.

'Get him charged!' she called again.

Denise stopped and called back at her, 'Rita, get your

clothes on. We need a word with you too.'

They took Hugh round and sat him in the back of the police car.

He was still angry and breathing heavily.

'Hugh. I shouldn't be saying this, but we agree with you, we are sure Rita did push Susan. We are just waiting on the forensic report to back this up. I am sure we will be arresting her before the day is out.'

Whatever emotions were coursing through him, they came to a head, and he suddenly broke down. He was showing the emotions she would have expected from Robin Wilson having his whole family wiped out in the course of a few days.

'This is all because we couldn't have kids and she didn't want me to have one.'

'Is Susan really your daughter?'

'What?' he said incredulously, looking at her as if she had lost her marbles.

'You said that out the back door, she killed your daughter, you said.'

'What? No. Susan wasn't my daughter, she was my girlfriend. Her baby was mine. We were keeping it a secret until the baby was born, then they were going to live with me.'

What an absolute plonker Denise suddenly felt. She suddenly realised in McCall's notebook it hadn't said HiS baby, it was just HS, Hugh Samson. There must have been a mark on the page that looked like an i. Now it started to make sense.

'Do you think Susan told her?' Denise asked, but now it seemed obvious.

'She must have. I think Rita suspected something though. Rita had been at me for months to get rid of her, but you can see why I couldn't. Rita would have been riling her, I bet she dropped the bombshell on her. It was her last day working, it was her last chance to do something, but I never expected her to stoop to murder.'

Harry had been sitting the whole time saying nothing, letting the Detective Constable take the lead. She knew these people after all. Denise looked at him and he just gave her a little smile. A gesture that said carry on; you are doing fine.

'Okay Hugh. I want you to get in your van and go home. We will deal with it. If you do come back near here, or even try to make any kind of contact with Rita, you will be arrested and charged.'

Hugh dried his eyes then got out of the police car. He looked up at the house before getting in the van and racing off.

Inspector Golder patted Denise on the arm.

'You did brilliant there.'

'Sure. All we have to do now is prove what we all think. Better give Rita another 5 minutes to get dressed. Seeing her anything but fully clothed is something I never want to see.'

Just then Rita's front door opened and 2 men in their 40's walked out. They hung their heads in embarrassment as they passed the police car.

'Another little sleepover,' Denise said, with a look of disgust on her face.

'Is that a regular occurrence?' Harry asked.

'Yes. Her neighbours wouldn't be surprised if she got a red light installed at the front of the house,' Denise said, then laughed gently at her own joke.

Rita answered the door then stood with her arms folded.

'I think it would be best if we had our discussion down at the police station, Mrs. Samson,' the Inspector said.

'Is he getting charged? You heard him threaten me.'

'We will discuss all that down at the station.'

'What for? He was doing all the shouting.'

'We don't want to talk about the shouting. We need to talk about the incident that happened on Friday afternoon at your shop.'

'Incident? You mean the accident,' she said, quick to try and correct him.

'You call it what you want, Mrs. Samson. If you want to get your things together quickly as you can.'

'Can I not make my own way down there?'

'No. We will give you a lift.'

The drive to the station took place in silence until they were driving past the Samson's shop. Denise leaned round and looked straight at Rita then dropped the latest bombshell.

'You probably haven't heard. Liz Wilson died last night. Looks like she killed herself by throwing herself under a train.'

Unsurprisingly, there was little reaction from her.

Outside the station a tall guy in his 50's was waiting impatiently.

Denise was at the door before Rita had managed to squeeze her big fat frame out of back of the car.

The guy looked round to make sure Rita couldn't hear.

'I heard you were working today. I need a word urgently.'

'Sure.'

'It's about Rita and the shop,' he continued whispering, before she was fully out of the car.

Denise started to get excited, she felt sure this guy had some evidence about Friday.

'Harry, you stay in the front office with Rita, I need a private word,' Denise said as she nodded toward the stranger.

Denise led the stranger through to the back office and invited him to sit, while she stood.

'I had to come and see you. This has been bothering me since Friday night.'

'Go on.'

'I went to the shop at about half past 3 on Friday. It was closed, which was very, very unusual. Rita is so greedy she would work a minute's silence. There was a note on the door saying "back in 15 minutes." I looked in the shop but there was no sign of life. Then I heard a scream. I stepped away from the entrance door to try to work out where the noise had come from. I thought it was from behind the shop, but I couldn't be sure.'

Denise didn't interrupt him, and he carried on.

'As I had 15 minutes to wait, I nipped into the pub for a quick pint. When I came out the ambulance was there, and all Hell seemed to have broken loose.'

'How long were you in the pub?'

'Not too sure, around 30 to 40 minutes, maybe an hour.'

'Right. You were right to come in. This is important information. I will need a statement from you. Obviously we have our hands full just now, as you can see we have brought Rita in. Could you come in tomorrow morning? Or we could come to you.'

'No. I would rather come in.'

'How does 9 o'clock sound?'

'Sounds a bit early. How about 10 o'clock?'

'Sure.'

'Sorry, I haven't even introduced myself. I am Detective Constable Denise Kelly.'

'Yes, I know. I am Donald Ford.'

'Pleased to meet you Donald. As you will appreciate we are

very busy with this just now, so it could just be P.C. Lambie in here tomorrow, but I will brief him on what you have told us, and he will take your statement. This could be very important Donald.'

'Good, hope I can help. If it's Billy, that's fine I know him well enough.'

Back at the front of the building Rita stood impatiently at the counter. Donald squeezed past, looking the other way as he did so. Harry was over at the fax machine reading the forensic report, which was still arriving, page by page.

Denise joined him and he pointed to a few things he had already seen.

'Think we will need to take her to Dingwall,' he whispered. Denise had to agree.

'Mrs. Samson. We will need to formally interview you. We can either do this voluntarily or if you don't agree then we will do so under caution.'

'Under caution? There is no need for that. Why would I not agree to speak to you? Of course, I will talk to you. I have done nothing wrong; I have nothing to hide, Inspector.'

She then fluttered her eyes at him and smiled.

'Unfortunately,' he continued abashed, 'we don't have the facilities here to conduct an interview properly. We will have to go to Dingwall.'

'Dingwall. Really? Could we not just do it here? Lock the front door or something.'

'No. I am afraid we will need to record it, to keep it all legal and above board, you understand. We simply don't have the facilities here for that. We will see you are brought back.'

'Well, I don't seem to have a choice, do I?'

THE INTERVIEW

Dingwall police station was dated but sported a modern interview room with a glass wall so events could be watched from the office next door while the others were oblivious to this.

Denise watched Rita through the glass as she sat in the room next door, waiting for it to begin. She seemed cool and calm. Not for long, Denise hoped.

They agreed Denise was too close to the case to be involved in the interview, so another D.C. was brought in to join the Inspector while she watched.

'Interview with Rita Samson. Present are Mrs. Samson, Detective Inspector Harry Golder and Detective Constable Alan Smith. For the tape, could you confirm your name and state for the record that at this stage you declined legal representation.'

'My name is Rita Samson. I declined legal representation.'

Through the glass, Denise was surprised at how clear it sounded through the speakers above her head.

'Can you just talk us through the events of Friday afternoon.'

'It was a normal busy Friday. We were starting.'

'Sorry, for the tape, who is the "we"?'

'I was in the shop with Susan Wilson. My husband was working in the morning but left at lunchtime to go to Edinburgh for the rugby. We were playing against Ireland.'

'Thank you. Carry on.'

'I think it was about half past 3 and I was in the front shop when I heard a scream. I hurried through to the back shop where it came from. Susan was lying on the ground at the bottom of the steps. She had been going down to the bins with 2 bags of rubbish.

That was when I noticed there was cooking oil on the top step. She must have slipped. I stepped over the oil and rushed down the stairs, being careful not to slip myself. Susan was knocked out cold, she had taken a nasty blow to the back of her head.

I phoned for an ambulance straight away. I went back down but there was nothing I could do; I don't know any first aid.'

The Inspector waited in case she had anything to add, but she had finished speaking.

'It takes over 30 minutes for an ambulance to get to Glenfurny from Dingwall and about 20 minutes from the Lawson Memorial. That is assuming they are available straight away. Did you not think about calling the local G.P. or going into the street and trying to get somebody who knew first aid?'

'I.I. I never thought. I must have been in shock.'

Denise watched and wondered how long it would be before Rita realised how much bother she was in and that she should have asked for a lawyer before talking.

'The shop had been open all day?'

'Yes.'

Denise had told him the nugget they got from Donald Ford about the shop being shut at around 3:30.

'What we are all wondering is, if she was going up the stairs, how did Susan manage to sustain a serious injury to the back of her head?'

'Maybe she turned as she fell, trying to stop herself. I don't know. As I said, I was in the front of the shop at the time.'

'We would have expected her to have injured arms too, if she tried to stop herself.'

'Not if she was carrying the bags of rubbish in front of her.'

'But surely they would have been thrown away as she fell to try to protect herself, or she would have landed on them. From the photographs, it looks like the bags were thrown out the way out sideways.'

'I don't think we will ever know; she can't tell us now,' Rita said matter of factly.

Denise thought she saw a hint of a smirk on Rita's face. Her confidence was growing but Denise was sure Harry was just baiting, playing with her, waiting for her to bite before winding her in, like an experienced angler.

'I think the evidence we have tells us a story and a damning one at that. You said the shop never closed but we have a witness who said the shop was closed at 3:30. At the time you said you were in the front shop, but the witness said they were looking in the shop when they heard Susan scream and there was no-one in the front shop at that time.'

'No, he must have imagined it, or he was wrong about the time.'

'He must have imagined he read a sign saying back in 15 minutes because you never shut the shop.'

Suddenly Rita raised a hand, as if she just remembered something.

'Oh, I meant to say that I locked the shop after I phoned for the ambulance. I didn't want anyone barging in when Susan was lying downstairs.'

'What if someone came in that could have helped?'

Rita just shrugged.

'Did you not think about phoning her parents? Her daughter was lying there, very ill. Did they not deserve to know?'

'Now you mention it, maybe I should have phoned Robin or Liz. They are nice people. I must have been in shock.'

The Inspector paused and looked at his notes before continuing.

'What, was there more than one scream?'

'What? No, just the one I heard.'

'Yes, well if she was unconscious she couldn't have screamed. So, you heard the scream when you were in the front shop. The witness looking in the front shop didn't see you or anybody in the front shop when he heard the scream at the same time.'

Rita shrugged again. 'He must have been wrong.'

'You know we haven't even appealed for witnesses yet. The witness we have came forward willingly. If 1 person saw the shop closed and a sign on the door there will be others.'

Denise saw her shake her head. She did it ever so slightly, but she had been trained in how to watch body language. She must have been thinking now she shouldn't have put a sign on the door.

'Onto the evidence. From the slip mark in the cooking oil, it was on the left-hand side of the top step. If Susan had slipped on it as you say, her left shoe would have been covered in oil.

'That would make sense, yes.'

'I suppose so,' Rita said indignantly.

'However, it is her right shoe that had a large amount of oil on it, there was none on the left shoe at all. How do you explain that?'

Rita never spoke but started licking her lips nervously.

'When her shoes were examined they were both knotted differently. The right one had a double knot, the left a single. I see you prefer a double knot yourself.'

All three present looked down at her training shoes which had double knots.

'I don't know what you are getting at,' she said huffily, crossing her arms in defiance.

'What I am getting at is you pushed her down the stairs as she was coming up them. Then you took off her shoe and rubbed it in the spilt cooking oil to go with your fabricated story about her slipping down the stairs. You messed up and took the wrong shoe off. Didn't you.'

Rita shook her head gently.

'You said you spilled cooking oil accidentally from a container. Where did you put the container afterwards?'

Rita's eyes darted to the left then the right, showing her guilt, Denise thought as she watched Rita's every nuance.

'I think it was left on the kitchen table.'

She licked her lips again.

The Inspector picked a picture from the bottom of his folder full of notes and turned it so that Rita could see it.

'This is the only open cooking oil container we found in the shop. The amount missing would equate to the same amount that had been poured on the top step. Can you account for this?'

For a moment Rita's mouth opened and shut like a fish in the water as she struggled for an answer.

'We know you did it, Rita. We also know why.'

The Inspector paused again to let that sink in before going for the jugular.

'All because the girl was doing something you couldn't and that was bear your husband a child. You couldn't face up to that. Everyone in the town would be talking about you because him becoming a father meant it was you that couldn't have kids.'

Rita cracked. She started crying and banging on the table.

'She shouldn't have told me. Bragging about it that afternoon. I didn't mean to kill her. I just wanted to kill the baby.'

'Rita Samson, I am charging you with the murder of Susan Wilson and the attempted murder of her baby.'

Denise leaned up and switched off the speaker from the other room. They had the result they wanted. She was only disappointed that Rita couldn't be held responsible for the third death she caused indirectly.

She continued watching without the commentary as Rita slumped in the chair, realising her sick and perverted life was over.

Harry turned to the glass wall and winked in at Denise. Result.

NO NEWS WASN'T GOOD NEWS

Next morning and Billy arrived early but Denise was already there.

'Is it right enough?' he asked as soon as he walked in.

'What?'

'That Rita Samson pushed Susan to her death.'

Denise nodded.

'Well, she has been charged with a count of murder and one of attempted murder. She is in custody in Dingwall right now.'

'What about Liz? Is it true she killed herself? There was a story on the news about somebody jumping in front of a train and one of mum's neighbours said he heard it was Liz.'

'Billy, I'm sorry but I am afraid it's true. Sad though it all is, our job now is to make sure we get enough evidence so that Rita goes down for a very long time.'

'Of course.'

'Are you looking forward to next week, Billy. Start of a new chapter, another 2 officers starting.'

'I like the way it is now, just us 2. We make a good team.'

'Yes, I think we do. I can only hopefully the 4 of us will make a bigger and better team.'

Denise put the tea out.

'Sorry, there are no biscuits, the shop is shut.'

'Do you think it will open again?'

'You will know better than me what the situation is with Hugh.'

They were interrupted when the door clanged as the postman appeared bearing mail.

After their last encounter he simply handed Denise the 2 letters and left quietly.

Denise looked at them. The first was addressed to Billy and looked official. Maybe the Advanced Driving course she recommended him for.

'For you Billy.'

Billy looked bemused as he opened the letter.

The other letter was addressed to Denise Kelly, Of no fixed abode. C/O Glenfurny Police Station, Glenfurny. She recognised the writing straight away. Obviously her ex-husband to be's attempt at humour. She folded it in half and slipped it into her shoulder bag.

When she turned round Billy was slumped in one of the armchairs.

'What's up?'

Billy looked at her as if he had been betrayed. Tears formed in his eyes. He held it to her as if he was glad to be rid of it.

She read it quickly.

"P.C. William Lambie. Further to our letter of the 14th, we have not received confirmation that you will be taking up the post at Dingwall police station as of the coming Monday, 25th April.

Please call our Personnel Department on receipt of this letter."

'Wow,' was all she could think to say.

'Why did you not just tell me?'

'I didn't know.'

He just looked at her.

'Honestly. This is news to me. I wouldn't have the power to be involved in decisions like this.'

'No, but you spoke to McKelvie often enough. He must have said something.'

'Honestly, he didn't mention you at all.'

'Well, that is me finished with the police. My mum needs me here. I will need to go back to the joinery work.'

'Could your aunty not help?'

Billy's eyes were filled with tears. 'My aunty can't get her out of bed every morning and help her get dressed. She can't stay the night to make sure she doesn't go wandering.'

'Billy, you have to believe me, this has nothing to do with me. God knows working with you was one of the main reasons I decided to stay here. You are a nice guy and a good cop. With my help you could get even better. Give me a chance to sort it out.'

Billy never spoke, just put his head down.

Denise swallowed as she saw tears land on the floor at his feet.

Denise called her boss, McKelvie. Her heart sank when his secretary said he was in meetings all day. She left a message asking him to call her as soon as he could.

The only other thing was to call the Personnel Department.

'Billy, why do you think you didn't get the letter?'

Billy sniffed hard before looking up.

'Mum would have binned them. She is really bad with her dementia. What did your pal McKelvie say?'

'He is in meetings all day, I left word for him to call me soon. I will try the Personnel number now.'

The number rang and was answered quickly by what sounded like a very young girl. She refused to speak to Denise, even though she identified herself as his boss.

'Billy,' she called him.

'Hello, I am Billy Lamont. Sorry, I cannot go to Dingwall on Monday.'

After that he just nodded as the girl seemed to be laying down the law to him, which was ironic. Then he slammed the phone down and barged past Denise.

'Billy! Billy, come back!'

By the time she said that he was round the corner and heading for the front door.

'Come back, that's an order!' she called but new it was futile, he was off.

Denise put her head in her hands, the joys of management.

Printed in Great Britain
by Amazon